THE ADVENTURES OF THE OMAHA KID

A Novel

BY

NATHANIEL ROBERT WINTERS

The Adventures of the Omaha Kid is a work of fiction. All incidents, characters and dialogue with the exception of prominent publicly well-known figures are the invention of the author. Where these real live public figures appear, the dialogues concerning those persons are entirely fictional and are not intended to depict actual events or to change the fictional nature of this work.

The Buffalo Publishing Company

First Edition 2013

THE ADVENTURES OF THE OMAHA KID

Nathaniel Robert Winters

Prologue

From the park across from my apartment came a very familiar sound. Opening the drapes, I smiled looking out at boys playing a pickup game of baseball. The pitcher went into the wind-up and a fastball flew from his hand towards the plate. The batter took a mighty swing. A loud "thunk" resonated from the metal bat and the sound played in my mind. I could almost see him out there...

Chapter 1 Brooklyn, New York
1954 - 1956

His parents named him Timothy Abraham Jacobson, the nickname; "Omaha Kid" would come many years later. He entered life at Brooklyn's Mount Sinai Jewish Hospital, one more infant crowding the hospital's maternity ward during the baby boom of the fifties.

Roberta and Larry Jacobson lived on Flatbush Avenue at the end of the elevated subway line in a small one-bedroom apartment when Timothy joined the family. The young family expected to find a bigger place as the baby and their savings grew.

Little Timmy, healthy and happy, displayed an enormous appetite. As an infant, about the only time he cried was when he was hungry and wanted to soak up more milk. By the time he was toddling, he drank milk in a 32 ounce Pepsi bottle with a nipple on top because he would throw a normal glass bottle against the wall from his crib smashing it and demanding "more milk!" His arm and his appetite were exceptional. The parents were more amused than worried about the demanding toddler.

With Timmy waddling around, the couple realized the apartment was way too small for the three of them. They had been struggling financially. Roberta was not working because the young boy needed her at home full-time. With the Korean War over, Larry had been laid off from his job at the VA hospital. He took some part time jobs but that barely covered their bills. They were running out of savings.

*

Beautiful and vivacious, nineteen- year- old, Roberta Corelli met the army veteran medic, Larry Jacobson, in a classroom. As they both started nursing school the two began dating. Soon they fell deeply in love. Roberta's family was conservative Italian-American Catholics. Larry's parents were Orthodox Jews. When she learned about her pregnancy, Roberta, despite trepidation told Larry. He was elated, immediately proposed marriage.

She threw her arms around him. "Oh, yes, yes, yes!" Her smile flew away; replaced by a worried look. "But what about our parents?"

Larry frowned shaking his head. "You deal with yours and I'll deal with mine."

*

"Son if you marry that girl you are dead to me and the rest of the family. You know Jewish law, no exceptions are allowed."

"Yea, I know Jewish law. It's a bunch of crap. Where was *our* God when Hitler killed millions of us in the concentration camps?"

"It is not for us to question his plan. Are you willing to give up your whole family and thousands of years of tradition for that… that Italian harlot?"

"Careful father you are talking about the women I love with all my heart."

"The woman you love is like Delilah in the bible and you are like Samson, the big war hero. Just because she is pregnant you don't have to marry her. Atone for your sins. Pay the dam girl. You'll see, give her enough money and she'll back off."

"You disgust me. I have not sinned. You're talking about a child conceived in love. This is the type of thinking I fought against during the war. Would you turn against your grandchild like the Nazi's turned against the Jews?

"Screw it. I'll make you happy. You never have to see me or that Italian girl, Roberta again. She will be my bride. We will have our child, your grandchild. Rip your garment, play your funeral game, pretend I'm dead. But I warning you, this will haunt you not me. Mark my words." Larry did an about-face, turned away from his father, family and heritage forever.

Roberta was saved the confrontation. Her furious family refused to even speak to her.

Still, Roberta was crazy in love with Larry and her unborn child. In spite of their families' open hostility, they eloped at city hall. As they boarded the train at Grand Central Station for their honeymoon in Niagara Falls, Larry told her, "We will make it on our own." She smiled, awash in his confidence.

*

The phone rang. Roberta answered, "One minute," she said, "It's long distance for you," and handed the phone to Larry. She listened to his side of the conversation with interest.

"That was my Army friend, Norm, I told you about. He's managing a clinic in Omaha, Nebraska. They need nurses and offered me a job. It's good money. Let's get away, forget our families."

"Yes, I know honey, but Omaha... Nebraska... can we get any further from civilization?"

"Hey I heard they have a sixteen-story skyscraper. Don't you know, Omaha's the new-New York."

The young mother looked at her boy. Tim's second birthday had been on February 10 and not one gift or even a card came from either family. Roberta's eyes fought back against the tears. She was tired of dealing with family prejudices, Catholic or Jewish. The boy needed a new start away from this nonsense. "Well, I guess we can't just stay here. Nebraska, really, that's somewhere west of New Jersey isn't it?"

Chapter 2 Omaha, Nebraska
August1957

Roberta drove the winding road along the Platte River. In the fields, ten-foot high cornstalks reached into the sky above the flat plains eliminating any view of the horizon. Roberta slowed down at each intersection to check the street signs. They came to the park near the edge of the river. She waddled over and found a comfortable place to rest on the grass, while her three-year-old son ran along the riverbank path. Feathery white wisps flew above their heads, seeds shedding from the cottonwood trees growing along the banks. When little Timmy had expended his energy, he came back and lay down next to his mother. Sweat poured off his forehead. It was a typically humid August day in Nebraska.

For a while they looked up at the sky and watched the cumulus clouds puff and rise into different shapes. "What do you see up there Timmy?" Roberta dreamily asked her son.

The boy pointed at a cloud and said, "That one looks like an elephant head."

The mother laughed and pointed, "Now that one looks like a giraffe with a long neck." After a pause she asked, "Timmy, do you know why mommy's tummy is so big?"

"Uh huh, you got a baby inside."

"Yes, sweetie, you're going to have a little brother or sister soon."

"Why?" Timmy asked.

Roberta smiled, "Because that'll make your mommy and daddy very happy."

"How come you're not just happy with me?"

"Mommy's very happy with you. I love you so very much and I always will. We just want another child to love also. When he or she grows up you will always have somebody to play with. Doesn't that sound like fun?"

The boy thought for a minute. "Okay."

"Thanks, that's very sweet of you. Now go play for a while before we go."

Timmy saw a man with a dog and ran towards them as fast as he could, tripped, fell forward and smashed his forehead on a rock. Blood streamed out of a gash just below his eyebrow. It spilled into his eye blinding him on one side and poured down on the front of his shirt. He screamed, rose, and finding his mother with his one good eye ran back to her. The pregnant nurse knew exactly what to do. She fished a handkerchief from her handbag and hugged the boy while pushing hard against the cut.

"It's alright honey. You're going to be fine." She kissed the top of his head while he continued to cry, hugging her, his body heaving.

Roberta came well prepared for this type of emergency and the handkerchief stopped the blood flow. She put three Band-Aids across the cut. Tim slowly ended his cry-and made kind of a cooing sound as he rested his head up against his mother's massive belly. Blood covered her green cotton dress. She didn't care. She felt needed and loved. She gave him a clean handkerchief and said, "Timmy, I need you to hold this tight against the cut. Can you do that?"

"I... I guess so," he said with his voice cracking.

"Mommy's very proud of you. Come on, let's get in the car and go home."

That day was one of the few Tim would remember from his Nebraska years. Just a week later, in the evening, Roberta went into labor. Larry drove her to the hospital where she gave birth to a healthy baby girl. Timmy, no longer the only child, gained a little sister, Linda.

Chapter 3 Omaha, Nebraska
November 1958

With harvest completed, fields of husks could be seen in every direction. Roberta and Larry drove home from a barbecue party at a friend's house out in the country. Susie, a teenager, who lived down the block, babysat for one-year-old Linda and four-year-old Timmy. The sun set, left a glow of orange above the stubbed fields behind them as they headed east on Highway 38.

Their 55 Chevy floated along the road, a workhorse serving as the family car for two years now. Its bench seat in front started to show some wear. In these days before seat belts and car seats, Timmy often sat in front next to the driver where mom or dad could keep an eye on him.

Larry driving behind the wheel said, "It's nice that you have reconciled with your family. I'm looking forward to meeting your brother Tony, Sophia and their kids."

"It will be sweet for Timmy to meet his cousins. I ordered a fresh turkey from the butcher. We can pick it up next week."

"Can you believe it's almost Thanksgiving already?"

Roberta said, "I know, time seems to be going so fast. May be we should go to
...LOOK OUT!"

A truck driver in the opposing lane had been blinded by the setting sun. He drifted right into the eastbound lane. The Jacobson's never had a chance to react. The two vehicles collided head on. Metal crashed and glass exploded. Roberta and Larry were killed in an instant, their bodies both thrown from the car. The blood from the two intermingled on the blacktop and ran down the highway. An ambulance came and the bodies were placed next to each other in the back, together one last time.

Chapter 4
Omaha, Nebraska   November 1958

A police car pulled up to the suburban house with the white picket fence just after dark. The officer rang the doorbell. Susie came to the door. She looked through the peephole to see the policeman. She immediately opened the door.

"Can I help you?" The teenager asked.

"Ma'am, can I ask who you are?" The officer asked calmly.

"My name is Susie, I'm the babysitter… is something wrong."

"Where are the children?"

"They're asleep."

"Maybe you should go get your parents. There's been an accident. I'll wait here."

Susie's eyes went wide. "Oh my God! Is everybody all right? Is anybody hurt?"

"I want you to go get your parents now," the policeman insisted.

The girl ran down the street. She came back with her mother and father.

"Officer, is something wrong?" Mr. Wrangle asked.

The policeman looked at Susie and nodded toward the father.

"Susie, maybe you should go home and wait for us."

The teenager looked frightened, but said, "Dad, I want to know what happened." The father nodded to the man in uniform.

"Sir, it is with my deepest sorrow to tell you that Mr. and Mrs. Jacobson have been killed in an accident."

Susie screamed.

Mrs. Wrangle said, "Oh Sweet Jesus!"

Timmy came out rubbing his eyes. The babysitter's father asked, "Susie, will you put him back in bed?"

Mrs. Wrangle said, "I'll do it. Susie you go home, we'll be there shortly.

The officer asked, "Do you know how to get a hold of the next of kin?"

"No, they're from New York. But I'll stay here and help you look if you'd like."

"That would be very helpful."

*

Mrs. Wrangle was there in the morning. She had a bottle fixed for little Linda when she woke up crying. Timmy came out of his bedroom looking for his mother and saw the neighbor with Linda in her arms.

"What are you doing here?" he asked, not remembering waking up during the night.

"Your mother and father had to go away for a while. I'll be staying with you today."

"Why?"

She ignored the question. "What do you want for breakfast?"

Timmy scratched his head with one hand and his butt with the other. His pajamas looked almost an inch too small. "I want my mommy!"

Sandra Wrangle looked at the little boy seeing tears emerging from his eyes, the nose sniffling, thinking this day is only going to get worse. "Would you feel better if your friend Susie comes over?" He nodded, lips pouting. She called home. "Susie, I'm going to need your help, come over as quickly as you can. I'll call the school."

*

During the day, relatives who had been notified about the tragedy started to arrive in Omaha. Tony, and Roberta's father Joey, were there first. Susie greeted them at the door. "Are you the Jacobson's?"

"No, I'm Roberta's brother, Tony…Tony Corelli. Thank you so much. Let me pay you."

"No, please I don't want any money. I'm so sorry."

He tried to hand her a twenty anyway.

She refused to take it. "No sir. Please, I couldn't." Susie got her jacket. "Our number is on the table. My Mom told me to tell you to call us if you need anything."

By that night Larry's side of the family had arrived, Larry's brother, Willy, his wife, May, and his parents. The two families greeted each other with civility, but the tension thickened. The young parents had left no will and a fight over everything ensued. What type of funeral would they have, Jewish or Catholic? How would the property be divided? Who was going to take the kids?

The first question was answered with the easiest solution. There would be a priest and a rabbi present, and the services would be held at a neighboring Protestant church, the minister being friends of the deceased. Larry was to be buried at a Jewish cemetery and Roberta laid to rest in a Catholic plot. No one seemed happy with this compromise. Each family had said that they should be buried together; but the religious doctrines of the local cemeteries would not allow this.

The division of the property in Omaha also was decided with a simple resolution. Everything would be sold and the profit would be divided between the two children to be put in trust until their eighteenth birthdays.

But who would take the children? Both families expressed a desire to keep both of the children. Heaven and hell played into contentious arguments. Voices were raised and lawsuits were threatened, but after two days of nasty haggling, they found a solution worthy of Solomon. Uncle Tony and Aunt Sophia would take Timmy home to Long Island. Linda would move in with Larry's brother's family, Uncle Willie and Aunt May in Connecticut.

Willie approached Tony. "What about visitation between Timmy and Linda. Do we want to get them together in the future?"

Tony thought about it for a few minutes. "Listen, I don't like you and you don't like me. These kids are so young; they won't even remember each other. So let's not prolong the agony. I say we let sleeping dogs lie and not kick over that can of worms."

Willie smiled at the mixed metaphors, but shook his head. "I don't agree. I think the kids should see each other." Tony looked like he was about to argue but Willie held up his hand. "Ok Tony I'm not going to fight over this. You think I'm a money hungry Jew and might sell Linda on the black market. My father implied that if Tim grew up with you he would be a Mafia gangster. I think we are all a little crazy. Let's agree to do the best we can for the kid we have."

"Amen, Willie. Go with God."

Willie couldn't resist. We are not going to bring God back in for this final negotiation are we? We may spend forty years in the desert."

Tony actually laughed for the first time in two days. The two men shook hands.

*

Tim would remember all the acrimony, even if he couldn't understand it. He would miss his sister later when he could barely remember her. As the two siblings boarded separate planes, Tim asked Uncle Tony if Linda could come to his birthday party.

"When is your birthday Timmy?"

"Next week, everybody knows that."

"So son we will have a party for you. Your cousins Junior and Maria will be there, won't that be fun?"

Timmy stated, "I want Linda, Daddy and Mommy all at the party!"

Uncle Tony looked at the boy and said sadly, "Your mommy and your daddy are dead. Do you know what that means?"

"Sure I know what it means. Mommy and Daddy can't be here but maybe they can come to New York. I still want them at the party."

Tony grabbed the boy's hand and gave it a loving squeeze. Tears streamed down the man's eyes.

Chapter 5   Lynbrook, New York
September, 1959

It was Timmy's first day of school. His first grade teacher was taking roll:

"Roger Agari?" "Here."

"Susan Borelli?" "Here."

"Lawrence Burton?" "Here."

"Timothy Corelli?" Silence. "Timothy Corelli?" Again no answer. "Is Timothy Corelli here?" The teacher tried one more time.

"My name is Timothy Jacobson."

His teacher, Mrs. Benden looked at her roll sheet again. There was no Timothy Jacobson on it.

"Timothy, do you know why my roll sheet says Timothy Corelli?"

"I live with my Uncle Tony and Aunt Sophia, they're the Corelli's. I'm a Jacobson."

"Where are your parents?"

"They are in Omaha, Nebraska."

"They live in Nebraska?"

"No ma'am, they are dead in Nebraska."

The teacher looked at the boy quizzically for a second. Then a look of understanding came to her face. She made a note on her roll sheet.

"Okay Timothy, I have you down as Corelli-Jacobson. Is that okay with you?"

"Okay, I guess so."

Mrs. Benden continued. "Kathryn Carson?"

*

The Corelli's lived in an impressive four bedroom colonial just south of Sunrise Highway. The neighborhood was populated by mostly nouveau riche Italian and Irish Americans. It was the Twentieth Century American dream, suburban living, just a half-hour commute to New York City on the Long Island Railroad.

Tim thought that it was okay living with Aunt Sophia and Uncle Tony, but he felt like he didn't quite belong. He missed his mom and dad, and his sister, Linda. Most of the time, he liked having a new brother that was almost his age. Tony Jr. and he played together all summer with lots of other kids from the neighborhood. They played stickball, Johnny on the pony, hoops, football and other games with any of the local kids that showed up at the school yard. Tim liked the eight-year-old, Maria. She showed him how to sneak through the neighbors backyard for a short cut to the school yard. Aunt Sophia ran the household completely. She had lot of strict rules he didn't like, but she was nice enough to him. The thing he liked least was he had to dress up on Sunday and go to church.

*

At recess that first day of school, Lonnie Libert, a big blond classmate, came up to him and teasingly said. "You're an orphan. You're an orphan."

Tim did not know what that meant, but he knew he didn't like it. "I'm not!"

"Are too."

"Take that back!"

"No! You're an orphan, so there," Lonnie stuck out his tongue.

Tim surprised the bigger boy and pushed him as hard as he could. Lonnie went flying backwards and got up making fists with his hands. He took a swing and Tim quickly ducked. The two boys wrestled to the ground. Many kids gathered around yelling and encouraging the fight.

Mrs. Benden came running up. "Stop this at once!" She got between the two boys with her arms out. They each retreated a step.

Lonnie said, "he started it."

"No, he did. He called me a bad word."

Mrs. Benden got between them. "Lonnie, what did you say?"

The taller boy just shrugged his shoulders.

"He called me an orphan,"

The teacher asked Tim, "Do you know what that word means Tim?"

"No."

"It's not a bad word. It means that your parents have died. That's not something to be ashamed of. Lonnie, you apologize."

"Do I have to?"

"Yes, unless you want to go see the principal."

"Sorry Timmy,"

"Okay, boys I don't want any more of this nonsense. You shake hands."

Both boys looked down at the ground, ashamed of their behavior in front of the teacher on the first day of school. The boys reluctantly shook hands. Lonnie said to Tim, "I really am sorry. Tell you what, I'll race you to the backstop."

"Okay, ready go."

The two boys took off. The teacher smiled and shook her head. To Lonnie's amazement Tim beat him by ten yards.

"Wow, Timmy you're really fast. I was the fastest kid in kindergarten last year."

Tim smiled. "Cool."

Chapter 6 Lynbrook, New York
November, 1963

A beautiful Indian summer day and 10-year-old Timmy beckoned but school kept him stuck indoors, in the classroom working on math problems. He looked out the window wanting to be in the sunshine playing ball. The clock on the wall didn't want to move. He daydreamed about playing Little League that summer. He played shortstop and proved to be team's best hitter. Line drives smacked off his bat all season long. After the last game all the kids got together for awards, and home run king, Roger Maris, showed up to sign autographs.

The bored boy looked back at his math book. "If a cookie cost $.37 how much change will you get if you paid five dollars?" He was writing down five dollars minus $.37 when an older student walked into the classroom and whispered something to his fourth grade teacher, Mrs. Levy. "Oh my God! The woman stood up. " Class listen closely. I have an announcement to make. President Kennedy has been shot. We are going to let school out early at two o'clock. Your parents will be notified. Go ahead and put your books away."

Becky O'Brien raised her hand. Mrs. Levy, a 33-year-old mother of two, was fighting back tears. "Yes Becky."

"Is... is he dead?"

"I don't know. I've told you everything that I know at this point." She had almost shouted at the child. "Sorry, Becky…I'm… just sorry." She took out a tissue and dabbed at her eyes smudging her make up. Mrs. Levy stood up. "Let's all sing a song." She started clapping her hands, getting the students clapping at their seats. The teacher started singing. The class followed her lead.

"This land is your land. This land is my land. From California to the New York Island…"

Tim tried to sing but his mind raced. Time seemed to stand still and he fought back tears. Some girls were crying but he was a boy. Boys don't cry. He didn't even remember crying when his parents died. Two o'clock couldn't come fast enough.

*

Tim didn't know anything about politics, but he knew about President Kennedy. There were kids like him living in the White House. As he walked home, he became more uncomfortable. The day seemed unreal reminding him of that night in Omaha, when his dreams were interrupted. It was a night he couldn't quite remember, but would never forget, the night he became an orphan. When Timmy got home, he went to his room, lay on his bed, and cried. He had not seen his sister Linda or his father's side of the family since they left Omaha. Uncle Tony and Aunt Sophia had adopted him, when he was seven, making him officially a Corelli. At some level, Kennedy's death represented the death of his father. More than he grieved for the President, he grieved for the loss of his parents. Mom, Dad, where are you, he thought, I need you so much.

That evening the family gathered in the living room watching the events of the day on television. They were devastated. Kennedy was the first Catholic president. The Corelli's identified with the young First Family. Maria had tears in her eyes as she watched Walter Cronkite show pictures and film reals of young Caroline and John-John.

Tim asked, "Uncle Tony, what happens now?"

"Lyndon Johnson is the new president."

"Does that mean that Jackie and the kids have to leave the White House?"

"Yes, of course."

"Well, that's just too bad." Tim recalled the day he had to leave his white house in Omaha. He watched the TV coverage for a little while longer, then excused himself and went up to his room. Tears streamed down his face. Wiping it with his sleeves, he got his baseball glove, and lay back on his bed. He played catch, throwing the ball up in the air then snagging it over and over. He looked at his poster of Mickey Mantle on the wall and said, "It's going to be a long winter, Mickey."

Chapter 7 Lynbrook, New York
April, 1966

The Yankees and the Mets played each other down in Florida. Uncle Tony promised to take Junior and Tim to Opening Day for the Mets at Shea Stadium. For the baseball crazy 12-year old kid from Omaha, spring stood as his favorite time of the year. Next week he would play in his first little league game of the year. Last year he showed everyone what an amazing hitter he could be and won an award as his team's best player.

So why did he have the blues? Easter Sunday arrived and Tim looked in the mirror to see a boy dressed in the most uncomfortable, itchy wool suit ever made instead of his baseball uniform. Aunt Sophia put Brill Cream in his hair and slicked it back, turning his black comb white with grease. Tim hated going to church. It was Aunt Sophia's favorite thing in the whole world. She wanted Tim to go every Sunday. She told her adopted son that his belief in the Catholic Church was the only way a half Jewish boy could find redemption. The more she preached to him the more he resented it. Tony was fine with him calling him Uncle Tony instead of Dad. Why did she insist that he call her Mom? She wasn't really his mother.

Maria didn't like church either. Tim felt close to his older cousin. She acted like she really was his big sister, coming into his room at night and reading sports stories to him.

When Aunt Sophia went up for confession Maria whispered, "Let's go."

Tim and Maria snuck out of the church. They ran to the pizza parlor and Maria bought Tim a strawberry Italian ice with money she had made babysitting. He wolfed it down causing an instant "ice cream" headache but it was a small price to pay. The two ran back and tried to sneak back into the church before they were missed, but Maria's mother caught them.

When they got home Aunt Sophia sent Tim to his room "No baseball today." He pouted as he stomped up the stairs. His aunt infuriated, screamed at the boy, "You little Jewish idiot, do as I say of your going straight to Hell! Is that what you want?"

How come his aunt's wrath always rained on him? Didn't Maria sneak out with him? She was a good girl before *you* came into this house. He knew his aunt would say.

He suffered in silence afraid to rock the boat any further. He really wanted to fit in somehow. But how could he be a good Catholic boy and accept that... woman as his mother? It just wouldn't be right, like he was forgetting both his parents. Besides, she's nothing like my Mother. My mother loved me! He tried to remember his mother but her face faded through his tears. Darn it, Darn it, Darn it! No one heard his silent screams.

Chapter 8 Adirondack Summer Camp
Lake George, New York Summer 1968

Rhonda Pastrovinsky's body was changing. She was reaching puberty, developing curves, going from an awkward tomboy to a pretty young woman. The Polish-American girl, who was always teased and treated badly by the popular girls at junior high, was now attractive. Boys began to look at her differently and she liked the attention. Here at camp, all the other girls wanted to be her friend.

Carol Simon, her bunk mate, said, "I think Tim Corelli's cute. Don't you?"

"I haven't noticed." Rhonda said as she brushed her sandy brown hair. In fact, Rhonda had noticed him looking at her, and when she looked at him he would quickly turn away. They had played this game a lot in the last few weeks, he trying to act like he wasn't looking at her.

"He won the camp tennis tournament and is so cute. I think he likes you," Carol stated.

"What makes you think so?

"Gloria said that Roger told her that Tim told him he likes you."

Rhonda shrugged her shoulders. "Oh well, there's just two weeks of camp left. So what if he likes me." Rhonda did like him but had no clue how to react to this news.

The Adirondack Summer Camp was located in upstate New York near the Vermont border. It was a summer haven for mostly suburban New York and New Jersey adolescents. The beautiful setting in the forested mountains by a large lake became the boys' and girls' natural playground. They could swim, canoe, play games and do all types of arts and crafts. Some could even plot their first romances. Large cabins provided dorms for the kids. Like aged girls were placed in the same cabin. Boys were grouped the same way on the other side of the mess hall.

*

The next day Rhonda decided to confront Tim. After breakfast she noticed him glancing over and walked up to him and said, "Hey Timmy, what's the deal? Why are you looking at me?"

"What do you mean?" he said, trying to be cool.

"Meet me in the trees behind the canoe dock in one hour."

"But I'm supposed to play tennis," Tim replied, as he noticed his palms-sweating and his heart starting to race.

"I've heard love is supposed to mean nothing in tennis," she said with a laugh, surprising herself with her wit. She walked away and could feel her confidence growing. Tim watched her go, his mouth agape.

*

Fourteen-year-old Tim was very comfortable on a ball field or a tennis court, but he didn't know how to deal with a pretty girl, especially *this* girl that he had spent the whole summer trying not to have her notice him sneaking glances.

He walked down the path into the forest above the canoe dock. The birch trees were in full maturity, white bark with green leaves hanging in bunches. Bees moved throughout the fertile flowers sucking the sweet nectar, summer in full bloomed. He came upon the object of his obsession, Rhonda, who he noticed was wearing pink shorts, her long legs ending with sockless tennis shoes. Her light blue tee shirt matched her eyes. His mouth went dry.

"Hi Tim," she said with a smile on her face.

"Hi Rhonda. Why did you want me to meet you?" He heard himself saying.

"Someone said that you like me."

"I… maybe… yeah… I mean I think I might." He felt her staring right through him.

"Do you want to kiss me?"

"Sure."

Tim closed his eyes and leaned forward. Rhonda stepped forward and kissed him lightly on the lips. He could feel the hair on the back of his neck standing up. Tim would always remember that first kiss fondly.

"What are you thinking?" Rhonda asked the boy.

"I'm not sure. Maybe we should try that again."

They kissed again, trying too hard, pressing too hard. Their lips just stuck together. "How is that?" Timmy asked.

"Maybe one more time, this time softer."

Their heads moved together slowly, lips joining softly, kissing and then kissing more. "I think we got it right that time." The nervous girl said giggling.

In the next two weeks, they would sneak off and kiss. It was puppy love. Timmy felt so wonderful, so horrible and so unsatisfied.

When camp ended, their parents showed up to take them home. They could not even kiss goodbye. As they drove south in separate cars, going their separate ways, Rhonda cried and Tim smiled.

Chapter 9 Lynbrook, New York
Autumn and Winter 1968

Tim realized that being a freshman boy in high school was like being the runt of a litter. Passing classes was the easy part. Finding a social niche was much more difficult. The freshman girls ignored him. They wanted to go out with older boys. He felt lucky if the older boys just ignored him. He watched as his friend Dick Howard got thrown in a trashcan by a couple of marauding seniors. Each day's Darwinian survival was a hunt to fit in or just not piss off a "bigger dog."

His biggest nightmare as a male freshman could be found in the boy's locker room. It had a smell he could never forget, a mixture of urine, sweat, some strange green peppermint shower soap and heat liniment. Tim had not grown for almost a year. Entering high school he was a little guy at five feet, four inches and 115 pounds. This lack of growth included the rest of his anatomy. As he stood in front of his P.E. locker, he realized he would have to take off his clothes in front of other guys. He could not remember being naked in front of anybody. The young athlete was not alone in his embarrassment. He felt really bad for another unfortunate freshman friend, Andy O'Riley, who took off his underwear in the locker room and having sat too close to a girl the period earlier was still partially aroused. Andy's nickname the rest of high school was "Boner." Please don't let this happen to me, he thought.

Tim found his refuge in sports. Too small for football, he decided to go out for tennis. Even without lessons he had been the winner of the summer camp tournament.

The novice found that tennis had many skills he could borrow from baseball. Hitting to the right side of the court to a righty's backhand was like hitting a pitch to right field. Hitting crosscourt was like pulling the ball down the line. The serve shared many properties with an overhand fastball. His natural speed and quickness allowed him to chase down balls which would be winners against a slower opponent. His weakness, especially against a bigger player, was his backhand. He could hit a natural slice to keep the ball in play, but to make it a powerful weapon he needed good lessons with someone who knew how to develop his natural talent.

Unfortunately for Tim, Mr. Schultz, the tennis coach was not the man to teach him the nuances of the game. The P.E. teacher just played occasionally with his friends. He took the job only because no one else volunteered. Not a major motivator or instructor, the coach left the boys to their own resources.

In spite of this lack of leadership Tim, as a freshman, was good enough to make the varsity team. He played number three singles and earned an impressive record of four wins and three losses against older, more experienced players.

*

"You know that right now you're the only freshman with a varsity jacket. While I was slaving away on the freshman football team, you were just out playing that sissy game," Lonnie complained to his friend as they walked home after school.

"You're just jealous," Tim replied.

"Damn straight!"

"Well, wait a couple of years and you'll get yours."

"Okay, fine, you SOB. I might just take yours now."

"Yeah, try and catch me," Tim said as he darted down the road.

Lonnie chased him for about half a block, and then stopped. He knew he could not catch Tim. "Okay, I give up. Keep your damned jacket."

Tim slowed down and Lonnie jogged up to him. "What are you doing for a winter sport?"

"I don't think basketball's a good idea unless I grow over the holidays."

Lonnie said, "I'm going out for the wrestling team. They were good last year."

"What do you know about wrestling?"

"They teach you. Why don't you try it with me? We could slam people out there."

"Yeah Lonnie, it looks fun on TV, but high school wrestling is hard and it's not fake."

"What would we have to lose?"

"How 'bout my head? Okay, I'll try it if you want to."

*

The sycamore and crabapple trees stood naked in front of Lynbrook High School. A thin layer of snow had fallen overnight as they walked to the first practice on a late November Saturday morning. In the locker room, they changed into their wrestling tights and covered them in sweats.

Coach Magley addressed the group. "Listen, nobody gets cut. If you're willing to do the work, I'll teach you the moves. This sport is not easy. If you're lucky enough to get into a match, you'll think that it's the longest six minutes of your life. There's the door, if you want to leave go now. Otherwise, let's get to work." He paired the kids off by weight class and started them exercising in ways not familiar to Tim. The 32-year-old coach went around the room watching the boys and talking to the new kids individually.

"Corelli, have you ever wrestled before?"

"Just my brother."

"That's not the same. I heard you're a good athlete. Stick with it and you'll learn a lot."

A month later, Tim found himself alone, faced off against a wrestler from Hewlett High School. It was a junior varsity match, but Tim was more nervous than before his varsity tennis matches. His mouth was dry and he could feel his body shaking. He closed his eyes and took a deep breath trying to calm his nerves. The wrestlers shook hands and the referee said, "Ready, wrestle."

The Hewlett boy shot in for a double leg takedown. Tim countered, throwing his legs back and grappling the boy's arm. He used all his strength, pushing the boy's head down while he applied a half nelson to turn his opponent onto his back.

"Pin him, Omaha!" Lonnie shouted from the bench.

The referee slapped his hand down on the mat. Tim had done it. He pinned his opponent in less then a minute. The wrestlers shook hands again and Tim turned, pumping his fist into the air.

The coach turned to Lonnie and asked, "What's this Omaha stuff?"

Lonnie shrugged his shoulders and turned his hands face up. "I thought our boy needed a good wrestling nickname. He used to live in Omaha, Nebraska so I'm going to call him *The Omaha Kid.*"

The nickname stuck. Throughout the rest of high school the other kids called Tim, "Omaha," short for the Omaha Kid.

Chapter 10   Lynbrook, New York
March 1970

Kristy Cullen wasn't just "in with the in-crowd." She headed the list of the in-crowd. The tall blonde senior cheerleader and teen tennis club champion exuded confidence. Already accepted to Radcliffe College, she dared to date a boy younger than her, a junior. But this boy was not just any junior. Tim Jacobson was the star quarterback for the Lynbrook High School football team.

*

They had met a year earlier, at the country club. Kristy had been looking for someone to play tennis with her after her lesson, and Tim practiced serves on the next court. He grunted and pounded another ball hard off the court and it smashed hard against the back fence. Kristy's peaked over.

She shouted to him, "I know you. You're on the baseball team at Lynbrook High."

"Yeah, I play shortstop." He had seen the attractive girl in the lunchroom but they had never met. As a sophomore, he was in the middle of a growing spurt and had reached six feet, 160 pounds.

"Do you want to hit some balls with me? I need a partner," Kristy asked.

"Sure, why not." He couldn't help notice her long legs under the short tennis skirt. Being new to the club, he had never seen her play tennis. She whacked a forehand to his backhand and he returned it with a wicked slice. She smashed a two-handed backhand with topspin to send the ball down the line to his forehand. Surprised, he used his speed to run down the ball and sent a forehand cross court right back to her. They sparred back and forth, she a year older and better trained. He was a natural athlete, with more power on his forehand side. After rallying for a while, they took a break to get some water.

"Why do you slice all your backhands?" Kristy asked, using a towel to dab the perspiration off her pretty face.

"I don't know. I guess that's the only way I know how to hit it. The shot just came naturally. It's worked well for me. I usually win my matches at school."

"Do you know how much better you would be if you could hit a topspin backhand to mix it up with your natural slice?"

He thought about it. He had a hard time hitting a passing shot if an opponent came to the net and hit to his backhand. "I've never really had lessons."

The girl said with confidence, "I'd be happy to teach you. After all you're going to play tennis next fall for Lynbrook."

"Actually, I'm thinking of going out for football next year."

Kristy said with her best cheerleader smile, "well that's even better. In the meantime do you want to learn a topspin backhand?"

He looked shyly at the beautiful girl in front of him. "Sure, that would be groovy."

They worked together on his backhand and hit balls often. Both players got better. A friendship ensued.

*

Tim went out for the football team that fall and when Head Coach Bellingham saw him throwing the ball to Lonnie running patterns, he said to his assistant. "Where did that kid come from? He's got a cannon for an arm."

"He said he played tennis last year and grew a lot. The boy can run too." Mr. Martin, the assistant coach said reading off his notes on a clipboard.

"Well we need a quarterback, Cummings graduated last year and is off playing for Maryland. Let's try this kid out and see what he can do. HEY CORELLI COME OVER HERE."

*

Tim earned the starting job going both ways, playing quarterback and safety. With Tim's scrambling ability and accurate passes, Lynbrook won ten games and only lost two his first year playing football. The kid was a natural at just about any sport he played.

After a win on the road at Elmont High, the football team and cheerleaders were riding the school bus back to Lynbrook. Kristi said to Tim, "Hey why don't we go out and celebrate. Maybe go to Long Beach and get something to eat."

"Just you and me?" He asked giving his tennis buddy a funny look. She had on her cheerleader outfit, actually holding her pom-poms. He was holding his helmet on his lap.

"Yeah, unless you want some others to come along."

"Kristi, are you asking me out?"

"Don't you think it's about time?"

He was surprised. Tim never thought to ask her out even though he thought she was beautiful and he really liked her. He was a junior and she a senior. It just wasn't done. "Okay, sure."

"Good," She said. "We'll take my Firebird, I'll pick you up at seven."

*

Their first dinner together wasn't fancy. They had pizza and cokes at Nathan's, the supersized "drive in" restaurant in Oceanside, which had a variety of food and attracted teens from all over the south shore of Long Island. Then the two drove to the beach and walked hand-in-hand along the boardwalk. The full moon glowed over the Atlantic. She shivered from the late evening ocean breeze. He snuggled with her, sharing his warmth. She stopped and turned to face him. Her blue eyes said "kiss me" and he did. She kissed back and then bit his lower lip, playfully teasing Tim, driving him crazy.

*

They sat together in the lunchroom conspiring. It was Friday night and her parents were going to dinner and a play in the city. "You're coming over tonight, right?"

"What time?"

"My parents will leave about seven. They're taking the train to Manhattan. They shouldn't be back until late." Kristy smiled suggestively.

"Okay, I'll be there about seven thirty." He couldn't wait to get her home alone.

"Perfect," she said and walked off shaking her hips, almost doing a dance.

*

Kristi met him at the door. She was wearing a sheer white blouse tucked into a black pleated miniskirt. He could see a frilly black bra showing underneath her top. Her bare feet showed her red painted toenails.

"God, you look good!" he said.

She giggled and produced a hand-rolled joint of marijuana. Worried about his standing on his school sports teams, he only got high with her, a private little secret.

He produced a small bottle of rum. "I hope you have some Coca-Cola."

Kristi turned on the TV, playing a movie he wouldn't remember. Then they turned to each other, smoking the joint, and sipping the rum and cokes. They started kissing tenderly at first, the passion building as she fell back on the living room couch. He started to fumble with the buttons on her blouse and she stopped him, stood up and undid the rest of her buttons, letting the blouse fall behind her onto the floor. She looked at him deeply with the pools of her blue eyes then seductively reached behind her and undid her fancy lace bra. He went to reach for her perfect breasts but she stopped him. He was surprised. They had gone this far before.

In silence, Kristy took his hand and led Tim up to her room, a place he had never been. She took off her skirt, revealing black underwear that had matched her discarded bra. She lit a candle and turned off the lights.

"Undress," Kristy whispered and pulled a Trojan out of her nightstand. His passion that had waited a thousand kisses exploded in bliss. After making love too quickly, they let their hands explore each other's moist bodies leaving goose-bumps in the wake of skin touching skin.

"That wasn't your first time," he said, not sure if he was making a statement or asking a question.

"No, you remember I dated David Taylor last year. We did it once, but it wasn't… well… like with you. This was special." She snuggled close, her head next to his ear. "Was that your first time?"

The junior didn't know if he should admit the truth, not wanting her to think he was immature, but finally he confessed, "Yes Kristi, you are my first."

She smiled and looked into his eyes. He saw pure love. Kristy kissed him again with a powerful passion, then playfully bit his lower lip and giggled. "Think you could go again babe?" She asked with a husky voice, reaching for him.

Just then they heard the front door open. Her father yelled, "Kristi, are you home?"

"Oh my God… my bra and blouse! They're in the living room… We left the TV on!" Kristy jumped up in a panic. The two scurried to get on some clothes as they heard footsteps ascending the stairs.

The door opened and Mr. Cullen stood there menacingly holding out a black see-through bra. "Young man, I think you should leave!"

Chapter 11 Lynbrook, New York
June, 1971

Dressed in a cap and gown, the Omaha Kid waited by the side of the stage. He straightened his tie. The principal announced, "Timothy Jacobson-Corelli." Tim raised his hands above his head as he walked up onto the stage. He shook the hand of the superintendent and received his diploma. A loud cheer rang out from the crowd. His Uncle Tony and Aunt Sofia were conspicuous in their absence. His cousins, Maria and Tony Junior, were in attendance. The siblings made sure they didn't miss their adopted brother's high school graduation. After John Zimmerman, the last graduate to receive his certificate was called, the administrator said, "I proudly present to you the Lynbrook High School Class of 1971."

"Where should we go to dinner?" Maria asked, after giving Tim a big hug.

"Well obviously not Dad's," Junior said. "How about Mesettti's?"

"That would be great," Tim said. "I'll meet you there with Sarah."

*

It had been a tumultuous year since the incident with Kristi. When she didn't show up for school on the Monday after the weekend they were found in the bedroom, he wondered how to get in touch with his girlfriend. He certainly couldn't call the house.   On Tuesday, Kristy still did not show up for her classes and Tim sought out her best friend, Lisa Moroney.

"I have a note for you," Lisa said with a frown on her face. She handed him a letter like it was contagious.

"Do you know where she is?"

"It's all in there."

The envelope was sealed with lipstick in the shape of lips on the back flap. He tore it open and read:

My dearest Timothy,

One last kiss, that's all I can give to you. I'm being sent away to a private school near Boston. I would be leaving for college next year anyway, but I will miss you greatly. Don't try to get in touch with me, at least not for now. I can't go against my parent's wishes. I'm not that brave. We don't really want to end up like Romeo and Juliet, do we? We never got a chance to say we loved each other, so I'll say it now. I love you.

With all my love,
Kristy

*

When word of his indiscretion reached his aunt, she was appalled. She screamed at Tim. "How can I face the girl's parents at church? I am so disgusted with you. You are an evil worthless son of a Jew. You need to go to confession for what you did to that girl."

"What I did? Aunt Sofia I did nothing wrong. We were in love."

"Sex out of wedlock is a sin. You know that. I've brought you up to be a good Catholic boy. Just because your dead mother didn't care about her soul and got pregnant with you doesn't mean you can sin. Hell fire awaits those who are unrepentant."

"You've got to be kidding me! Haven't you heard that there's a sexual revolution going on? Nobody my age believes that sex is a sin. What I did with Kristi was beautiful." He had raised his voice level. Tim was angry, upset about losing his girlfriend. And what the hell was she saying about the sins of his mother. He was in no mood to be lectured by this...this *guardian*. Who did she think she was telling him what to do! She wasn't his real mother...my real mother loved me! Adolescent rebellion kicked in full throttle. He thought about bringing up what he heard about his cousin, Maria, in college, but he didn't want her to get in trouble.

"Young man this is not acceptable behavior in our household. You will go to church with me, confess, and do your penance!"

"Hell no!" he said defiantly

The woman appeared outraged. She yelled, "Maybe you won't be allowed to play football in the fall so you won't meet cheerleader sluts. Go to your room!"

Tim went to his room, very angry. He took out his new Sports Illustrated and tried to read but was far too upset to concentrate on the pages. He loved Kristy, like his mother, father and sister. Now they were all gone. What good was it to love someone, damn it. He hurt deep inside his gut. Tears flowed. He wanted to scream but what good would it do?

His uncle came home and he heard his adopted parents talking downstairs, but he couldn't hear the words. Tony Senior came up and knocked on Tim's door.

"Come in."

Uncle Tony stood over him as Tim looked up from his bed. "Son, you need to make this right. Your aunt is very upset. I know how young boys are, what happened is not that big a deal. Go to church and confess, make your Aunt Sofia happy."

Timothy looked at him defiantly. "It may not be a big deal to you, but it is to me. I love that girl. This confession stuff is bullshit! I won't do it."

"In that case, you're not playing football in the fall."

"You know that could keep me from winning a scholarship."

"Well then, the answer is simple, go to confession."

"Maybe, I should go live with my Uncle Willie, Aunt May and my sister."

It was Tony's turn to be angry. "Why you ungrateful little snot! We haven't heard from them in years. I've heard they moved to California, so good luck finding them. Besides, if you won't go to confession just try their crazy religion."

"So, now you're an anti-Semite like Aunt Sophia. No wonder you haven't heard from them!"

"You know me better than that." Yet Tim could tell his words about anti-Semitism strung and he knew he hit too close to the truth.

*

Discomfort descended on the house. Tim spent as little time as possible at home over the summer. He played tennis, went to the beach and stayed out late, hanging out with his friends, avoiding his aunt and uncle. When the vacation ended, everybody at school was amazed when the star quarterback did not show up for football practice. The coach tried to talk to him at school, but Tim told him he just didn't want to play football.

In October a letter arrived from Kristy

Dear Tim,
You will always be my first true love but it is time for us to move on. I have a new boyfriend in college. He's nice. You would like him. I hear you're not playing football and I'm disappointed. I would be sad to think that I had anything to do with that. Be true to yourself. Live life to its fullest.

> Yours with love,
> Kristy

It seemed like a weight had been taken off his back. His guilt dissolved. He felt free for the first time in quite a while. That night he told his aunt that he would go to church with her and make confession. On Sunday the family, with the exception of Maria who was away at college, all dressed up and went to church.

Tim missed her greatly. If she had been here maybe it would have all been different. When it was his turn, Tim entered the confession box.

"Father, what I say to you cannot be repeated to anyone, right?"

"That is correct my son."

"Forgive me father for I have sinned. It has been two years since I have made a confession."

"What do you have to confess?"

"I have trouble believing in all this hokus pocus."

"That is normal. Even the Saints had their doubts."

"Well, I'm certainly no saint."

"So, what else would you like to confess my son?"

"Nothing really."

"That's all right. Look into your heart and see if you find your faith. If you do, I will be here."

"Thank you, father."

He left the confession box and came back to sit down with his adopted family. He smiled at his aunt and uncle. The next day he went out to football practice. Lynbrook had lost two of their three first games, but with their star player back they only lost one of their last six.

*

In February, Tim turned eighteen. He registered to vote as Timothy Jacobson, not Corelli. Being in a rebellious mood he made sure his aunt and uncle knew about it. He also started dating a Jewish girl from Hewlett. Sarah Freeman who was totally different from Kristi Cullen. She was tiny, at just five feet and weighing 95 pounds. He had met her while out with his friends at the Oceanside Nathan's after a Friday night high school basketball game. She had short dark brown hair and the only makeup on her pretty face was red lipstick. She wore a bright paisley minidress and knee-high boots. Sarah was waiting to get some French fries in front of him and he was holding one of Nathan's famous hot dogs.

The petite high school junior turned and looked at Tim's dietary choice. "You're not really going to eat that thing. Do you know what they put in a hot dog?"

"I don't think I want to know, but I like 'em."

She giggled. "You're kind of cute in a dumb jock sort of way," Sara said with an amused look on her face.

"Is that supposed to be a compliment?"

"Absolutely, I'll even let you sit with me if you buy me some French fries. I've got the munchies." She looked up at him, a sweet smile on her face.

Tim looked into her dark brown eyes. Her pupils were dilated and the whites were almost as red as her lipstick. "Oh my God! You're stoned, aren't you?"

"She giggled again. "Wow, you're smart for a dumb jock."

"What makes you think I'm a jock?"

"Are you kidding me with your short hair, those biceps and that body?"

"Okay you sweet talker, the fries are on me. I'll even buy you a coke."

"Nope, I never drink soda or eat meat. It's bad for you. But you can buy me an orange juice."

"Tell you what. I buy it for you if you let me have a hit of what you've been smoking."

She looked intrigued. "I'm surprised you're interested, wouldn't think you're the type. You have a car here?"

"No. I'm with friends."

"I have my daddy's Mercury out back in the lot. Let's blow this joint and go smoke one after we get our food."

"Okay, let me stop and tell my friends. Where do you want to go?"

"Long Beach, maybe we can watch the submarines racing."

They smoked the joint in the car and turned the music up loud. She played her Grateful Dead cassette tape and her head bobbed in rhythm. Tim was not used to being stoned and he giggled.

"What are you laughing at?"

"Just laughing, you're funny. He went to kiss her and she let him.

She smiled and one eyebrow rose slightly. "You know what Jocko, I'm curious about you. You really aren't the kind of guy I usually go out with, but there is something…It's like you have this quiet inner rebellion like James Dean in the movies. Yeah, I like it."

They kissed again and Sara tickled the upper part of his mouth with her tongue. "Will you go to the city with me tomorrow to see some artwork?"

"I have wrestling practice tomorrow, but I'll go Sunday." Tim was having a good time, this girl was fun.

"It's a date, Jocko. Then, maybe you can teach me to wrestle." Sara giggled some more.

They dated for the rest of the year.

*

In the spring after batting .452 and hitting 12 home runs at the cleanup spot for Lynbrook High School baseball team, Tim was offered a full athletic scholarship to the University of Miami for baseball and Penn State for football. He was also drafted in the third round by the Oakland Athletics and offered a $50,000 bonus to sign. Uncle Tony and Aunt Sophia wanted him to take one of the scholarships, so of course he signed with Oakland. His aunt and uncle were still angry with him and his resentment could barely be contained. The three barely spoke. He didn't bother to invite them to his high school graduation and they didn't bother to come.

*

After the graduation ceremony Tim and Sarah walked hand-in-hand to her dad's Mercury Cougar. He zipped out of the gown and placed it with the funny square hat in the trunk.

"You are going to let me drive tonight. After all it was my graduation."

"No way, my Dad would kill me."

"And you would never do anything your dad wouldn't allow, like going to Manhattan for the Grateful Dead concert two weeks ago. Then you dropped LSD while you were there, so I had to watch you to make sure you didn't get lost and couldn't find your way home."

"Yeah, I would never do anything like that. Okay, you drive." She threw him the keys.

He was happy to have the opportunity. He had his license but his problems with his adopted family left him with no car to drive. They cruised down Peninsula Boulevard towards the Italian restaurant. Tim glanced at the Sara and saw her face wearing a frown.

"What's the matter? Smile, this is supposed to be a happy occasion."

"It's just with your graduation… I'm realizing that you will be leaving soon."

"You know what the song says, 'live for today.'" One side of her face lifted up in a smile. "That's better," he said. "By the way, will you take me to the airport when I go?"

"Of course, I will take you. Do you know where you're going yet?"

"No, but I should find out in about a week."

"You know what? After dinner let's go down to the beach and stay out all night," she suggested.

"Okay cutie. I'm game if you are." Tim was happy to spend one of his last nights on the Island with this wonderful nymph and not in the now uncomfortable house in Lynbrook.

Chapter 12 Modesto, California
Summer 1972

It was Tim's first professional at bat, in the second inning of a game against the Stockton Ports. Tim dug in the batter box, took a practice swing and let out a deep breath. It's just like high school, no reason to be nervous, he told himself. Tim saw the first pitch, expecting a fastball. He swung, but the ball bit down and away, a nasty slider and the bat missed it by a foot.

"Strike," the umpire grunted. Tim stepped out of the box, took another deep breath, stepped back in and stared intently at the pitcher. He thought, okay, look fastball and adjust. I can hit this guy. He's got nothing.

The righty went into the stretch, checked the runner and fired. The pitch exploded high and hard. The bat hit the underside of the ball and it flew, spinning towards the left field bleachers. Three hundred and fifty feet later the ball smashed into the aluminum bleachers, took one bounce, and found the glove of a young fan. Tim took a hop step away from the plate, and tossed his bat aside. He knew the ball was gone the moment he connected.

"Way to go Tim," the third-base coach said as he slapped him a high five as he came around the diamond and headed for home.

Tim continued to play well, smacking three singles, stealing a base and scoring two more times. In the ninth, he took the field with his team up by one run. The first hitter sent a searing line drive down the third base line. Tim dove to his right snagging the ball saving what would have been a sure double. The next batter hit a line drive to his left. He dove again, finding the edge if the ball peeking white out of the web of his glove, like an vanilla ice cream cone. Two outs and the crowd stood and cheered. The pitcher worked the count to two and two. He went into the wind-up and threw a fastball on the inside corner. Crack! The ball smacked off the bat coming right at Tim. All he could do was raise his glove to protect his face. He felt it before he heard it smack into his glove. A smile appeared behind his catch. He looked at the sphere in his mitt and held it tightly. It was a keeper. He made all three "put-outs" in the ninth.

He wondered, what were the odds? His teammates mobbed him. It was his first baseball game as a Modesto A. The Omaha Kid was making quite a name for himself.

*

Tim had arrived the day before on July fifth, jetlagged and bleary-eyed. He had flown from New York to San Francisco. Then he waited an hour and a half for a connection to the little turboprop that would take him to the small airport in Modesto. Tim got his suitcase and was greeted by a gray-haired, middle-aged man wearing shorts, tennis shoes, white socks, and an Oakland A's T-shirt.

"You're Tim, right?"

"Yeah. You Coach Reins?"

"Yup, that's me all right. How y'all doing? Your flight all right?"

"My flight? It was fine, but long. What's up now? Do I go to my apartment?"

"No time for that, we have a game tonight. I don't think you'll be in the lineup but we have practice and the manager wants to see you. We'll get you situated later, don't worry."

It was 5:30 PM West Coast time. Tim had been up since 6 AM on the East Coast and he was tired but excited. He was wearing jeans, a T-shirt and a light jacket. It had been cold in San Francisco. They walked out of the small air-conditioned airport and onto the street. The heat hit him like a blast furnace.

"Holy crap! It must be a hundred degrees!"

"Actually 102, get used to it kid. Welcome to the Central Valley. This is just normal everyday summer weather."

The New Yorker squinted from the bright sunlight in a cloudless sky. He looked over his left shoulder and saw nothing but open farmland. To his right he saw a few buildings and beyond there were rows and rows of trees lined up in what was some kind of orchard. Boy I'm really out in the sticks, he thought. "Isn't this California? Where are the buildings and the beaches?"

"You're right in the middle of the state son, lots of farmland. No beaches for a hundred miles."

Dust-filled, hazy smog hung in the air. Tim felt like he could almost taste it. The baseball park was a few blocks from "downtown" Modesto, behind a public golf course with seats for about two thousand fans. The coach introduced him to the manager, Ralph Hawking, a former shortstop for the Kansas City Athletics.

"Just put your suitcase over there. Take locker number nine. It's got your uniform in it. See you out here for infield practice in fifteen minutes."

Tim sighed. He was tired. Taking a deep breath, he strolled to his locker and changed into his uniform. When he left the club house, he couldn't believe it, the air felt even hotter than at the airport and yet his shirt felt dry, not like at home. On Long Island when it was this hot, the sweat would make his uniform heavy. He remembered that old saying, "it's not the heat it's the humidity." Maybe it wasn't so humid but it sure the hell was hot.

"Go ahead take third base rook." Ralph Hawking said, "Let's see what you can do."

Fungo bat in hand, the manager started slapping ground balls at Tim. A confident fielder, Tim ate the balls up and made strong throws to first base. Then Mr. Hawking bunted the ball to him. He came in, one handed the ball and fired a strike sidearm to the first baseman. Tim felt light headed and fell to his knees.

"You okay son?" the manager asked.

"I'm...just a little dizzy," Tim shook his head from side to side, trying to clear it.

"Go ahead and get some water," The manager laughed. "You'll get used to the heat soon enough. By the way, you got any trouble with black fellows?"

"No sir." In truth, Lynbrook was a white community. Tim's experience with black people was mostly as domestic help or as opponents at sporting events. He never had a black friend.

"Good. Hey Johnson, come over here. The new kid's your new roommate."

The six-foot four-inch first baseman came over and shook Tim's hand after the newbie drank from the water fountain.

"I'm Nate, Nate Johnson. Good fielding out there."

Tim looked up at the tall black man and smiled. "How long have you been here and how the heck do you handle this heat?"

"Been here since spring training, so I'm used to it. Just don't get dehydrated. Where I'm from, the Southside of Chicago, it's different. The humidity just soaks right through you. This dry heat's not as bad."

The manager looked over at his new rookie. "Hey, Jacobson, you go by Tim or do you have any nicknames?"

"Most people call me Tim, Mr. Hawking, but back in high school some kids called me "Omaha," short for the Omaha kid."

The Skipper scratched his head. "I thought you were from New York. Why Omaha?"

"I spent a few years in Nebraska. It was just a stupid nickname from my high school wrestling team. Never mind, forget about it. Tim's good."

"No, no. Charlie Finley loves nicknames. He thinks it sells tickets. The Omaha Kid works, might even get you to the majors quicker."

Tim sat on the bench and watched the A's lose 5 to 4. Roger Shaffer played third for Modesto and booted a ground ball leading to the winning run. Roger also went 0 for 4 at bat. Tim sensed he had an opportunity to start.

After the game that first night, Johnson drove Tim back to the apartment in his 1968 Ford Fairlane. Nate put a cassette tape in the audio system and Janis Joplin stated singing.

"This white girl has soul," Nate said, "What music do you like to listen to?"

"Um...Jimi Hendricks, great guitarist."

"Is that the only black guy you could think of?" Nate's smile let Tim know he was kidding.

"Well, yeah, off the top of my head. Should I have stuck with Motown?"

The first baseman glanced at Tim and cracked up laughing. "You're all right, man. I hope you can hit, because I think you're going to be a good roomy."

The small, shabby one bedroom apartment was furnished with a dingy couch and two beds that looked like they came from the Salvation Army. Dark, water-stained curtains covered the unwashed windows.

"Welcome to the minor leagues, Mr. Omaha Kid. That's your bed over there."

Tim stripped down to his underwear, crawled into bed and slept well past noon. Johnson woke him in time to go to the ballpark.

Jo Lynn and her friend, Cathy Trancis, were ball-girls for the Modesto A's. The two tall beauties' unpaid jobs were to sit on stools down the right and left field lines and catch or chase foul balls. Once the ball was captured, the girl would pick out a youngster in the stands and give him the souvenir. They would also cheer for the home team by holding up signs like, "Make some noise!" Dressed in matching yellow hot pants and sleeveless kelly green Modesto A's uniform tops, they would also dance between innings to loud rock or country music coming from the loudspeakers.

After signing autographs, Tim and Nate flirted with the two pretty ball-girls after games. Jo Lynn said, "Tim you're my favorite player. Your swing is so awesome. It reminds me of when Joe Rudy played here."

After a rare Saturday afternoon game, the players asked the girls if they would like to get something to eat. Excited, the young ladies agreed. The four drove downtown in Tim's new red Mustang convertible, bought with some of his bonus money. The top was down, it being a typically hot summer evening, when they pulled into the A&W Drive In. A waitress came to the car on roller-skates. She dressed in short shorts and a tee-shirt tucked in tight that had the A&W logo across her chest. She smiled and asked, "Can I take your order?" The four ordered and the waitress attached a tray to the window and skated away.

"I heard you're students at U. C. Davis," Tim said to Jo Lynn, who sat in the bucket seat next to him, her beautiful long legs bent in front on her tanned slim body.

The girl gave a conspiring glance at her busty blond partner in back next to Nate. In fact, that fall the seventeen-year old girls would be seniors at *Davis High School* in Modesto but she answered, "Yah, Davis students, that's right."

"Do you have a major yet?"

"No, just takin' general classes," Jo Lynn said. The ballplayers, also still in their teens, easily believed the girls were college freshman.

The waitress skated back the car and delivered the food.

After eating, Nate asked, "Do you girls want to go back to our place and party?"

Jo Lynn looked at Cathy who nodded, "Sure."

Tim said, "Great, let's stop and get some beer." The drinking age was 21, but Nate knew a store that always sold beer to Modesto A's players.

They arrived at the apartment, dishes piled in the sink. The girl didn't seem to care. They each grabbed a cold beer. Rock music pumped from the speakers. They drank, danced and before long the four found themselves in the bedroom with clothing coming off. Tim was on one of the beds, kissing Jo Lynn passionately and caressing her, only her frilly panties still covering her young body. He was naked, quite aroused; but he stopped for a moment. Moans could be heard over the music. He looked over at the other bed through the dim lighting. Nate and Cathy were making love. Tim watched fascinated, skin on skin, black on white. He returned his attention to the girl in his bed, exploring, probing. He went to get a condom out of his nightstand when Jo Lynn stopped him.

"I'm on the pill," she whispered trying hard to catch her breath.

*

The roommates spent a lot of time with Jo Lynn and Cathy. The two ball-girls were at every home game and it just seemed natural for them to continue to date.

Tim and Nate fell in naturally with each other. The suburban white kid and black city boy quickly became best friends. When they were alone on the road at night after games, they would talk about everything and nothing, politics, religion, race relations, childhood stories, their families, nothing was taboo.

One night Nate asked. "So Omaha, what are you going to do about Jo Lynn? She is real sweet on you."

"I don't know. I like her, but it's not like I'm ready to settle down or anything. I'm not in love with her like I was with my girlfriend, Kristy, in high school."

"Cathy told me she wants to get her hooks into you," Nate said.

"Hey, I'm just trying to have a good time. Hopefully she's in for the ride."

"You sure she's on the pill?"

"Why would she lie about that?"

"Man, I thought you New York boys were street smart."

Chapter 13 Bakersfield, California
August 1972

Tim didn't know how Bakersfield got its name, but after playing in the Southern Central Valley city, he believed it must be because everyone baked from the heat. The scoreboard thermometer showed 104 degrees at game time.

The farm team for the L.A. Dodgers' record reflected their awful play. They had lost their last eight games and, with the heat, the home club's player's tempers were ready to explode. The Modesto team punished the locals; the score read 14 to 2 in the eighth. The few hard core fans, fueled by beer, booed the inept play of the home team.

Tim hit two homeruns and Nate one when the first baseman came to bat in the top of the inning. The first pitch came right at his head. Nate ducked and sprawled to the ground. He jumped to his feet and pointed the end of his bat at the pitcher.

"Come on ass wipe. Try throwing that weak shit over the plate."

The pitcher unnerved by Nate's reaction to the bean-ball reared back and delivered a fast ball belt high. Nate's bat smashed he ball over the bleachers in centerfield, a tape measure home run.

"Anything that flies that far should have a stewardess on board." He yelled loud enough for the pitcher to hear, flipped the bat and did an agonizingly slow trot around the bases. As he came around third the opposing pitcher waited for him in the baseline, glove off, fists at the ready. Nate jabbed with his left and punched the player right on the nose. The pitcher went down like he had been hit by George Foreman.

The benches emptied and the players faced-off. Like most baseball brawls there was some pushing, shoving and cursing, but no real fighting. The umpires took quick control, throwing the pitcher and Nate out of the game. But the remaining fans were turning into an irate mob.

When there were three outs and Modesto took the field, the A's were pummeled with all types of debris, thrown from the angry fans left in the stands. In light of the score, and fearing for the visiting team's health, the umpires cancelled the ninth inning.

After the game, Tim and Nate laid uncomfortably on their beds at the Motel 7. The air conditioner was unable to keep the room cool. Nate soaked up his sweat with a towel.

"Let's get out of this dump and find a place we can get a cold beer."

"I'm with you. I think I saw a bar just down the block when the bus driver dropped us off."

The roommates walked up the street, passing other cheap motels until they were in front of a neon sign with the words "The Angry Bull." Just below, also in lights, blazed a picture of a cowboy riding a bucking bull, steam coming out of the animal's nostrils. Old pickup trucks, one sporting a Confederate flag on the back bumper filled the parking lot. The place screamed "redneck bar-stay away."

Tim said, "Do you think we should chance it?"

"Hell yeah, I'm hot and thirsty."

Tim knew they made a mistake the moment they walked into the saloon. Four young men dressed in Bakersfield Dodgers tee-shirts and baseball caps with the blue D logo played pool on the table in the front of the bar. A few other people scattered around the darkly lit room. Merle Haggard's *Proud to be an Okie,* wined on the jukebox.

"Hey Chuck, look who just walked into our damn bar," a big blond pool player said. It's that nigger from the A's that started that fight at the game today and the Jew boy Jacobson."

Nate and Tim each started to back out of the bar as the four shit-faced locals took one step toward the pair, pool cues in hand. Tim looked to the bartender for possible help but he just watched, a twisted evil cruel sneer of a smile on his face.

The door to the bar opened and six more Modesto Players walked into the bar led by the catcher, Bakersfield local, Pete Morgan bat in hand. Pete said, "I thought you guys might need some help when I saw you leave the motel." He then turned to the pool players. "You good ol' boys don't want to get the shit kicked out of you. Do ya?"

The redneck loudmouth stopped in his tracks. "That you Pete? No, I don't have no shit with you." The other pool players retreated back to the table."

"Good, you boys just stay over there and you get to keep your teeth." Pete said.

Nate was tempted to smash Pete's bat over the bigot's head, but he took a breath and let his red hot anger simmer, then cool. His desire to play ball in the majors was greater than his rage.

*

After winning Sunday's game, the A's were happy to get out of the inferno of Bakersfield and board the air-conditioned team bus back to Modesto. Pete took a seat right behind Nate and Tim. "The next time you boys want to go to a bar for country music, you guys might want to invite me along."

"Yeah, you all can tell your kin folk that I'm only half Jewish." Tim said, joking back with his teammate.

The big catcher snorted a laugh.

Tim was quiet for a minute and without the smile said, "I owe you one, thanks Pete."

"We're teammates; I know you got my back."

Chapter 14 Modesto California
August 1972

When Tim came back from the road trip, Jo Lynn was waiting for him at his apartment.

"Can I stay here tonight?"

He could tell she had been crying. "Sure. You ok?"

She shrugged her shoulders. "My asshole father got drunk again. When I didn't get him something to eat fast enough he smacked me with his belt. I hightailed it out of there, didn't know where to go. Came here." She showed him her bruise, a big welt on the top of her right leg. It was turning a nasty black and blue.

"Ok, that's fine. You can stay the night, but you need to report that SOB."

"Are you crazy? He'd kill me.

"What does your mother say?"

"She's been into lots of drugs lately and don't care. She's more scared of him than I am. Most of the time she just ain't around."

"At least you will be out of there when college starts."

"Tim, I'm not really in college. I'm going to be a senior in high school. I just wanted to be with you. So when you thought that I was in college, I just went with it. "Sorry."

Tim didn't say anything for a while.

"Are you mad at me?"

"Yeah, a little, but I guess you've dealt with enough crap tonight."

"Please forgive me." She kissed his neck and reached for him. They made love and then she curled up with him in bed. Nate came in, looked at the two of them nodded and said nothing. In the morning, after Jo Lynn left, Nate turned to his roomy and said, "Yup, she's getting her hooks into you."

*

That Monday the Modesto A's finally had a day off. Tim, Nate and the two ball-girls went out to Woodward Reservoir about a half hour drive outside of Modesto. The lake was nestled in low, dry-grassy hills, with a few tall oak trees dotting the countryside. The trees provided the only shade from the hot valley sun.

They arrived at the lake in the early afternoon Tim paid the entrance fee at the ranger station that had a small café and general store attached. The temperature-approached the century mark and the cool lake water looked very inviting. The four claimed a good spot under a big oak tree with a blanket and striped down to their bathing suits. The girls wore tiny string bikinis that barely concealed what they needed to cover.

"Race you to the water," Jo Lynn yelled, already sprinting ahead of her companions. The four dove into the water and wet and giddy, they splashed each other. Soon they played *Marco Polo* and the game where the girls get on the guys shoulders and they try to knock the other couple down. Jo Lynn pulled Cathy down and they stopped playing because they were laughing so hard and thought they might inhale water and drown.

Tim asked Nate, "Have you heard the stereotype that black guys can't swim?"

"Of course."

"I can see you're a good swimmer. Where do you think that comes from?"

"I don't know. Maybe it's because most black city families can't afford to go to a pool. I learned at the YMCA."

Tim challenged his roommate. "I'll race you to the buoy."

"Okay, go." Nate took off. He was a strong swimmer and forged ahead, but Tim had spent many summer days at Long Beach swimming in the ocean. He caught his buddy and his strong stroke swept him past to the marker.

When Nate reached him way out in the lake, treading water, he asked, "Is there any sport you're not good at?"

"Fishing, I suck at fishing, no patience."

"Good 'cause I'd like to think I could beat you at something."

"Boxing, I saw how you brought down that Bakersfield pitcher in one punch."

"Yeah, but you're a lot quicker than that shithead ever was. You would duck."

"Speaking of ducks, they swim pretty well, don't they?"

"You mean the birds, what the hell do they have to do with this conversation."

"Nothing, I'm just going to *duck* out and beat your black ass back to shore." Tim took off leaving Nate chuckling.

When they were all back on dry land, Tim and Jo Lynn wandered off to get a coke at the small café they passed on the way in.

"Have you always lived in Modesto?"

"Yup, I'm a native. My grandparents came out here during the depression from Oklahoma, when my father was just a little kid. You know that dust bowl thing we learned about in school. They were called Okies and worked in the fields for years before the Mexicans took over. My grandma was half Cherokee Indian, so can't no one can call us poor *white* trash."

"Jo Lynn you're not any kind of trash."

"Oh you're such a sweet talker." They laughed.

"I just meant to say, you are a smart girl with great potential."

"Thanks." She kissed him. "Tim, did you have many girlfriends before me?"

Tim told her about Kristy and Sara. "What about you?"

"When I was a sophomore I hung out with my friend Lisa who lived down the street. We would listen to records and get stoned when her parents were at work. Her older brother Ralph was the quarterback for the Davis High School team. I thought he was good looking. Well, I guess he thought I was cute because one night when we were both high he made a pass and started to kiss me. I couldn't believe he would want me. He could have had any girl in the school but he picked me. That is when I knew I could be sexy. We went out for a while but when he graduated he took off to L.A., wanted to make a movie or somethin'. He said he'd call, but never did." She shrugged her shoulders. "After that, there was no one special until you."

*

Daytime temperatures in the low nineties signaled a cooling trend. By evening, the game time weather would feel comfortable with the thermometer in the dugout reading 84 degrees and a slight breeze blowing in from right field. The cooler air came in over the pass from San Francisco and the ocean ninety miles to the west.

Unlike the weather, Tim's hitting stayed hot. He batted .361 with eleven home runs. The Omaha Kid and the daughter of an Oklahoma immigrant had been dating for eight weeks. Outside the clubhouse, Jo Lynn told Tim to meet her after the game.

After another two hits, a single and a double, Tim showered then went to change at his locker. Nate combing his afro while looking in the mirror said, "Man, if you were any hotter they would have to call the fire department."

Tim smiled. "Yea, it was a good night."

*

Tim was still smiling when he walked out to his car to meet his girlfriend. He went to kiss her but she turned her head offering just her wet cheek. The girl had been crying.

"What's the matter?" he asked.

Jo Lynn face wrinkled in trepidation. "I'm… I'm pregnant," She said, her voice cracking.

"What? How? I thought you were on birth control."

"Yeah, well, maybe I was doing it wrong…or skipped a day. I don't know."

"Are you sure? How do you know?"

"Well, I was late. So I went to the free clinic."

He looked into her eyes and saw desperation. He felt panic. What are we going to do? His mind raced. Holy crap! Not now, things were going so well.

She asked, "What are you thinking?"

"Do you want a baby? Would you keep it?"

"I do if you love me. Tell me you love me."

Did he love her? He wanted to say yes, hold her in his arms. Instead he sighed. "Jo Lynn, I'm only eighteen, just starting the minor leagues. I like you, maybe with time… but I … I'm not ready for a wife and a baby."

"Oh, my God!"

"I… I'll make things right. Send you money for the baby when I leave town."

Her face changed from a look of helplessness to one of hate. "No, fuck you, asshole! I don't want your damn money!" Her tears streamed down.

"Jo Lynn, please I want to help… you."

"Don't bother. I'll take care of this."

"You mean an abortion?" He felt guilty, took a step toward her. He wanted to reach out somehow support her. But she stepped back.

"What would you care? I said I'll take care of it! I never fuckin' want to see your sorry ass again!" She turned and walked away.

He was stunned. He wondered, should I go to her? He froze unable to move as she walked away getting smaller, until she was gone out of his life.

He thought, well, I'll see her tomorrow. She'll calm down. Then we can talk.

*

When Tim got to the ballpark the next day, he put on his uniform and went out for warm-ups. He looked for her but Jo Lynn wasn't there. He found Cathy behind first base talking to Nate. They were horsing around, like nothing unusual happened.

Tim walked up to Jo Lynn's friend and asked. "Did you know Jo Lynn was pregnant?"

Cathy gave him a look of doubt. "No I didn't. But I'm not surprised she told you that one."

"What do you mean that one? You don't believe it?" Tim asked.

Cathy said, "I don't really know. We had a falling out. We haven't been talking since I told her my parents didn't want her sleeping over any more. She was really pissed off. But before that, she told me she had a plan to keep you."

Nate said, "I told you she was going to get her hooks into you."

"Son of a bitch! Yesterday she pulled off quite an act if she's not pregnant. I'd give her a damned academy award." He thought, Hell, that's why she said she would take care of it.

Tim walked off towards the locker room. He did not know whether to be relieved or angry. What's the truth?

Ralph Hawking poked his head out of his office and yelled, "Tim, come over here."

Oh no! Tim thought, am I in trouble because of Jo Lynn?

The manager smiled at him and gave him the good news. "It's September, the major league rosters have expanded. You and Nate have been called up to Oakland."

Tim drove by Jo Lynn's house before he left town. He wanted to say goodbye and find out for sure if she was really pregnant. He parked the car and toyed with the idea of going up and ringing the doorbell. Screw it, he thought, she said she didn't want to see me again. If she needs me she knows where to find me.

Chapter 15 Oakland, California
September 1972

In the two months Tim had played for Modesto, he had not left the Central Valley, having had a game almost every day. They had traveled to games by bus as far south as Bakersfield and north to Redding, going from hot to hotter, but never had seen the other side of the coastal mountains. As he drove to Oakland he felt the temperature drop thirty degrees. The eastern side of the Bay glistened beautifully in the sun, while to the west, the San Francisco fog hugged the bay. He got off the freeway at the Coliseum exit and drove directly to the player's gate. Nate followed right behind as they had caravanned over the Altamont Pass.

The guard looked at Tim's player pass and said, "Welcome Mr. Jacobson, you can park over there. He pointed to a gate.

The lot sat empty at in the midmorning. The Oakland A's would not play until evening. Nate caught up and the equipment manager gave them-uniforms and assigned them each a locker. Tim unfolded his shirt. He was given number 64, usually anything above 50 was assigned to a short term rookie, but it was the back of this jersey that was so interesting. Instead of his name, *Omaha Kid* was printed on the back.

The clubhouse attendant shrugged his shoulders when Tim looked at him. "It was Mr. Finley's idea." Tim held it up for Nate and they both got a good laugh.

Tim and Nate walked out onto the field. Three decks of seats planted in concrete stared back at them. Tim had been to Yankee Stadium with his uncle and spent many a day at Shea Stadium, home of the New York Mets, but looking up from the field to the thousands of empty seats of the Coliseum sent shivers down his spine. Every blade of grass in the newly mowed lawn lined up like soldiers standing at attention, bright green and uniform blazing in the sun. But when Tim went over to third base and examined the infield, he was surprised it wasn't in better shape. He found divots in the infield grass. He then remembered that the baseball team shared the field with the Oakland Raiders during the autumn and the divots in the grass were a result. He made a mental note, there might be some bad hops.

After checking into the hotel, the boys realized they had hours before they had to report for the game. "Let's go explore," Nate suggested.

"I think we better stay on this side of the bay. I remember watching the news in Modesto. The Bay Area traffic can be a mess. We don't want to get stuck on the Bridge and be late to our first major league game. I turned down a couple of college scholarships to sign with the A's. I'd like to see what I'm missing. Let's go check out the university at Berkeley."

"Ok, scholarship boy, do you really think I want to hang out where people go to school? Is that really the best we can do?"

"There should be lots of pretty coeds."

"Good point."

*

A half-hour later they were walking up Telegraph Avenue toward the University. Even the city boys from New York and Chicago had never seen anything like this. The avenue looked like a street fair. Along the sidewalk lay blankets filled with arts and crafts and other trinkets for sale. Hippies, professionals and students mixed in great masses, moving to the rhythm sounds of guitarists playing on each corner, their cases open collecting spare change.

The two ball players crossed over to the University and were greeted by a collection of bongo drummers pounding out a beat in front of one building, while protesters held signs and chanted slogans on the steps across the commons. Students walked by, oblivious to the distractions, and headed for classes.

"You're right. There are a lot of pretty girls here." Nate said, as he hid behind his sunglasses to watch the coeds pass by dressed provocatively in skimpy shorts or miniskirts and light tops.

Out of the corner of his eye, Tim noticed a pretty young girl that looked familiar. She had dark brown hair and a face he knew he had seen before. He quickly scanned his mind but couldn't place her. He tried to look again but she was gone. They were walking back to the car when it came to him; the girl looked very much like the black and white photographs of his mother. Boy that was weird, he thought.

*

Tim and Nate each had a couple of slices at Blondie's Pizzeria.

Tim, his mouth full, said, "This isn't bad. It's almost like a New York slice."

"You call this pizza. In Chicago, my boys would laugh at this little pathetic excuse for a meal. It ain't pizza if it ain't deep dish."

"Are you kidding me, deep dish is ok, but it's not real pizza. You should have to hold a slice with two hands and the cheese should drip into your mouth."

"If we ever get to Chicago, I will show you what real pizza is."

"I haven't checked the schedule. Do we play the White Sox or the Yankees?"

"I don't know, but it would be amazing to play in front of my boys."

"Yeah, it would be cool."

*

Tim put on his uniform and sat on the bench, spellbound, as his childhood heroes arrived: Reggie Jackson, Joe Rudy, Billy North, and Captain Sal Bando, the reigning third baseman. The Omaha Kid watched the others with a nickname, Vida "True" Blue, "Campy" Campaneris, "Blue Moon" Odom and "Catfish" Hunter, change out of their street cloths and put on the jerseys bearing their monikers. His arm showed goose bumps and his heart raced. This was really the big leagues. Tim realized he probably wouldn't play. The A's were in the middle of a pennant race, needing the starters to be on the field for the stretch run. He was there with other minor leaguers that made up the expanded roster to get a taste of what it may be like when, and if, he arrived again.

It was mustached reliever, Rollie Fingers that approached him first.

"Hey, Omaha Kid, I hope you can hit as good as you are at getting attention."

Reggie added, "Yeah, rookie, don't you know getting attention is *my* job!"

Both men had smiles on their faces, but Tim still felt intimidated. "What's going on?" He wanted to crawl into his locker.

Joe Rudy the outfielder, who had grown up in Modesto, flipped him a copy of the Oakland Tribune sport section. "Don't worry kid. We know this was Charley Finley's idea."

There was the article, including a banner headline, on page one of the sports section:

THE OMAHA KID COMES TO OAKLAND

Tim Jacobson reports to the big club as part of a group of rookies that should help the A's as the pennant race heats up. Tim also known as "The Omaha Kid," is an infielder who has been smacking the ball around. He played third base for Modesto, Oakland's single-A farm club. The "Kid" earned his nickname because he was a teen rodeo star in Omaha, Nebraska roping bulls and riding bucking broncos. Tim, a poor orphan, spent his early childhood in the slums of New York City, before he escaped to the rodeo. He can also ride roughshod on pitchers, batting .352, which leads the California League. With seven homeruns, the young Mr. Jacobson shows good power to all parts of the field.

The article continued, moving to another rookie.

"What kind of bullshit is this? More than half of this is invented."

Reggie laughed, "Only half? You should see the shit they print about me."

Oakland won that night when Jackson homered in the eighth to give the A's the lead. Catfish threw eight innings, giving up just one run. Fingers was brought in for the ninth and got the save. Tim never left the bench but he would remember this game for a different reason.

After showering and changing into his street cloths, Tim attacked a roast beef sandwich from his first big league post game spread. The reporter who wrote the story about him stopped by for a quote.

"Quote this. That story was a bunch of crap."

"Listen kid, Mr. Finley gave me that story. You can thank me when he gives you a major league contract."

The reporter then walked over to Jackson's locker. "Reggie, how did it feel to hit that homerun?"

A clubhouse security officer came over. "Mr. Jacobson, there are two young ladies waiting outside the gate to see you. The pretty one said it's important."

"Did they give you their names?"

"Nope, and I didn't ask."

Tim grabbed his bag and walked outside. He immediately recognized one of the girls. It was the brunette he had seen earlier at Berkeley.

"Hello." she said sticking out her right hand to shake. "My name is…"

"Linda." He finished his sister's sentence.

*

The three, Tim, Linda and her friend Josie went to the dining room in the Airport Hilton Hotel where he was staying. It was not far from the Coliseum, and a good place to spend some time together. First Linda called Aunt Mae to check in and say she was going out to eat with her friend. She was safe and would be home later. For now, she kept Tim a secret.

"How did you find me?"

"From the article in the Oakland Tribune. Were you really a rodeo star?"

"No, and as you know, I did not live in a New York slum."

"How are Uncle Tony and Aunt Sophia?"

"Last time I saw them, they were fine. But I haven't talked to them for a while; we're kind of on the outs."

"What's that about?" Linda asked between bits of a slice of apple pie. Her friend was drinking a milk shake. After eating at the post game spread at the ballpark, Tim was not hungry and just sipped a cup of decaf coffee.

"That's a good question. I don't know. Maybe it's about religion, or just me trying to live my life…well, it's complicated."

"I think I understand. In our family religion kept us apart."

"So Linda, were you brought up Jewish?"

"Yes, I was brought up that way and sometimes I feel Jewish, but I think religion gets in the way of people. You know like that song from John Lennon 'imagine there's no religion, and no war too.' Well something like that."

Tim smiled. "So how have you been doing? And what the heck was a 16-year-old doing at Berkeley today?"

"You saw me at Berkeley…today?"

"Yeah, I was there with my friend Nate and saw you. Of course I couldn't place you at first and then you were gone but you look so much like Mom, it stuck in my mind."

"Really, I look like Mom?" Linda unconsciously whisked her hand through her hair.

"Yeah, you really do, just like her pictures."

She smiled and looked like she was thinking for a second. "I'm actually a senior at Berkeley High School. I skipped a grade. I'm taking a special advanced placement class at the college, pre-med."

"So you got all the brains from the family," he said with a laugh. "I was wondering about that with Mom and Dad being nurses you know."

"So you didn't do well at school?" she asked her brother.

"I did okay. As a matter of fact, I was offered a couple scholarships but I was more interested in sports. I picked baseball over college."

"Looks like you made the right choice."

"Well so far, knock on wood." Tim rapped his knuckles on the table.

"Timmy it's so funny seeing you all grown up. In my mind you're just a little boy."

"Yeah, and you were just a baby."

They finished eating and Tim looked over at Josie. "We must be really boring you."

Josie said, "Are you kidding me? This is one of the most amazing things I've ever seen."

Tim asked, "Can I take you girls home? Do you need a ride?"

"No, we will be fine. I have Uncle Willie's car. But we should be getting back. I'm going to tell them about you, if that's okay, have you over for dinner."

"That would be great. Let me give you my phone number here at the hotel." They got up and he paid the bill.

"Just one request at dinner, don't bring up religion," Linda suggested, and they laughed.

*

Linda dropped off Josie and made her way to her home in the hills of North Berkeley. It was almost midnight when the girl unlocked the front door and entered the house. Uncle Willie was watching TV after a long day at work. He had waited up for Linda. He heard her come in as he sat on the couch in the living room.

"Sweetie did you have a good night?"

"Yeah, Unks, I had an exceptional night." Unks was her pet name for him.

"Oh no, did you meet a special boy?" He asked, teasing her.

"Actually I met a very special boy," teasing her uncle right back.

He smiled. "Do you want to talk about it?"

"Not tonight. But I have something important to tell you and Auntie in the morning."

"It's not about The Omaha Kid is it?"

"Unks, how did you know?"

He laughed, "Don't you think I can read a newspaper?"

"God, I can't get anything over on you can I?"

"Well I hope when you *really* do meet a different kind of special boy, you remember that. When can we meet Timothy?"

"He wants to see you. Can we talk about it in the morning?"

"Of course, I'm going to bed too. Good night Linda."

"Goodnight Unks, love you."

The two Jacobson children had very different upbringings. Even though Linda's aunt and uncle never officially adopted her, she felt very much at home with her guardians. Being just an infant at the time of her parent's accident, she did not remember her mother and father. It's hard to miss something you never knew. Her family moved to Berkeley in 1962, when her Aunt Mae was offered a professorship in philosophy at the University of California. This provided the young girl with a strong female role model. The move planted her in one of the most progressive cities in the United States. Her Uncle's career as an architect provided stability and an example of a successful two-income family.

With the move to the west coast, away from the influence of their religiously conservative parents, Aunt Mae and Uncle Willie left the traditional Orthodox Judaism behind. They joined Berkeley's progressive Reform Temple, giving Linda a religious base but the freedom to find her own spirituality. She had her Bat Mitzvah Ceremony on her twelfth birthday and had been an infrequent guest at the Temple since dabbling in Buddhism.

The greatest difference between the siblings' family lives was that Linda felt totally at home with her aunt and uncle. She felt that she was loved unconditionally. The couple never had other children and Linda became the center of their attention. They may have spoiled her at times but they were also demanding about her school work and she was expected to get good grades. She thrived under these conditions. She was socially well-adjusted and performed-at the top of her class.

She went to bed that night with a smile on her face. Deep down in her subconscious, something had been missing from her life. Her brother, Tim, was the missing link to her biological mother. She didn't understand how, but she felt like an electrical circuit to an empty spot in her heart had been completed, the loose wire was now connected. Her pillow was wet with tears of joy.

Chapter 16 Oakland, California
October, 1972

In October the A's clinched the Western Division Pennant on the second to the last day of the regular season. Tim and Nate hadn't made it to New York or Chicago. The last few weeks of the season Oakland played against teams on the West Coast. Before the final game, Manager Dick Williams approached his rookie third baseman.   "Jacobson, sorry you're not going to be on the playoff roster, but I'm giving Bando the day off and starting you at third base. Show me what you can do, Rook."

"Thanks, Mr. Williams."

Tim looked at the lineup card. He was batting sixth. Nate batted fifth. He went up to his roommate and slapped him on the back. "You and me, let's get 'em."

The A's went down in order in the first inning. In the second, the lead-off hitter walked, but Nate struck out. As Tim approached the plate, he noticed butterflies dancing in his stomach. The stadium lights illuminated the field so much better than the skimpy lights of the minor league fields. It created a bright daytime from the twilight. He took a fastball in on his hands that the umpire called a strike. He looked back in surprise.

The catcher said, "Rookie you should know better than to show up the umpire. You better swing at this one." Tim knew he was being set up, so he took the slider outside. The count was one and one when the pitcher went into the stretch, checked the runner and delivered a 90 mph fastball on the outside corner. The Omaha Kid took a step and his bat swished, connecting with the ball on the sweet spot sending a line drive down the first base line into the corner of the outfield. He cruised into second as the runner scored. The crowd of 21,291 stood and cheered the rookie's first major league hit.

Tim walked his next two times at bat and Williams sent up a lefthander to pinch hit for him in the ninth. Nate, who had played in a few games before, got his third major league hit in the fifth.

*

The two went to an Oakland jazz club after the game to celebrate. It was next to the bay at Jack London square. Tim walked in, looked around and realized he had the only white face in the room.

Nate peered over at Tim and laughed at his buddy's look of discomfort. "Now you know how I felt at that redneck bars in the central valley."

"I'm all right here but maybe we should call Pete back in Modesto to meet us. I'm sure he would feel right at home in this place."

They both laughed at the thought of, their friend, Pete the country music loving catcher in this club. Tim relaxed feeling more comfortable with the distinctive flavor of the establishment knowing Nate was by his side. The band was playing some serious blues as the lead switched back and forth from the electric guitar to the saxophone. The teammates walked up to the bar. Nate ordered a seven and seven and Tim a rum and coke.

"Can I see some ID gentleman? "The bartender asked.

Another man behind the bar dressed in a classy three piece suit said, "It's ok Joel, that's Nate Johnson and the Omaha Kid from the Oakland A's, I got this." He poured the cocktails and said, "Sorry guys, I'm Tommy, the manager, this drink on me. Welcome to my club. You have any problems, just let me know."

The two ballplayers were treated like celebrities as patrons bought them drinks. They were introduced to the band and in a room backstage the drummer offered them each a line of cocaine. Nate had snorted the drug before and he showed Tim how to suck it up his nose with a rolled up $20 bill. Tim felt amazing, like he did earlier standing on second with his first hit.

Tim said, "This feels really good but can't this ship really screw up a career?"

Nate shook his head. "I personally know four other Oakland player that do this stuff all the time, bennies too. Help with the day games after playing a few nights in a row."

"But it's addicting isn't it."

"Just got to be careful that all.

"Which players?"

"I can't tell you that. You know I can keep a secret."

"Even with me."

"Expecially with you. I don't want you getting in trouble."

"I can see where someone can get addicted to this. It feels amazing."

"By the way, buddy, I'm cleaning out my locker tomorrow headed home for Chicago. What about you?"

"I'm sticking around for the playoffs, going to stay with my sister in the East Bay. I'll probably stay here and work out with the team. I'm hoping for an invite to the major league camp for spring training."

"Yeah, me too." Nate looked around the room. "So this will be our last night together. Let's make the most of it. Do you see those two hot chicks over there? Let's go see what they're doing."

"Really, me and a black chick in this club? You trying to get me killed?"

"Hey, I didn't have any problems with the honkies in Modesto. Don't worry man, you're with me."

Tim laughed. "Ok, I'm game."

They walked over to the two young ladies who were dressed disco fashion, each in a bright minidress, showing lots of cleavage and lots of jewelry.

"Can I buy you drink, ladies?" Nate asked.

The boys had a good time that night. They did not get back to the hotel until late the next morning.

When Tim woke up late in the afternoon, Nate was gone. His head felt like an eggbeater had scrambled his brain. And he wished someone would get the elephant off his forehead. The pain was intense. His mouth was dry and in spite of just waking up he had no energy. It was like he had the flu, only worse. Man, I better lay off that shit.

Chapter 17 Berkeley, California
Winter 1972-1973

Staying with his Linda, Uncle Willy and Aunt Mae proved to be a revelation for Tim. He didn't know a family could be like this, calm. In his childhood home there was lots of fighting and screaming. He fought with Junior. Junior screamed at Maria. Uncle Tony and Aunt Sophia often exchanged verbal salvoes. Both adults yelled at the kids. Tim thought the quarrels signified normal behavior, until this winter.

Outside, storms would rage all the Northern California winter, but not inside the Jacobson household. The quiet felt almost unnerving.

Tim found he enjoyed his sisters company. She had school and he spent his days working out at the A's training center. Weekends and evening they were often free to spend time together. They took hikes in the East Bay hills, played tennis, and went to movies or music shows. The two spent more time together then many romantic couples, maybe they were trying to make up for the lost years.

Sitting at breakfast on a Sunday morning in February, just before Tim's twentieth birthday, brother and sister relaxed after breakfast. Sipping coffee Linda asked, "What do you remember about Mom and Dad?

"Little, I barely remember them. I can see Mom's face, maybe from seeing pictures in the house. I do remember one day, before you were born, I fell down and cut my head. Mom took care of me. I remember feeling safe in her arms." Tim pointed to his head." See I have this scar above my eyebrow. Wow, I have thought about that memory of her for years. What about you? Do you have any memories?"

"Nothing I was a baby, remember."

"Of course I know you were a baby but I just wish I knew more about them. Uncle Tony and Aunt Sophia never talked about Mom and Dad. It was like the subject was of off limits."

Linda suddenly smiled. "Let's ask Uncle Willie." She strolled out of the room and came back a few minutes later their uncle. She poured him a cup of coffee.

"Linda says you two want to know about you parents. I only met your Mom once. She really was beautiful and sweet too. She lit up the room. Unfortunately I never really got to knew her. Larry took her to one party before they eloped and... After that they were no longer part of the family."

"Tell Tim about Dad."

"He was my big brother and I idolized him. War hero, boxer, no one messed with me because they knew he was my brother.'

"He was a boxer? Tim asked.

"I thought that might interest you. He was quite athletic. He never made it big but he made some money betting on and winning golden glove fights in Brooklyn during the Depression. He moved as quick as a whip and he packed a powerful punch.

"Then the war broke out an even thought he was only seventeen, he joined the Army. He scored so high on the entrance exams they made him a medic."

Tim got up and refilled their cups. "I did hear from Uncle Tony that my Dad was at D-day."

"That was only the beginning. His unit fought all the way into Germany. Many of his friends were killed. Later he was called in to help survivors of Buchenwald Concentration Camp. It messed him up mentally for a while. Then he met your mother.

"Linda I always meant to show you this letter. I was waiting for you to be old enough to understand. I'm not proud of...well you'll see."

They read the letter together.

Dear Willy,

Don't sweat it. I know you are only listening to Dad about not talking to me. They sat Shiva like I was dead. I know the tradition. I just think it's wrong. Roberta's not Jewish but we love each other. We are married now and that's, that! Anybody who doesn't like it can go to Germany's concentration camps and find out what prejudice really looks like.

I was in a bad way after the war. It was like I was lost in big fog. I couldn't feel anything, couldn't relate to anybody, not even you. I kicked around Philly then Boston getting odd jobs and such. I dated some girls had some fun but I couldn't stay with anyone. I didn't even tell you, Mom and Dad when I came back to Brooklyn. I signed up for nursing class on the GI Bill but I wasn't sure I could do ok. Remember I didn't finish high school.

When I walked into that classroom and saw Roberta everything changed. I could feel something again, something powerful. It was love at first sight. I know that sound corny but that's what happened. It was like she was in Technicolor and the rest of the world was in black and white.

I had to know more about her. I followed her home from a distance. She got off the elevated subway line and some construction workers started whistling at her, saying stuff like "Come bring that stuff here sweet baby." and "Hey beautiful, shake them melons over here." I almost gave myself away. I was going to kick some butt but then Roberta yells right back, I'll never forget what she said, "Hay Danny, why don't you show me your IQ is bigger than your shoe size." I was mesmerized. What a woman. I asked her out for coffee the very next day. I couldn't believe it when she said yes. Somehow she fell in love with me. I am such a lucky SOB!

I'll tell you the first time we were, you know together, I thought I was looking at God's greatest work of art. I felt closer to God that night than I ever did in a temple.

Now we are going to have a baby. Tell Mom and Dad that. They are going to be grandparents.

Please sneak away and come see us.

Your loving brother,
Larry.

Linda looked up at her uncle mouth agape.

Staring the hand-written paper, Tim said. "This is amazing."

Willy volunteered, "I sorry to say I never wrote him back. I never saw him... alive again. It's something I really regret."

"Oh Unks." Linda cried, tears streaming down her face. She ran over a hugged her uncle.

Later in the day Tim reflected on the letter. His father was so in love. I felt that way about Kristy but I guess we were too young. We were not ready go against our families' wishes. Will that ever happen to me again? Will I see a girl and immediately know that I'm in love. Will I ever feel like my father felt when he walked into that classroom?

He daydreamed about growing up with his parents and Linda behind the white picket fence in Omaha. How would his life be different? He could never know.

Chapter 18 Arizona and New Mexico
Spring 1973

Ballplayers are like traveling musicians or the military. They always keep a bag packed. In the spring of 1974, Tim's home was A's training camp in Arizona. He had been invited to the major league training camp. Against the dry desert environment the grass of the field glowed, a sunlit inviting green oasis.

It was his first spring training, having joined the club during the season his rookie year. Tim took his turn at infield practice on one of the many diamonds around the complex. Coach Reins from his Modesto team hit fungo drills to a collection of minor leaguers from different levels of the A's farm teams. Nate Johnson was conspicuous by his absence.

"Ok, double play drill, go to second," the coach said, and slapped the ball to Tim at third. He made a strong throw, leading the second baseman to the bag, who pivoted and fired to first.

Tim's Modesto manager, Ralph Hawking, appeared with his uniform too tight and a fat belly pouring over his belt. "Hey Omaha, come over here."

Tim jogged off the field and over to his former boss. "How are you doing Mr. Hawking?"

"Come over here, away from everyone. I have something important to tell you." They walked away from the field to the metal fencing surrounding the field. The minor league manager took a deep sigh, "I know how close you were to Nate Johnson, but he won't be here."

"Was he traded?" Tim asked.

"No, he died," Hawking said with his head faced down.

"What?" Tim said, taking two steps back like someone had hit him in the mouth…"How?"

"Drug overdose…sorry Tim."

"Oh fuck… no! Son of a bitch!" Tim yelled, and all the players turned to look at him.

"I know, son. Take the rest of the day off. Report back tomorrow."

*

Tim slept restlessly that night. He dreamed that he was driving at night in his Mustang with his sister Linda. "So, how have you been Tim?" she asked in an unfamiliar voice. He glanced over and the girl had turned into his mother. Headlights lit up the windshield and a truck came out of nowhere. There was no sound as the metal scrunched and the windows smashed. Tim was then above the car, which was no longer his Ford, but a 1955 Chevrolet. An ambulance arrived and the medics pulled a body from the car and placed it on a gurney. Looking down he could see Nate Johnson's pale lifeless face, eyes wide open unblinking and staring at him. In spite of being in the dry Arizona desert, Tim woke covered in sweat

*

Tim felt like a zombie as he went through the motions, trying to concentrate on the task of winning a job as a major league ballplayer. For the first time in his life he couldn't hit a baseball and his average dropped below .200. He made uncharacteristic mistakes on defense. He woke up in the middle of the night and looked at his new roommate snoring across the room. He didn't know the guy at all. He needed desperately to talk to Nate, to someone. He threw on his sweats and snuck out the door well past curfew. Walking felt better than lying awake staring at the darkened ceiling. The next day he continued his slump going hitless. In the ninth he booted an easy grounder letting in the winning run.

"Nice play Mr. Omaha Kid," the losing pitcher, John Martin, shouted sarcastically at him.

"Fuck off asshole." Tim shouted back.

The two faced off but Coach Reins got between them. "Martin go cool off. Tim, come with me." The coach took him aside. "I watched you play ball all summer I know you can play. You are trying too hard. Relax, let the game come to you."

"Yeah, Tim said. Thanks." He knew that was not the problem.

His cousin, Maria, just graduated from college with a degree in psychology. He decided to call her. After Tim explained his situation to his cousin, she said she wanted to help. Maria had always felt a bit maternal towards Timmy and she caught the next plane to Phoenix.

As soon as she got there, he started to hit. It felt so good having her there with him and they stayed up talking late into the night.

"I know Uncle Tony and Aunt Sophia did their best, but I always felt like an outsider. If I totally accepted them as my parents, I felt like it would have been somehow disloyal to my biological parents, especially my father and his side of the family, the Jewish half. And…Aunt Sophia with her religious crap didn't help. I also think I was angry about not being able to see my sister, Linda. Does this all sound crazy?"

"No, Timmy. It is quite normal that you would have repressed feelings about your parents. I would like to explore that with you. And my mom, she even drove *me* crazy with her religious stuff.

"By the way, how amazing was it that you found your "other" sister?" Maria intentionally used the word other, implying that she was his sister also.

"It was so amazing. I couldn't believe it. Linda and I had a great reunion. You would really like her. Seeing my Aunt Mae and Uncle Willy after all these years proved really interesting. They were all real nice to me.

"You wouldn't believe it. Maria, my Uncle Willie had a letter from my father about meeting my mother. It was amazing to read. They were so in love."

Their conversation went on over many days. Tim talked about feeling alone and told her how angry he was when Aunt Sophia called Kristy a slut. "I truly loved her," he said.

"I understand. The way it ended must have been difficult. But you're going to have a heck of a story to tell your wife someday."

"Yeah, I guess so." He laughed.

"What about that girl Jo Lynn, the one you got pregnant."

"I'm not sure she was pregnant. Nate thought she was making it up as a trap. If she really was you know... knocked up, she got an abortion. I tried to call her, but she moved out of her house. I can't find her. She said she never wanted to see me again and I guess she meant it. I do feel a bit guilty about that whole mess."

"Well you can't change it now so, unless you hear from her, it might be a good idea to let it go...your guilt also. She made choices about this and it was really her's to make."

"Yeah, I think you're right." Tim was quiet for a few minutes lost in thought. "Maria, it's...you have been so helpful."

She smiled and took his hand. "I think I understand how hard you took it when you heard your roommate died."

He looked out the window, like he was looking for Nate. "I miss him."

"I know." She kissed his cheek where a tear ran down.

They were silent for a quite a while. Finally, Maria said, "you have to make peace with my mom and dad or you'll never feel whole. Of course they made mistakes with you, but to go forward you may have to let the pain go and move beyond. Let your guilt go."

"My guilt? I didn't do anything wrong."

"You don't feel any guilt about Kristy being sent away? Getting caught having sex in her house?

"You think I should get in touch with Kristy to apologize?"

Maria said, "I don't think she blames you. It's about how *you* feel. I actually think you'll feel better and forgive yourself if you can forgive your aunt and uncle."

Tim thought about what his cousin said for a while. He wiped a tear and said, "Maybe you're right. How did you get so smart?"

"Me, I'm just faking it. "So, you'll call my mom and dad?"

"I promise," he said holding up three fingers like a boy scout.

"I think my work here is done. I love you Tim, call me if you need me. Actually just call me often. I love hearing from you."

*

By the last week of spring training, Tim had been on fire, raised his batting average to .302 and had hit eight home runs in the elevated dry Arizona air. The local papers reported that Oakland's management was impressed with the hard hitting infielder, but the defending World Series Champions had Sal Bando at third and Bert Campaneris at short. Where would they play the Omaha Kid? Rumors of trades for different players appeared daily in the sport sections of the Tribune, Chronicle and Examiner. The day before they broke camp, Manager Dick Williams called Tim into his office.

"Tim we really like you. But there's no place for you on the big-league club to play. You've been traded to the Dodgers. You need to report to their triple-A club in Albuquerque. Thank you for your service. Maybe I'll see you in the World Series. Good luck, son."

Just like that, Tim was no longer an Oakland Athletic. He was a member of the Dodger system, an infielder for the Albuquerque Pacific League Team. He turned in his uniform, packed up his gear, loaded the car and took off for New Mexico.

On the drive from Phoenix to Albuquerque, Tim felt like he was in a Road Runner cartoon. Red sandstone mesa cliffs rose up next to the roadway and they reached to a blue sky that seemed to go on forever. The sun beamed brighter. Of course, he had to stop at the Grand Canyon and look down the 5000 feet to the Colorado River. He felt incredibly small.

After a night in a motel in the middle of nowhere and driving all day, he arrived at the biggest city in the Land of Enchantment. Tim asked for directions at a gas station, and found his way to the front of Tingley Field, home of the Albuquerque Dukes. He reported to the manager, Steve Monroe.

"Welcome aboard Tim," the manager said. You can go to the clubhouse and get your new uniform. You will be number 15. Oh, and Jacobson, this is the Dodger organization. Things are done the right way, the Dodger way. No more of that Omaha Kid crap, okay?"

"Fine with me Mr. Monroe, I just want to fit in."

The Dukes had purchased a dive motel and turned it into apartments for players. This was still the minors so there were two beds to every room. His new roommate was there watching TV when Tim arrived with his bags.

"Hi, I'm Charlie Wright. You must be Tim Jacobson, Monroe told me you were coming. Didn't you play for the A's, third base right?"

"That's right, was up with them during their pennant drive. Didn't get to play much. What position do you play?"

"Catcher, been in the minors five years, never had my cup of coffee."

"Well you're in Triple A. Maybe you'll get up this year. Were you here last year?"

"Nope, Richmond Virginia, I was traded here by the Braves."

"Well I guess we're both starting out fresh."

"Hey, I'm going out with some of the boys. You want to join us?"

"No, I need to make a phone call that's long overdue."

"Girlfriend?"

"No, to…my parents." It sounded funny when he said it, but he realized that his aunt and uncle were the only parents he was ever going to have.

"Okay man, see you later," The catcher said.

Charlie walked out the door, leaving Tim alone staring at the phone on the desk. He picked it up and dialed the phone number he knew so well. "Hello," the familiar voice said on the other end of the line.

"Uncle Tony, it's me, Tim. I'm… I'm sorry for the way I left."

The phone was silent for a minute. Tony's voice broke as he said, "It's good to hear from you son. I've waited a long time for you to call."

"I'm in Albuquerque."

"I know you're playing for the Dodgers. I never could forgive them you know, for leaving Brooklyn." Tim laughed.

They talked for an hour, laughing and crying, catching up. Finally Tim asked, "Can I talk to Aunt Sophia?"

"No. She's too angry. She doesn't want to talk to you."

"Okay. Tell her… I'm sorry."

"I will. Goodbye for now. Call again soon."

"Yeah, soon. Bye."

The next day Tim went out to one of those Hallmark stores and bought a card. It had a picture of a beautiful colonial house in the snow on the front and was blank inside. It wasn't quite like the house he grew up in but was somewhat similar. It reminded him of home, something he didn't have anymore. He wrote inside:

Dear Aunt Sophia,

I am sorry for the pain I have caused you.

You deserved better after you and Uncle Tony gave me a home.

I miss you.

Love,
Tim

*

May 15th was a night game. It was a cold evening on the New Mexico plateau. Snow could be seen on the peaks of the Sandia Mountains, to the east. Tim could see his frosty breath as he jogged out to third base in the top of the first. He was having another great year so far, only a month into the season. He was sure that if he continued playing well and hitting Triple-A pitching, he would be called up to the Dodgers soon.

The first hitter for the Portland Beavers was a speedy centerfielder, Carlos Cisneros. Tim played in, ready to pounce if the left handed batter lay down a bunt. With the count 1 and 1, Carlos slapped a pop up back behind third base, in foul territory. Tim turned and raced after the ball at full speed. His foot hit a broken sprinkler head and his ankle bone exploded, like the glass windshield in that '55 Chevy his parents were driving almost two decades earlier. He caught the ball, and then tumbled, rolling in pain.

The trainer ran out to the field. One look and he knew it was bad. The joint was already discolored and swollen. When he touched it Tim screamed, sucking in his breath. He had to be carried off the field by teammates. He was unable to put any weight on the leg without sending jolts of pain throughout his body.

At the hospital, he was given a pain injection and the staff took x-rays. "Tim, you're done for the year," the doctor explained.

Chapter 19 St. Petersburg, Florida
Spring 1976

After two long years, three surgeries, opiates, bed rest, bad daytime television, rehabilitation, and physical therapy, Tim was finally back at spring training, playing the game he loved. Dodgertown at Vero Beach, Florida was a huge complex that included a minor league stadium, six full baseball diamonds and other practice fields. For many years, the Dodger facility was considered to be the best in the world.

Tim was enjoying working up a sweat, fielding one ground ball after another. Then he went over to the batting cage where his hands became bloodied and then blistered from batting so many balls. Unfortunately, he felt like something was missing. His natural baseball rhythm had not returned and his timing was off. The scouts were saying that he had lost a step. Even playing in minor league spring exhibition games, Jacobson was batting only 204. Every night he iced his swollen ankle, but he hid the stiffness from his manager because, just like a pitcher with a sore arm, a fielder with a bad wheel was useless.

As the major league club was packing up to go to Los Angeles, management called Tim in for a meeting. The Assistant General Manager, Victor Bishop invited him to sit down. "Mr. Jacobson, I think we have been more than patient with you. The club has waited for two years for you to recover from your injury. I'm sorry, but we are releasing you. You are free to find another team."

Tim expected this. He knew he had not completely recovered. "Mr. Bishop, you will hear from my lawyer tomorrow. We believe there was negligence by the club in Albuquerque."

The Dodgers settled with Tim's new attorney, Lonnie, his childhood friend, quickly and quietly. His future medical requirements would be handled through worker's compensation and he would be paid an annuity of $500,000 over five years. If he signed another major league contract with any other club within those five years, the annuity would be adjusted accordingly.

The Omaha Kid was a free agent. Unfortunately, he had no offers. He was considered damaged goods, his dream dashed.

*

It all happened so quickly. He felt lost, not knowing where to go. Tim decided to turn north, back towards his nest. After three days of coffee, diners, and cheap motels, he crossed the Verrazano Narrows Bridge to Long Island, pulled towards his childhood home. Yet he didn't go immediately to Lynbrook.

Nostalgia led him down the road past what used to be Nathan's in Oceanside. The mega-large drive-in was gone, replaced by other small fast food establishments that one could find anywhere in the USA. He then cruised on to Long Beach. Tim spent many a summer's day imitating the words of the Drifters song *Under the Boardwalk,* "on a blanket with my baby, that's where I'll be." He thought about his days and nights as the high school sports star with Kristy, his cheerleader girlfriend. The beach town looked sadly different, rundown. Tim walked along the boardwalk and looked dreamily out at the ocean alone with his memories. Finally, he found his courage and wheeled his car to his childhood home.

He rang the doorbell and felt like a Fuller Brush salesman or one of those religious missionaries that come to people's porches dressed in suits and tried to sell redemption. What were they? Mormons, Seventh Day Adventists, Jehovah Witnesses? He couldn't remember them all, just that his Aunt would tell them all to go away. Would she do the same to him?

"Who is it?" The woman's voice came from inside the door.

"It's Tim."

The front door opened and there was Aunt Sophia. "I'm not sure I want to speak to you," she sighed. "I guess you can come in."

Tim smiled. He thought the hardest part would be getting in the door. "You look good." he said, but older, he thought. Crow's feet appeared next to her eyes and gray gathered at her temples.

"You think you can go off for three years and then turn up here like nothing happened."

"I'm sorry. I think we both have stuff we wish we could have done better. I thought of you all the time and what you and Uncle Tony did for me."

"Don't you understand how a mother loves a son? I didn't give birth to you but I raised you the best I could. I wanted the best for you and I wanted you to be a good Catholic boy."

"But you didn't think I was a very good Catholic boy."

"No, but I cared for you. Went to all your ball games, took you to Sunday school, to church, PTA meetings."

"Yes, I owe you a lot. I came to thank you. You didn't have to take me in." His voice broke when he said, "I love you, Aunt Sophia."

"Oh, now you tell me," she laughed, tears streaming down her eyes.
"Do you know what you need? A good meal."

"I was worried there. I thought you were going to say confession."

The woman smiled and said, "All in good time."

Chapter 20 On the Road
Summer 1976

Uncle Tony offered Tim a job with his restaurant chain, but the former ballplayer felt like New York was no longer home. California called to him in the form of his sister Linda. She was graduating from college at UC Berkeley, not in the spring, but after summer session, in August. Then she would start medical school in the fall at Stanford.

"I'd love you to come to my graduation," she told him at the end of a long-distance telephone conversation.

"I'll be there," he promised.

Tim planned his trip like it was his farewell tour to baseball. First, he went to Philadelphia to see the Phillies, then on to Pittsburg and the Pirates. He spent the fourth of July at Wrigley Field in Chicago and when the Cubs won there were glorious fireworks. He stayed in town for the White Sox. Next, he went back down to St. Louis for the Cardinals and a visit to a jazz club. He met old minor league friends in different cities playing now in the majors with various levels of success. It was as if he was trying to purge himself from the game by going to all the places in which he had expected to play.

On July 21st his Mustang crossed the Platt River into Omaha, Nebraska. It had been almost twenty years since the accident. Timmy didn't know what drew him to this city that he remembered with so much pain. It took him a while to map out the course to his childhood house. The white picket fence was still there but it looked so much smaller than he remembered.

There were two cemeteries to visit, one Jewish for his father and a Catholic one for his mother. He had never been to either one. He spent about an hour at each, leaving a pebble on each gravestone. He didn't shed any tears. He knew he wouldn't find his parents at those sites, only their markers. As he drove away through the corn fields that reached to the heavens, he felt empty, unsatisfied. The Omaha kid did not think he would ever be back.

*

Tim did find his parents in the face of the young woman with the funny square cap on her head. She had her mother's hair, nose and lips, her father's dark brown eyes and thick eyebrows. The graduate, his sister, Linda, daughter of two nurses, was going to be a doctor. He felt a certain amount of sibling pride, despite having been separated for so many years.

Many of his father's side of the family were in attendance and they greeted the prodigal son warmly, but he could tell there was a sense of unease, like he was part of a dark family secret. Linda though was enthralled that he came all the way across the country to be at the ceremony. She invited her brother to stay with her at her apartment in Berkeley until she moved to Palo Alto the next month. Not knowing what he was going to do next, he accepted. The next day he checked out of his hotel and moved to his sister's living room couch

Chapter 21 Berkeley and
North Lake Tahoe, California
Autumn 1976

Dear Mom,

I just met the man I'm going to marry. He is
Linda's brother.
His name is Tim, and he is a dream, tall, dark, and so
good looking.
He was a professional baseball player but he had to
leave the game because he had a major ankle injury. He
is mostly better now and is staying with us. (Don't
worry, he is on the couch.) Tim has not asked me out or
even done anything to let me think he likes me. Yet the
two of us have stayed up late talking, and he listens.
Can you believe it, a man who listens? I think he has a
great sense of humor; he jokes all the time.

I want him to fall for me. But you know that
Linda moves out at the end of the month, and of
course, he will leave with her and I will lose my chance.
He just came out here from New York for his sister's
graduation. So, I have an idea. I want to invite them up
to the cabin at Lake Tahoe before she starts med school
at Stanford. What do you think? Would that be all right
with you and Dad?

Love you,
Jenny

*

At Jennifer Canon's family cabin near Squaw Valley, Tim Jacobson fell instantly in love, not with the girl, but with the Sierra Nevada. Devoid of his allegiance to baseball and its daily duties, he felt a new freedom. The mountains with their clean pine scented air and primitive forests, called to him like a fastball right over the plate.

Jenny, Linda and Tim spent a long weekend playing together. They rafted down the Truckee River on the first day. Getting up early on the second morning, they bicycled along Donner Lake, then up the old US 40 highway to the summit. After a snack while enjoying the view, they screamed back down the curves at breakneck speeds.

For Tim, the best day was hiking on a mountain trail above the ski resort. They followed a creek up from Squaw Valley and found clear waterfalls flowing below the chairlifts. Moving above the mixed hardwood tree laced creek bed, they crossed into thick fir and pine forest losing the view of the cliffs but surrounded by the grandeur of the big trees. The trail climbed even higher above the timberline. Where Indian paint brush, wild dandelion and other ground flora bloomed yellow, purple and red fighting to grow in every crack of loose soil among the mica and quartz speckled granite cliffs. They climbed up the sheer switchbacks, putting one foot in front of another, stopping periodically to catch their breath, fighting the thin air and the exertion of ascending the steep rise. Then, finally, Tim felt an amazing exhilaration as he reached the peak and looked down to see the valleys below and Lake Tahoe shimmering in the distance. He had never seen anything like this.

That night, after going to a club for dinner, rock and roll and shots of tequila, they fell back into the cabin, which was very luxurious. All the houses in the Tahoe area were called cabins. Jenny decided to make her play for the object of her affection. She put a Nat King Cole album on the stereo and curled up on the couch next to Tim.

He started to ask. "What are you d…" when she put her finger on his mouth.

"Shush," she said tilting her head towards him, her long brown hair falling in front of one of her brown eyes. Linda took the hint and quietly left for her bedroom.

Tim kissed her.

"Why did you wait so long to do that?" she asked breathlessly. "All those nights we stayed up late talking, didn't you think I was attractive?"

"I think you are beautiful, but you're Linda's roommate. I thought it might get weird."

"Don't worry, she's moving out at the end of the week," Jenny reminded him.

"Maybe I should leave and come back next week."

"The hell with that!" This time she kissed him passionately. When the kiss ended, she smiled at him. "Do you know how long I wanted to kiss you?" Jenny took him by the hand and led him to her bedroom.

*

The early September light filtered into the room as the sun slowly peaked above the mountains. Jenny inhaled and with eyes still closed filled her nostrils with the musky smell of his body. She smiled and ran her fingernails lightly through Tim's chest hairs.-He awoke and held her, then kissed her forehead. His mouth was dry and pasty, so he avoided her lips. A dull ache filled his sinus cavity, the result of too much tequila the night before.

"I'm going to move here," he declared.

"California?" She asked hopefully.

"Yeah, but here, the Lake Tahoe area."

Jenny frowned. "I was hoping you might want to stay in the Bay Area. I have another year until I graduate from Berkeley. Don't you want to see more of me?"

"Yes, sure, absolutely, I can come visit you. Linda's going to be in Palo Alto. You can come up to your cabin and see me up here."

"So can I call you my boyfriend or are we just dating."

Tim hadn't even that that far ahead. He knew he liked her a lot. She sure was pretty and they had fun together. "Ok, Jenny you can call me your boyfriend. I guess I have a girlfriend." He laughed and hugged her. "I really didn't expect this."

She giggled and kissed her new lover, finding his lips. Breakfast would have to wait.

Chapter 22 Lake Tahoe, California
January 1978 to February 1979

Lake Tahoe gave off an aquamarine blue glow in the bright sunshine. Tim never tired of the view looking down the thousands of feet below the summit of Alpine Meadows Resort. The two skiers stood at the top of the steep ridge above beaver bowl. Tim could feel his adrenaline pumping as he adjusted his goggles. His ankle did not hurt encased in the cast-like structure of his ski boot. It had snowed all night and four feet of new powdery white snow blanketed the Sierra Nevada playground. The now cloudless sky was as blue as the lake.

Tim was skiing with Steve who he met in the Bar of America in Truckee. The two became good friends and often skied together. Tim's new pal had moved to the mountains a year earlier after a stint a college at Sacramento State. Steve shouted so his voice could be heard above the hailing wind, "Go for it!"

Tim turned his shoulders downhill and floated on the feathery, white powder. His knees pumped like pistons as the long skis turned in a rhythmical back and forth, like a metronome keeping time for a pianist playing a Beethoven symphony.

"Hell yes!" Tim shouted as his skis created little avalanches, flowing down the slope in front of him. Steve followed and caught up to Tim as he stopped just above the timberline to catch his breath.

Steve went first this time, picking his way through the tall Ponderosa pines. The green branches hung burdened, covered with a heavy layer of snow. The needles tossed snowflakes at the two friends as they darted around the tree trunks in the forest. Below the trees they jumped down to the groomed trail of machine-packed snow that led to the ski lift. They flew, almost becoming airborne as they tucked to gain speed. Finally, just in front of the lift, they turned sharply using a hockey stop to dig in their edges, throwing up a wave of white. There was no line on this early weekday morning, so they mounted the chairlift to take them back to the top of the world.

Tim had become a mountain man. A crusty snow encased beard covered his face. At Tahoe City, he worked as a bartender serving the flatland tourists that invaded every weekend. His job left him free on weekdays when the mountainsides were less crowded to hike, fish and bike ride in the summer and ski during the winter.

*

Jennifer and Tim continued to be a couple throughout the school year, seeing each other as often as possible. But with her in classes and he working weekends, their meetings became more infrequent, yet still very passionate. The distance tested their relationship. They passed the test. June came and Tim attended her graduation.

There was a party at Jenny's parent's house in Walnut Creek. Linda, Tim and Jenny found they were alone in the living room after all the other guests went home. Mr. and Mrs. Canon said good night and retreated upstairs. Jenny poured a new batch of margaritas continuing the celebration.

Linda asked, "So what does the honors graduate in literature do now?"

Jenny looked at Tim. "How would you feel if I moved up to the cabin to be with you? I have a job offer at the Truckee Hotel."

"Wow that would be great. We could be together all the time. Would your parents let us live together up there in their cabin?"

"I actually asked them that very question. They would like you to keep your apartment for appearance sake, but they know you are going to be at the cabin all the time."

"The sooner the better, babe."

"And Linda, if you could take a break from your studies, you could come up and hang out any time.

By July the two were living together.

*

Winter invaded with Tim and Jenny nested comfortably in the cabin. They spent their first Christmas and the New Year's Eve festivities together and Tim was happy to have a partner to share these events with him. February came and the skiing conditions remained excellent.

After a full day on the slopes, Steve and Tim had a quick beer in the Chalet. Steve headed to Tahoe City while Tim turned toward Squaw Valley for a quiet evening with his girlfriend. Jenny cooked chicken and dumplings for him. He poured her a drink.

"I'm thinking of going to graduate school next year to become a teacher." Jenny said. She waited for him to comment, and then continued. "I'm thinking of Reno or San Diego. What do you think?"

"I think it should be your choice," Tim said with a smile.

"It's my choice. That's all you have to say!" Her voice got louder.

"Why are you getting angry? Of course it's your choice. You would get upset if I told you what to do."

"So Reno or San Diego, you don't care?"

"I'd love to visit you in San Diego."

"God, you're infuriating," she said gritting her teeth and sucking in her breath.

"There you go using those big words, showing me that UC education." He smiled teasing her, doing his best to get her to laugh and put an end to her growing anger. He wasn't sure he understood why she was upset with him.

Her voice cracked. She said softly, almost a whisper, "Tim, you know I love you, don't you."

"Yes."

"Do you love me?"

"I *believe* I do."

"You believe you do. After all this time is that the best you've got? Tim, something is missing here."

"Jenny please, let's not fight."

"Really? We have been together over a year. You haven't asked me to marry you. You never even told me you love me."

"Jenny, you know I care about you. Come on let's not do this."

"Why didn't you insist on Reno? You don't care if I move away. Do you?"

"I do."

Her voice softened and she begged, "Tell me to stay with you."

He didn't answer for a second. Jennifer started to cry big tears falling down her cheeks. "Oh my God! You don't love me. Tim, why not?"

Tim felt like she punched him in the gut. "I want to love you. But I don't know. There is something wrong, not with you, but with me." He realized that he hadn't really been in love since his lost childhood sweetheart, Kristy. "Maybe with more time...I...could..."

She stared at him, mouth open, tears continued to run causing her eye make-up to run black streaks down her face. She saw him differently, like something inside him was broken, not just his ankle. Her anger left, replaced with a deep sadness.

"I do love you Tim. I thought..." Her back stiffened. She stood up straight. "You need to leave, now."

"Jenny please, I want to be with you. You are wonderful."

"Sorry, it's not enough."

*

Linda called her brother. "Tim, what is the matter with you? How could you do that to Jenny?"

"I didn't do anything, I didn't want break up with her. But I couldn't lie to her. I owe her that much. I couldn't just tell her what she wanted to hear. I wanted to love her but Sis, something was missing."

"Something like you having a screw loose. She is smart and beautiful. I love her, almost like a sister. Hell if I was gay, I'd marry her."

He laughed but said with sadness in his voice, "I have no answer for you. I didn't want to hurt her. I care about Jenny a lot. I just wasn't in love and I'm not sure why. She is a great girl."

"You are going to look for a long time before you find another Jenny. And she loves you."

"You're right."

"I think you need therapy."

"Really, you think I'm that hopeless. What about you? You're not exactly ready to settle down with anyone."

"I'm younger than you and just started medical school. I'm not ready for that type of relationship." She refused to let him off the hook.

"By the way, how are you doing? How's school?" He tried to change the subject.

"Hard, but I like it."

"Ok, you finished giving me a hard time?"

"I guess so, for now."

"Ok sis, I love you."

"Yeah, me too, but you're still an idiot. Bye."

"Bye," he said and hung up the phone.

*

Steve and Tim stopped at Alpine's mid-mountain chalet for lunch on their third run down the mountain.

Tim asked his friend, "Do you think I was a fool not telling Jenny that I loved her?"

"I think I'm the wrong person to ask. You know me, Mr. Love 'um and Leave 'um. But if you didn't love her what else could you do?"

"Yeah, but even you admit that Jenny was special."

"Yes, but I am not sure guys are supposed to be monogamous and be with one woman for life. Look at JFK, he was married to the perfect wife, Jackie, but did he kick Marilyn Monroe out of bed? Hell no!"

"Well…"

"Remember the Crosby, Stills and Nash song, 'If you can't be with the one you love, love the one you're with,'" Steve said adding to his point.

"Great, I'm getting love advice from a rock and roll band."

*

Tim decided to call his high school buddy and attorney, Lonnie, who was married with two kids. He explained his confusion about the break up with Jenny.

Tim asked his longtime friend, "Are you happy being married?"

"Well, I can't give you a simple answer. I think I'm happy, but I'm so busy, away from the kids too often. Marriage is hard."

"Do you ever think of straying?"

"I did once, with a client, but I felt so guilty. I don't think I'll ever do it again."

"Does Betsey know?"

"Hell no!" And I want to keep it that way."

"Well, she won't hear it from me."

"Are you still confused?" Lonnie asked.

"Yeah, I think I'm missing a piece of my heart or something. Jenny is amazing."

"Sorry buddy, I don't know what to tell you."

"Oh well. Say hello to your family for me. We'll catch up again soon."

"Just go get drunk."

"Yeah, maybe. Be well buddy. Bye."

"Bye, Omaha"

Chapter 23   North Lake Tahoe
and Reno
Spring 1979

Tim played shortstop and the opposing batter smacked the ball into the hole towards third. He raced over, backhanded the ball into his glove, planted his damaged ankle and fired a strike to Steve at first, nailing the fast runner by a full step. It was only a club softball team, but Tim felt like his old self, before the injury.

"Nice play Tim. I would have liked to have seen you play for the A's," Steve said as they jogged off the field.

"It feels good to be able to go into the hole like that again. My leg feels the best it has since before I hurt it. Are we still going to Tahoe John's for pizza and beer?"

"Yeah, but I can't stay too late. I have to be at work early tomorrow at Squaw." Steve was completing his first year on the ski patrol.

"Were you able to get me a ski pass?"

"Yeah, I have it for you, but you need be there early. Even north facing slopes get slushy this time of year."

*

The sun shined brilliantly on a beautiful April morning. Even early in the day, wearing just a light jacket, Tim felt warm. Bright rays of light beamed onto his sun block coated face as he approached the bottom of the KT22 lift. There was a small line of people ahead so he called, "Single."

"Single," a woman replied in front of him.

Tim stepped up to the young lady who was wearing tight ski pants and a matching vest over a white turtleneck sweeter.

"Hello," Tim said as his gloved hand grabbed onto the chair and he was hoisted into the chair and towards the top of the mountain.

"Hello, it is a good lift, yes?" The woman said with what he thought was a French accent. "It is my first time here."

"It's hard coming down this way, expert only. I hope you can ski well."

"Yes. It is ok."

"Are you French?"

"Yes, I am sorry my English is not so good, always."

The young woman's pretty face was tan. Her blond hair was gathered in a ponytail and mirrored sun glasses hid her eyes.

"Is it your first day skiing at Squaw Valley?"

"It is first time in California. I come from Reno this morning."

"Were you there to gamble?"

"Gamble? What is this word? Oh I remember. No, no gamble, to play tennis."

"All the way from France to play tennis in Reno, Nevada?"

"Yes, I play in professional tournament."

"Oh, you must be good."

"Maybe, not so much. I did not win." she said and laughed. "Do you play tennis?"

"I did, many years ago."

"Not so many, you are still young, no?"

They were coming to the top of the lift. They skied off the chair and around a rocky outcropping. The slope was very steep and full of big hard packed moguls.

"Are you ok with this?" he asked.

"Yes, you come with me, ok?"

"Sure." Tim was worried that KT22 might be too challenging for her until he saw the French woman turn her skis down the ridgeline and bounce into perfect rhythmic turns. He followed, trying to keep up.

The early morning run was still icy and they stopped to catch their breath. The girl said, "That snow was not so good, yes? Ice on top."

"I know a good spot for this time of year. The back side of Shirley Lake has good corn snow."

"What is this corn snow? Corn is to eat, no?"

Tim laughed. "Yes, corn is food but it is also a type of snow in the spring. It's good skiing, you'll see. My name is Tim. He put out his gloved hand to shake. She smiled at him and shook his hand.

"I am Brigitte, Brigitte Muldaur."

"Follow me Brigitte."

They took off and had a wonderful morning skiing and talking on the lifts. They took a break for a snack at High Camp.

Tim said, "You are an amazing skier."

"Thank you, my family has a house in the Alps. You are good also, yes?"

"Thanks, but I could barely keep up with you."

"I must go now. I have to practice tennis this afternoon and I leave Reno tomorrow. You come to play tennis with me now?"

"I'm afraid I wouldn't be able to play well enough to challenge you. It has been a long time. I don't even have a racquet."

"Yes, that is ok the hotel barrows racquets like they barrow my skis. I practice every day. It will be fun, no?" Her blue eyes challenged him.

He shrugged his shoulders. "Why not? I don't have to work tonight. Let me get some stuff. Do you want a ride?"

"Yes, that is good, I took bus from hotel."

*

They hit tennis balls, rallying for about an hour in the warm Reno spring sunshine. The game came back to him quickly like riding a bike. His ankle felt good. He was much stronger than his high school playing days and while he could hit the ball with more power than the woman on the other side of the net, her consistently brilliant shot-making ability kept him at bay. He thought that she looked beautiful in her short, white, pleated tennis skirt and matching blouse that was damp and clinging to her from perspiration.

"Let's play some points for real," Brigitte said. "Two games, no add. Ok."

"Sure, you serve first."

Her topspin and slice serve was hard to handle and she went up 40 to love, but then she left one short and he blasted a winner. The girl smiled.

"40-15," she called and then served to his backhand. Tim hit a slice back. With good disguise, she came under the ball dropping it just over the net. Showing his speed, he got to the ball but topped it out. She won the first game.

"Ok, you serve. Hit hard," she said.

Despite her warning, he hit a relative easy serve to her forehand and she smacked a clean winner. I'd better bring it, he thought but he was out of practice and his first serve was long. On his second serve, she hit another winner just on the line. He aced the next two serves one to her backhand the next to her forehand. "30 all," she said. They split the next two points. "Forty all, no add so it is match point. No pressure," she said smiling, trying to psyche him out.

He hit a hard serve to her backhand and came in behind it. She sent a two handed topspin lob back over his head. Brigitte held her hands over her head like she had just won Wimbledon. They both laughed.

Tim came to the net to shake her hand, but she kissed him on each cheek, "That is how we shake hands with good friends in France."

"I like your way better."

Evening was falling as the sun sank early below the mountains to the west.

"Let us go get some dinner. Did I say that correct?"

"The dinner part, say 'Let's go get some dinner,' and then it's, 'Did I say that correctly?'"

"Correctly," she repeated.

"I'm all sweaty. So, maybe something simple, like a pizza place," Tim suggested.

"No, I would like to take you to dinner at my hotel. You can use my shower room."

"But you're the guest in my country. I should buy you dinner."

"You were my practice partner. It is business, no?"

"I'll tell you what, let's go Dutch."

"Dutch? Do you want German food?"

Tim laughed. "No, Dutch is an American expression for we each pay for our own food."

"Really? I never heard that. Dinner will be charged to my hotel bill, so you have no worry, please."

"All right, if you insist."

After cleaning up, the two went to the main dining room in the Hilton. Tim looked at the menu and was suddenly glad she was paying. The prices did not match his bartender salary.

"Do you know what you want?" he asked.

"Yes," she said looking intently at him.

He matched her stare with a smile then signaled the waiter, "Please go first."

Brigitte said, "I will have the shrimp salad with a glass of white Burgundy, then the petite fillet with vegetables and a glass of red Bordeaux."

"How would you like your steak?" the waiter asked.

She looked at Tim. "He means how do you want it cooked?"

"Red. Is that right?" She asked.

"I believe she means rare."

"Very good, and you sir?" the waiter asked.

"I'll have the same but I would like my steak medium well and the baked potato." He turned to her, "I usually drink beer. I hope you don't mind"

She said, "I like beer also, but in France we match the food with wine."

"I know, I work at a bar. I have just never really tried to do that."

"So you will try it. Yes?"

"Yes," he said with a smile, and turned back to the waiter. "I'll have the wine she's having."

She reached out for his hand. "This is nice. But you must do me one more thing."

"Yes?" he asked.

"Americans eat so fast. In France, we eat slow and enjoy our food. Can we eat more slow?"

"It will be a pleasure."

It was almost two hours later, they finished dinner, sharing a dessert with coffee and brandy.

Tim followed Brigitte to her room to get his things. She turned on the television. "I need to use the toilet. I will soon be out, you wait. Ok?"

Brigitte came out of the bathroom wearing a black negligee with stockings to match. She shook out her blond hair and came across the room to Tim. Brigitte whispered in his ear, "Remember in France we go slow and enjoy."

Chapter 24 Northern California
Summer 1979 to Autumn 1980

The smell of wet leaves carried on the light breeze and the trees on campus blazed in color. Tim admired the beauty of the yellow, orange and red foliage flying around him as he walked, tennis racquet in hand. A blond cheerleader walked by, with a big "S" emblazed on the chest of her cardinal red outfit, looking a lot like "Supergirl" from the comic books that Tim read when he was a kid. It was a typical autumn Saturday at Stanford, with the UCLA football team due to play at the stadium that afternoon. Tim would attend the game later. This morning he was headed for a match with John Rollston, a student from the number one ranked college team in the country. Since Tim had won the open tournament at the Palo Alto tennis club, he had been invited by the coach to work out a few times with the college tennis team.

Even months later, the day and night Tim had spent with Brigitte seemed like a happy dream and the vision of her lingered. He could not get the French woman out of his mind. That morning when he woke up next to her, his senses were filled with the smell of her hair, the vision of her sleeping face and the feel of her body next to his. Their day skiing, playing tennis and making love awakened something deep inside of him. As Tim drove her to the airport, he realized he didn't want her to go. They said their goodbyes. She told him to visit her if he ever came to France and then kissed him on each cheek. Then she was gone, sent off with little more than a French hand shake. He'd watched her plane take off with his hand to his cheek where her lips last touched him.

*

Brigitte awoke in Tim a new passion for the game of tennis. He started to play and practice again, often. In July he entered a tennis tournament at Squaw Valley. To his great surprise he won easily (6-2 6-3) in the finals. His quickness, and powerful forehand, made up for a lack of experience. A month later in Reno, he met with more success, winning another amateur tournament. When he won again in Sacramento, he decided to move out of the mountains to Palo Alto, where he could play tennis year around and be close to his sister.

He found an evening job tending bar at the White Rabbit Tavern on University Avenue pouring drinks mostly for the older students. During the day he played tennis, turning it into his main occupation, as he had with baseball. Like baseball, his first year he was in the minor leagues, playing and winning tournaments all over the southwest. He won in the desert at Palm Springs, then near the beach in Orange County and between rain showers in Portland. He came in second in the greater Los Angeles open, losing in the finals (7-5, 4-6, 4-6) to the number 20 ranked player in the country. He was good and getting better. He even won a little prize money along the way, although not near enough to quit his evening job.

*

Tim destroyed John Rollston that fall day, (6-1, 6-2) returning the student's hard serves easily, hitting winners all over the court.

"You were unbelievable today." John said as he shook Tim's hand. "I'm glad my Coach didn't see that."

"Thanks, my timing was good," Tim replied humbly, wiping the sweat from his forehead with a towel.

"Are you going to the football game?"

"Yeah, I'm meeting my sister and her friend. Want to come along?"

"No, I'm meeting a couple of guys from the tennis team, but maybe we will see you there."

"Sounds good, thanks again for the match."

Chapter 25 California
and New York
December 1980

The phone rang in Tim's apartment at four in the morning. He woke out of a deep sleep dreaming about playing guitar with the Rolling Stones. "Hello?" He managed to say groggily.

"Tim, its JR. Dad's sick. He's in the hospital."

He was instantly awake. "What's wrong?"

"It's his heart. They need to do a bypass."

"How are your mom and Maria holding up?"

"Not so good. They're worried sick."

"I'll catch a flight today if I can, if not tomorrow."

"That would be great. You can stay with Cathy and me."

"I would like that. We have a lot of catching up to do."

"Oh, and Tim, Joey told me, he would like his uncle to stay for Christmas."

"Let me see what I can do."

It was too early to call travel agents or anybody else, so Tim decided to try and go back to sleep. He couldn't, upset and ruminating about his uncle's condition. He thought that it might be a good idea to ask his sister to go with him. He waited until seven o'clock and called her.

"Hello, Linda."

"Hi Tim, what's up besides you so early this morning?"

"How would you like to spend winter break with me in New York?" He explained the situation to his sister then said, "I know you haven't been back East since you moved out here with Aunt Mae and Uncle Willie, come with me. My treat, what do you say?"

"It's tempting, but I have a lot of studying to do."

"Can't you take that with you? It time you faced Mom's side of the family, the crazy Italian side, instead of Dad's neurotic Jewish side. And you know New York during the holiday season is awesome--Macys, Bloomingdales, 5th Avenue, Times Square, We could even go to a Broadway play."

"What are you, the Chamber of Commerce?" She gave his proposition some serious thought. "Let me make some phone calls. I'll call you back."

"Ok, but I need to know this morning. I have to get tickets and we would need to leave by tomorrow."

*

They were about halfway through the flight, over Nebraska, when Linda asked her brother, "Why did you want me to come?"

"Two reasons. I thought it was time for my side of the family to meet you, to know that you are ok and to ease their Catholic guilt, especially Uncle Tony. I think he always felt bad about not fighting for you. You know, especially now that he is sick."

"Ok and the other reason?"

"I wanted to spend Hanukkah with you. We never got to do that."

"Oh, that's sweet. Do you even know what it is?"

"Not really, something about a festival of lights, and that menorah thing."

Linda laughed. "Yeah, that menorah thing. There are nine candles, one for each of the eight day holiday, plus a special lighter candle. It's not even a major Jewish Holiday but with Christmas in December, American Jews made it a bigger deal."

"So what is it about?"

"To make a long story short, the ancient Israelites were defeated by another tribe who desecrated the Temple in Jerusalem. They ran pigs through the place and made a mess of things. When the Jews finally defeated the bad guys, they wanted to clean up the Temple. The first thing they did was to light the eternal flame but there only was enough oil to burn for a few hours. The miracle and the symbol for the holiday was that it burned for eight days."

"Cool. Of course that brings up the whole pig thing. Why are they so bad to eat?"

"It's called being kosher. Much more than just pigs were considered unclean. Also you can't eat milk with meat, no shellfish and a lot of other silly rules. It was kind of like the first pure food laws combined with a religious respect for what you are eating."

"I always wondered about that.

"Tim?"

"Yeah."

"Did you ever wonder what we would be like if Uncle Tony took me and you went with Aunt Mae? You would have grown up Jewish and me Catholic."

"Of course I thought about that, especially when I was a teenager and in full rebellion mode."

"I wonder, would I still be going to med school? Would you have played baseball?"

"I would have always played baseball." Tim said with a laugh.

"I'm serious."

"I guess it all goes back to that whole nature, nurture argument."

They just stared out the window for a while lost in thought, looking at the clouds.

*

Tony Jr. and his wife owned a lovely and spacious four bedroom Upper East Side condominium complete with a doorman in front. By living in Manhattan, the younger Corelli was able to be close to the offices of the business he owned with his father. Besides the six family Italian restaurants, the company had expanded under the leadership of Tony Jr. to include a franchise of fast food drive-ins serving pizza, calzone and meatball hero sandwiches located in New York, Chicago and Los Angeles. To Tim, the younger Tony was still Junior, but his workers and friends now called him JR. He greeted his adopted brother and Linda at the door.

Tim made the introductions. "Linda this is Junior…Sorry," he said with a teasing smile and winked at his cousin, "this is JR and his wife Cathy. That little guy standing behind them is Joey. This is your long lost cousin Linda."

"Joey, say hello to your uncle and cousin," JR said.

The boy stood behind his mother and waved shyly. "Hello," was all he managed to say.

"Uncle Tim was about your age when he came to live with Grandpa, Grandma, your Aunt Maria and me."

"Really?" the boy asked.

Tim smiled at his nephew. "You remember me don't you? I saw you about a year ago."

Joey shook his head up and down. "I remember you Uncle Tim," but he still did not venture away from his mother.

His father picked the boy up and took him to the guests. "Shake hands, Joey."

When the introductions were complete, Tim asked, "How's your Dad?"

"Not good. He is in the hospital and surgery is scheduled for the end of the week. Excuse my manners. Let me show you to your rooms."

*

For the next few days Tim and Linda stayed busy. The first day Cathy took Linda shopping in Manhattan while Tim and JR went to visit Tony Senior in the hospital. Tim's Aunt Sophia was already there. Tim was amazed how bad his uncle appeared to be and how old his aunt looked.

The Californians spent the next few days doing the tour, which included--the Zoo in Central Park, Rockefeller Center, The Empire State Building, Wall Street, the Staten Island Ferry past The Statue of Liberty, and even a Broadway play, Neil Simon's, *The Odd Couple*.

Maria came in from Princeton and Tim spent the day with her. She was just finishing her PhD thesis in Psychology. The two reminisced and shared stories about growing up together as they drove out to Long Island to pick up her mom and visit the hospital.

It had been a long time since Tim had been in his childhood home in Lynbrook. With the children out of the house, Aunt Sophia had turned the place into a shrine. There were pictures of the Virgin Mary, various saints and Jesus throughout the house. The living room had been turned into a Christian sanctuary with a huge wooden image of Jesus hanging on the cross.

"What in the world?" Tim whispered to Maria.

"I know." She whispered back, "I'll talk to you about it later."

It was a short visit with Tim's Uncle Tony, doctor's orders. He was not doing well and needed to rest. The surgery would take place the day after Christmas. Maria and Tim left Sophia in the hospital. She wanted to stay in the hospital chapel and would get a taxi home.

On the way back to the city Tim asked, "What is going on with the house?"

"Mom's gone a little off the deep end. She believed Dad was having an affair a year ago and she thought that by turning the house into a shrine she could guilt him into stopping."

"Was he?"

"Probably, JR and I don't really know."

"It's very creepy, weird."

"Yeah, that's the official psychological term we use for it."

"You know, the thing I miss most about New York is this. I miss the talks with my big sister."

"I miss you too, Tim." She leaned over and kissed his cheek.

"Are you coming for Christmas at Junior's place Thursday morning?"

"I'll be there.

*

That night at sunset was the beginning of Hanukkah. At JR's condo, Linda lit the first candle of the menorah saying the same magical Hebrew words that her tribe had been chanting for thousands of years. It sounded foreign and strange to Tim, but not any stranger then the equally magic words of Latin that he heard at Mass growing up. When she finished she wished her reunited family a happy Hanukkah. Hugs were exchanged and Linda gave Joey five silver dollars and various different coin shaped chocolates.

"What did you think of that Joey?" Uncle Tim asked.

"I think Christmas is more fun."

Linda said, "Well I guess it's a good thing Santa comes tomorrow night. Were you a good boy this year?"

"Yup," Joey said and looked longingly at his Dad for confirmation.

"Don't worry buddy. Santa wrote me a letter saying he was coming."

*

Christmas morning Tim was awakened by his nephew tugging at his hand. "Uncle Tim, Uncle Tim, Santa came, get up!"

Tim thought he would never get to finish his dream about the Rolling Stones. "Ok buddy, I'm coming."

JR, Cathy and Linda were already gathered around the tree, drinking coffee and wearing robes. The bell rang and Joey ran to the door to escort his Aunt Maria into his home. Notably absent was the boy's grandmother Sophia who had decided to skip present giving and spend the morning in church praying for her husband.

It was Linda's first celebration of Christmas. Every year on this day she felt a little left out, being Jewish in the overwhelmingly Christian country. She never had Santa come to her house.

JR said, "Linda you are the guest. You get the first gift." He held out a present for his cousin.

"That's no fair!" Joey yelled.

His mother quickly silenced the boy. "Joey where are your manners!" Santa would be disappointed."

The gift giving continued, each taking a turn. Tim gave Linda silver earrings from Tiffany. For his nephew, he got a baseball autographed by his former teammate and at that time, New York Yankee, Reggie Jackson. After the presents were exchanged, Maria, JR and Cathy left to go out to the Island to meet their mother for Mass and then be in the hospital to see Tim's Uncle Tony. That left Linda and Tim behind babysitting.

"I hope you enjoyed that," Tim said to his sister as Joey played more with the boxes than the toys that came in them.

"It was really sweet. I'm glad I came. Thanks for bringing me."

*

The doctors pronounced the operation a success but Uncle Tony grimaced with extreme pain. They had to crack his ribs open to get to the heart. Morphine dripped into his veins. He contorted his painful body to look at Linda and Tim sitting at his bedside. Knowing that their uncle was safe, the siblings scheduled a flight back to California the next day.

"You look so much like your mother. Oh Roberta forgive me." A single tear made its way down his cheek. "I can't believe you're all grown up." Tony weakly tried to sing. "You were a beautiful baby and baby look at you now." He laughed at stealing the song lines from his youth but it hurt to laugh. "How have you been?"

"I've been really good Uncle Tony. I love living in Northern California. The Bay Area was an interesting place to grow up. You have to come out when you are feeling better. I'll give you the special tour."

"Did you go to your prom?"

"Of course, I had the normal American childhood."

He didn't know how to ask. "Are…you Jewish?"

"Yes Uncle Tony, I'm even circumcised."

"What?" He almost sat up.

"Sorry, I was just kidding, they only do that to boys."

"Please don't make me laugh. It's painful. I hear you're going to be a doctor."

"Yes sir. I know what you are thinking, just what we need, another Jewish doctor."

"Will you stop with the jokes." But he couldn't resist giving her a smile. Uncle Tony looked deeply into his niece's eyes. He felt like he was looking at his sister. "Your mother would be so proud of you."

"Thank you. That means a lot to me. Merry Christmas, Uncle Tony."

"Happy Hanukkah to you. Please give my best to your family back in California. Tell them I'm sorry if…"

"Uncle Tony, you don't have anything to be sorry about. It all worked out fine."

"Yes, but there is one thing I'm very sorry about. Not seeing you grow up. I should have reached out to you. I should have never let you and Tim not be a part of each other's lives. Your parents would have definitely not approved of my behavior." The effort and emotion of this simple apology left him exhausted. But tired as he was, he smiled at his beautiful, intelligent niece and winked. "Maybe it was better that I wasn't around you to screw you up." He tried to laugh at his bad joke, but again his sore ribs protested. "There, I'm glad I could tell you I'm sorry. You know, guilt was a heavy burden to carry around."

Linda bent down and kissed her uncle on the cheek. "Get well Uncle Tony, and if you don't come sooner, I promise I'll invite you when I graduate from medical school."

Chapter 26 North America
Winter 1981

The sun would not come over the horizon to greet the New Year. Rain poured down in the Bay Area on New Year Eve and the forecast predicted the deluge to continue throughout the week. For Tim this evening appeared to be just a very busy work night. Even if he didn't have to tend bar, he refused to find a date for the night. The tall, handsome bartender in a college town did not have a shortage of opportunities to meet and go out with attractive women. He dated often, but for Tim, New Year's Eve was not a night for a casual date. As he dressed for work that night, he had a feeling that this year something pivotal in his life would take place.

He felt himself thinking of the one woman that still entered his dreams. Brigitte Muldour. He tried to call her home in Marseille, but he kept getting the machine telling him in her sexy French voice to "Leave a message." He said hello and asked her to call but never received a reply.

With the New Year came the new United States Tennis Association's tennis rankings and Tim was informed he was 89th in the country. Being in the top 100 meant he would be invited to second tier professional tournaments. On January 10, he received notification that he was invited to the Coca-Cola Vancouver Open, played indoors at a hockey arena, starting January 21. Unfortunately, at this level, he had to pay his own way to tournaments. Luckily, he had a flexible schedule and an understanding boss.

*

He won his first four matches on the indoor hard courts, all in straight sets, using his powerful serve as a weapon. In the finals he played Barry Long, the number ten ranked Canadian.

He tossed and turned all night before the match. He played out the match in his mind over and over. His lack of sleep left him exhausted and he lost the first set 2-6 with the crowd cheering wildly for the local twenty-two year old British Colombian. Then Tim got hot and reeled off 8 games in a row to take the lead and went on to win the match 6-2 in the third set. The winning check paid little more than his expenses.

Next up was the Cincinnati Indoor Tournament in February. He had a harder time reaching the finals with two higher ranked players taking him to three sets, but on Sunday he cruised to a 6-3, 6-4 win over another long shot.

*

Tim walked into The White Rabbit, on the next Tuesday night for his shift. With his Canadian adventure, he hadn't been at his job in over a week.

"Surprise!" People yelled in unison, and then sang, "Happy Birthday." Stunned by the reception, he looked around the room. There was a mix of his friends, tennis partners, people he knew from the bar, a couple of girls he had dated. Steve had come from the mountains and even a couple of his old baseball teammates showed up. After his initial shock wore off, Tim toured the room saying hello. Linda was there with a big smile on her face. She had organized this party in between her homework assignments and classes at med school.

"I bet this is your fault," he said to his sister.

"Guilty as charged."

He gave her a big hug and a kiss on the cheek. "Thanks and don't you ever do this again."

"Nope, you only get one surprise birthday party from me in a lifetime. By the way, congratulations on your big win."

Then she continued, "I have another surprise. You have to see this. Look where I underlined." His sister handed him a section of the San Francisco Chronicle. It was a part of Herb Cain's column from Monday:

...

It's hard to believe but the Omaha Kid is back. Remember Tim Jacobson of the Oakland A's? No, can't blame you. He only played in one game. Tim batted once officially as a Major league player. He doubled and never made an out. So the hit gave him a career batting average of 1000. The next year, he was injured and had to give up the sport. The twenty-six year old Palo Alto resident is back, not in baseball but in professional tennis. He won tournaments in Vancouver and Cincinnati and is scheduled to play at the Cow Palace in March.

...

"You must be back in the big time if Herb Cain is talking about you. What's next, running for mayor?"

"Funny girl, but I must say this is pretty cool."

*

After his last win, Tim was ranked 27th by the U.S.T.A. He received a letter inviting him to play in the qualifications tournament for the French Open in Paris during May. If he won this preliminary tournament he would then get to play in the French Open the following week, one of the four most important tournaments in the world. It was an amazing opportunity to get a chance to qualify for this Grand Slam event. Tim was shocked. He stood looking at the letter with open mouth.

"Yes!" he screamed. He had never been out of North America and had never played on a clay surface like the courts at Roland Garros.

The day after his invitation, he tried to call Brigitte to tell her that he was coming to France and would like to see her. He was quite surprised when she, and not her machine, answered the phone.

"Bonjour."

"Brigitte hello, it's Tim from California. Remember me?"

"Of course. I was going to call you. I am just back in France so I just heard your telephone messages. I was traveling with tennis so much. Last week I was in Japan. Sorry, maybe my English is not so good."

"No your English is great. Listen, I have been invited to play in the French Open Qualifier, so I'm coming to Paris and I want to see you."

"Yes, yes that is wonderful. I have happy news also. I am getting married this summer."

Tim was crushed. He managed to say, "Congratulations… so maybe I won't be seeing you."

"No, no. I want to see you too. We are friends, no? My good friends, Paul and Cynthia, I think can host you. I will send you the address and phone number in Versailles."

"No, I wouldn't want to impose."

"Yes, you must stay with them or I will not be happy. They are tennis people. They have a lot of rooms in the house and own a tennis club. Please. I want you to meet Michel, my fiancée."

"Well, maybe, I'll see."

"Tim, you must come. Say you will be with them."

In spite of his disappointment about her marriage plans, he smiled at her words. He did want to see her. "OK, send me the address. Thank you."

"Come soon to practice with me."

"I'll see what I can schedule. I still need to get a passport."

"Ok, much good."

"Ok, Brigitte, goodbye for now."

"Goodbye Tim. I will see you in Paris."

He hung up the phone and just stared at it. "C'est la vie," he said out loud trying to be cool with the idea that Brigitte was engaged. He thought about it and he felt his gut churning. "Son of a bitch."

*

Tim started the San Francisco tournament at the Cow Palace with a hot streak winning his first two matches. On Wednesday evening, he faced the unenviable task of a match with the U.S. Open Champion, John McEnroe. He never played against such a highly ranked opponent. Each player held serve in the first six games and with the score tied 3-3, McEnroe sliced a second serve to Tim's backhand. "Out," yelled the linesman.

"That was in!" McEnroe shouted. The linesman just continued to point out. Tim's opponent then walked up to the referee and said, "You saw that in right?"

The referee said, "It was too close to overrule, love-15."

McEnroe shouted, "Are you crazy? That was clearly on the line!"

The ref repeated, "Love – 15."

McEnroe went ballistic, screaming, raving and ranting. The formally friendly crowd started to boo. Tim was left just standing on his side of the court. He thought the ball might've hit the line but he wasn't sure and it wasn't his call. He had seen McEnroe do this on television, but to have it happen to him was very intimidating. Finally, John sullenly dragged himself to the baseline and then smashed the next serve up the line for an ace. He raised his fist and looked angrily at the referee. McEnroe spun his next serve out wide right on the line, pulling Tim way off the court and he easily volleyed the return for a winner. McEnroe held serve and went on to win the match, even though the fans had turned against him. If Tim did hit a winner during the match McEnroe pouted and stomped like a child not getting his way with his mother. Hey give me *some* credit, Tim thought, I can hit some good shots.

Tim lost the match and worse, he had lost his concentration. It was the least fun he ever had on a tennis court. When Tim and John shook hands at the net they didn't even look at each other nor did they say anything.

Tim was disgusted with his effort. His ability to keep his cool when playing athletics had always been a strong point, going all the way back to his days as a high school wrestler and quarterback. He was determined not to let this happen again.

Chapter 27 New York
Spring 1981

In April, Tim departed for France, first stopping in New York. He briefly saw his family, spending the night before his first international flight with his cousin and confidant, Maria, the now Dr. Corelli, PhD. Maria lived and practiced in Hewlett, New York, not far from Lynbrook.

"So you think you are in love with Brigitte, this Frenchwoman."

" I haven't been able to get her out of my mind and it's been over a year."

"Tim, it's not love. It's just a fantasy. It was just one day, for gosh sakes. She was beautiful, exotic and fun. I get it. But you probably never even heard her fart."

He laughed. "Yeah, but if she did, it would've smelled good."

She laughed with him. "But seriously, one day is not love, it's infatuation. Did you ever wonder why you have never fallen in love with anybody available?"

"What are you trying to get at?"

"You tell me."

"Oh, this is one of those psychology things, where I figure out what's wrong with me."

She smiled. "You have a problem with self-examination?"

"Ok, tell me your theory."

"Well, let's look at the obvious. You fell in love with a woman you only knew for a day, and might never see again, when you met and dated many women who were available. You have even lived with Jenny, who Linda thought was perfect for you, and you let her walk out of your life. Maybe you are afraid to love. It's a classic case for people who lose a mother when they are young.

"Well, maybe I just wasn't ready to get married," he said defensively. "What about you? You're not married."

"Tim, this isn't about me."

"Why not Maria? I'm not one of your patients."

She sighed. "I'm way too complicated. We can play with my love life another time."

"Oh really? My flight doesn't leave till tomorrow. We have time."

"Let's talk about your match with McEnroe. What did you learn?"

"No, I'm ok with that. You're trying to change the subject."

Maria looked at him intently, quiet for a moment. "Tim, if I tell you this you can't repeat it to anybody."

"What, you're gay? The rumor that you slept with another girl in college was true?" She didn't say anything, just smiled. "Oh my God, you are."

"I have a girlfriend."

"Really? How long…"

"About a year."

He was not totally surprised, heard rumors, especially when she was in college, but flattered that she trusted him enough to tell him. "Well I know why you would be in the closet. Uncle Tony and Aunt Sophia would have a cow."

"Really, you can't tell anyone, not even Linda."

"Don't worry Maria. You know your secret is safe with me. I'm happy for you, if you're happy."

"I'm happy. At least I think I am."

"Can I meet her?"

"You already have, her name is Sara Freeman."

"My Sara Freeman?" Now he was surprised with his mouth wide open again.

"That's my girl."

Tim laughed out loud. "Holy shit! Sara wow!" He thought about his old girlfriend, warmly. "So, Sara and you...You know Uncle Tony and Aunt Sophia will never accept this relationship. She's a Jew."

They both laughed until tears rolled down their faces.

Chapter 28 Paris, France
Spring 1981

Tim landed at Charles De Gaulle Airport in the middle of a rainstorm. April in Paris, the rainy season lingered. It rained when he left California, rained in New York and now in Paris. Was it an ominous sign? He dismissed the thought.

Tim took the Metro to downtown Paris, then a commuter train to Versailles. Brigitte and her friend Cynthia Perrine were at the station to greet him. He remembered the French greeting, offering each cheek for an exchange of kisses to both women during introductions. They showed him to the awaiting large black Mercedes sedan.

"Nice car," Tim said.

"This? It is not so nice, it's like a taxi," Cynthia stated. The woman spoke with almost no French accent, sounding more like an American than someone speaking the King's English. She was a pretty blond, in her late twenties. She wore a short skirt and high heels, showing off her legs.

"This is considered a very nice car in America." Tim said. "What do you think is a nice car?"

"Something more unique, like a Ford Mustang, so cool and hard to find here."

Tim shook his head. "That car would be no big deal at home, must be the tariffs."

They pulled up to a lovely large gated French Country style home, with a cottage in back and a separate three car garage. A stunning statue of naked woman carved from marble poured water out of a carafe into a fountain. The flowing water introduced the ornate garden leading to the front door.

"You will be in the main house. Brigitte is staying in one guest bedroom and you shall have the other. We are happy to have you stay with us."

"That sounds wonderful. Thank you very much."

"No need to thank me. Any friend of Brigitte is a friend of mine. We are childhood friends. My husband and I always have guests during the French Open."

Brigitte said, "Tomorrow we practice on clay courts. That will be good for you and me. Ok?"

"Not too early, ok? It is still afternoon here but I feel like it's night time, you know, jetlag. " He tried not to stare at Brigitte seated next to him. She also had on a short skirt and high heels and her white blouse clung to her body. Did he notice a smirk on her face?

"Of course, I know this jetlag," Brigitte said.

At dinner Tim asked, "Where are your men, Michel and Paul?"

"Michel is in Germany, he is international banker. Then he is into Japan," Brigitte answered then looked at Cynthia.

"Paul is in the United States with the French Davis Cup Team. He is a trainer for young Jonick Noah. He will be back next week."

Tim raised his wine glass. "Thank you again for hosting me. This dinner is delicious." They had salad, baked chicken in a wine sauce, with roasted red potatoes, green beans and a pear tort for dessert.

"You are most welcome Tim. There is no need to say thank you anymore. It is my pleasure having such a lovely young American in my home. I hope you don't mind but some of the local players at the club would like to play against you this week. Would that be all right?"

"That would be great. I need the practice. I've never played on clay."

He turned to Brigitte. "I was surprised you were engaged. When did you meet Michel?"

"I know him my whole life. He is like older brother. We have been expecting to marry from our families."

"Does he play tennis?" Tim asked trying not to stare at the woman.

Brigitte giggled. "He tries but...how do you say?" She looked to her friend for help.

"He has two left feet," the host replied.

"You speak English so well," Tim said to Cynthia.

"Thank you. I lived in Portland, Maine for a year, an exchange high school student. See, now you are my exchange student."

The three talked for a while then Tim asked, "Do you mind if I excuse myself and go to bed. I'm still on New York time."

"Yes of course. Let me help you get settled," Cynthia said.

He could hear the pitter patter of the rain falling on the red tile roof of the house. Shortly after his head hit the pillow and he was almost asleep, he heard creaking and the door to his room opened. There, standing in the doorway was Brigitte, wearing a red negligee and black silk stockings. Was he dreaming? No, he didn't think so. His fantasy woman tip toed over to his bed, pulled back the covers, got in and kissed him.

"What are you? Why are you? Aren't you engaged?" Tim stammered.

"Tim, you want to ask question or do you want to make love?"

He answered by kissing her back passionately, hands reaching desperately for her body. She giggled. "Remember Tim, go slow."

*

The sun peeked into the window of the guest bedroom and awakened Tim. His nose opened up before his eyes and he could smell his lover next to him. The smell was a wonderful mixture of her perfume, her musk, and her sexuality. He opened one eye to find her head curled just below his shoulder, a lock of her blond hair over his outstretched arm. She stirred, stretched, blinked awake and looked back at him, smiling. She kissed his neck. "Good morning," she whispered.

His hand went to her breast, as if by feeling a part of her body, he knew last night was not a dream. "Over the last year I have had many fantasies about you. I thought of you all the time."

"You say sweet things."

"What was that, last night? What is this?"

"This…this is fun."

"What about Michel, are you in love with him?"

"We love each other, we are not in love."

"What does that mean?"

"I mean love, it is complicated. We travel a lot, me all the time. He has other lovers, and so do I, but we are home for each other."

"So I am just a fun interlude."

"Interlude, I do not know that word."

"I am just a good time."

"Let me tell you story. My parents work in French movies. He is actor, she is editor. They been married and divorced twice. After second divorce, they lived in houses next to each other for me. They are still good friends, they have love, but are no longer in love. Do you understand? I would rather be with someone I can love always, than be with some I am in and out of love with. I like you so much but I do not want to fall in love with you. I will marry Michel. Is that ok? We can stop this if you want."

What did he want from her? He wondered. Whatever it was… this felt too good to stop. Maybe a bittersweet love was good, like a piece of dark chocolate. A little part of her was better than nothing. He said, "Ok, Brigitte lets enjoy the time we have together. Like Humphrey Bogart said in the movie, 'We will always have Paris.'"

She looked at him questioningly, and then remembered. "*Casablanca*, see my parents were movie people."

He shrugged his shoulders, and then kissed her. "I know, go slowly." He started to kiss the rest of her body.

*

Tim was glad he had come to France early. Playing tennis on clay was very different than the American hard courts. The surface took away some of the power game, but with his speed he could run down more balls. He easily beat the club players, so he worked on his consistency, spins and drop shots. He watched the French players slide on the clay, something very unnatural for an American hard court player to learn. He couldn't quite get the hang of it. He noticed his footwork was even more important on this slow red surface. One thing played to his advantage, the softness of the clay felt easer for his ankle. The joint finally seemed healthy. The top professionals he would play against in the French Open had coaches and trainers. He had to get in the best shape of his life and figure out the tactics on his own.

After tennis each day, Brigitte, Cynthia, her husband Paul took turns taking their American guest to see the sights of Paris. He felt like a great explorer visiting The Palace at Versailles, the Louvre Museum, and Napoleon's Tomb.

At the Eiffel Tower Brigitte said, "I bet I will win you up all the stairs."

"Are you serious that's an amazing amount of stairs."

"Good for training." She replied.

"What are we betting?"

"She winked at him. "We will think of something. No?"

"Ok go," he yelled and took off.

They were both in top shape and her shorter legs gave her an advantage as they pumped up the metal stairway, the sound of their feet banging all the way. His completive nature took over and determined to win he started taking two steps at a time. He tripped and fell. She scooted past him laughing. They reached the finish line, the third level at the top of the landmark with Brigitte just a meter in front. Both were covered in sweat and sucking air, but they didn't care, the race being so exhilarating and fun. She raised both hands above her head in victory and said, "you must do something special for me later."

He was all smiles, "I think we will work something out."

The other tourists who took the elevator looked at them like they were crazy.

After a change of clothing they went out into the Parisian night. The two ravished an exclusive dinner and drank champagne on the right bank of the Seine River. Stuffed they moved to the left bank for a trendy burlesque club.

The next morning, Brigitte left to play in a tournament in Spain. Paris lost most of its romance without her.

He allowed himself a brief break from his training schedule to take a train alone to the one place in France he felt compelled to visit, Normandy, where his father had come ashore to this country a generation earlier. The Omaha Kid meets Omaha Beach. How ironic he thought.

He was so young when his father died. They were never able to have that talk. What did you do in the war Daddy? Since he knew that his father was at D-day. He read extensively about the battle. It was one of the only links he had with his father. The monuments and cemetery left him feeling awed. He looked down from an old pillbox and could imagine the medic come ashore, bullets cutting down the invaders as they struggled through the waves and up the beach head. Tears filled his eyes "Thanks Dad." He said to the empty beach. He was grateful that he was able to visit this beautiful countryside during a time of peace and freedom.

*

Brigitte came back the day before the qualifying tournament began. They made love in the afternoon, which helped to calm his nerves. Brigitte being a French tennis team member with a good ranking did not have to qualify. She was already entered in the Open.

"I have special way to calm your stresses in your matches this week."

"What is that?"

"When you have important point, think sex with me. Every match you win you get something special." A seductive smile covered her face as her fingernails raked his chest.

Tim laughed. "That idea may help my nerves but not my concentration."

"Maybe, help your desire to win." There was a mischievous twinkle in her eyes.

"You have such a strange and sexy mind. Are all French women like you?"

She giggled. "Maybe a little, but maybe not so much."

*

In Tim's first match, he won the first set 6-4 against a Spaniard Don Cardoso, but fell behind a service break in the second. He had a break point to pull even and the crowd started cheering loudly. Tim could feel his nerves tightening his muscles. He took a relaxing breath and thought of Brigitte's naked body. A smile came to his face and he actually laughed out loud. The Spaniard served into his body. Tim calmly took a step back, centered the ball on his racquet and stroked a winner up the line. He won the next 9 points and easily closed out the match.

He had dinner with his new friends in Versailles, and they toasted his success. After he retreated to bed that night, Brigitte came into his room. She was dressed all in black, wearing long leather boots, a short leather skirt, a buttoned down blouse and long gloves. His lover so sensuous stripped off her clothing, dancing to saxophone jazz music while he watched her from a chair. Naked, the beautiful Brigitte helped him off with his clothing. Out came a warm bottle of scented olive oil. She spread the oil all over his body massaging his sore tired muscles. With every inch of skin covered, their bodies entwined to make fervent love.

*

Tim won his second match and his reward involved liquid chocolate, whipped cream and a lot of licking. After his third win, Brigitte was absent from the Versailles house. No one knew where she was. He was exhausted, so he excused himself and went to his guest room. He lay down to a bed full of jelly beans. As he laughed, Brigitte came out of the closet wearing nothing but a wicked grin and dove in to bed.

*

He need one more victory to make the French Open. That morning Brigitte said, "Tim this is the last night I can stay with you. Michel arrives from Nice to watch me play the tournament and I must go to him.'

"Are you sure that is what you want to do?"

"Yes." She said simply. She smiled. "No regrets ok?"

Tim took her hand in his and kissed it. "Ok."

"Good, because I have special reward tonight when you win today."

"You mean if I win."

She smiled. "You will win. I feel it."

*

Tim played a young, powerful 6'5" Australian, Roger Newton. His serve was the fastest Tim had ever seen, but Australians learn to play on hard courts and grass, much faster surfaces than the red clay of the French courts. Tim's time practicing in France paid off. He spun the ball, used drop shots and lobbed his way to a 6-4, 6-4 win.

This time Tim's hosts and Brigitte came to the match to cheer for him, not satisfied to wait for him in Versailles. After he showered and changed Tim went up to meet his new friends. Champagne corks popped, the celebration of his victory launched. More much bubbly was poured over his head than into his mouth. A stunning redhead joined the party.

Brigitte made the introductions. "Tim Jacobson, this is Yvette Dumont. She is good friend of mine from the tennis team. I have told her all about you and she wanted to meet."

He kissed the new girl on both cheeks. "Nice to meet you Yvette."

"Congratulations, you play so good." Yvette said, ~~raising~~ her wine glass in salute.

Brigitte, evil smile on her face watched the introductions. She said something to Yvette in French. Yvette said, oui, smiling and looking at Tim. Brigitte leaned over and whispered in Tim's ear, "I told you I had special surprise for you tonight. Yvette will be joining us. You know we French invented 'menage a' trois'."

*

The problem for any qualifier winning a spot in a grand slam tournament is the seeding. While top players are placed by their world ranking, the qualifiers are unseeded and are picked randomly to play the best players in the world. Tim's reward for making it into the draw was a match against Sweden's Bjorn Borg, who in 1980 was the number one player in the world and four times French Open champion.

They played on center court. It was a beautiful sunny day and the red clay almost shined, spotless before the warm up. The huge crowd rooted for the champion. No image of Brigitte could settle his nerves. Yet Tim played well, after losing the first set 3-6, he held serve throughout the second, forcing the world's number one ranked player to a tie break. Tim won the first two points but his nerves betrayed him, and he lost the tie breaker and second set. In the third set, the champion relaxed and got a little too comfortable. Tim raced in front and won the third set in the best of five. The French crowd stood and cheered for Tim excited with the play they tried to rally the underdog. Tim rode the ovations to a 6-4 fourth set win, but Borg was too steady and too experienced to be unnerved. Tim, never having played in a Grand Slam, hadn't ever-played a fifth set and the match continued into a fourth hour. The energy he used to come back left him little in the tank. The champ used his famous two handed backhand to pass his overmatched challenger twice in the fifth game of the last set. Borg closed the match winning the last three games. The spectators rose in a rousing standing ovation for both players.

At the net the gracious Borg said, "Tim, that was a great match, I'll see you again." As they shook hands, the large crowd rose again and cheered.

Tim collapsed in a chair in the locker room. He struggled to replenish his liquids. Exhusted, he took a cold shower and readied himself to leave. Before he could go, he was handed a sealed envelope. Inside was a card with the letterhead of the All England Tennis Club:

"To Mr. Timothy Jacobson,
You are hereby invited to
The Championships
To be played at
at
Wimbledon, England.
Starting June 20, 1980

Chapter 29 London, England
June 1980

Losing in the first round of the French Open actually gave Tim an advantage at Wimbledon. He had two extra weeks to practice on the grass courts of England. His former baseball agent had come back on board and arranged accommodations and practice courts in London. He thought about entering a grass tournament. Instead, his new French connection, Paul arranged an exhibition match with the 18 year old French phenom, Jonick Noah, on grass courts in Oxford, England a week before the big tournament started.

Each player earned $10,000, which Tim badly needed to offset his expenses. The experience would help both players. Young Noah played mostly on French clay and Tim on American hard courts. Tim beat Noah in a competitive three set match, 6-4, 4-6, 7-5. Tim could tell that the kid was going to be a special player as he danced around the court, his dreadlocks flowing. The two practiced together for a few days, Bob Marley wailing in the background. Tim enjoyed the company of the teenager and marveled at his athletic skill.

*

The morning he was to play ~~that~~ his first match against Gunther Kruger at the All England Tennis Club, the London fog burning off quickly. The dawning sun glowed orange and gold through the dwindling cloud layer. The foggy summer morning reminded him of Palo Alto and the San Francisco Bay Area.

He met Brigitte briefly for a coffee, and the traditional Wimbledon strawberries and cream snack. She had made it all the way to the third round in Paris, before losing to the great Chris Evert. When they finished eating, the two hugged and wished each other luck. She was due to play just after him.

Brigitte reminded him, "Remember when you are nervous, think of me." She smiled and winked. He laughed.

By the time the taxi deposited him at the Wimbledon player's gate, the sun was peeking above the stadium. The grass courts appeared pristine, unmarked, awaiting the best players in the world to leave their footprints. Scheduled to play on court 14, he needed to walk out early to Center Court and look into the empty stands. Chills ran down his spine.

*

Tim looked across the net at Gunter Kruger. The 6'5" blond with an impressive serve and volley game appeared to be a natural for this surface. Wimbledon is played on grass, the antithesis of the slow French clay courts. The ball skips off the grass and stays low favoring the style of the powerful player who serves hard and moves to the net to volley, hitting the ball in the air before it can bounce. For the most part, the player who showed aggressive play had the advantage.

They competed four hours and ten minutes, going all out for each point. On the break, while changing sides, Tim poured water down his throat and on his face, the two exhausted players returned to the court.

The referee announced the score, "Mr. Jacobson leads eight games to seven, fifth and final set." The English Championships had no tie breaker in the final set. One had to win the match by two games. Tim was ahead by a game, but he had to break the German's serve, something he had only done twice in the whole match. Gunter had held serve in twenty-seven service games.

Kruger blasted a serve to Tim's backhand. Tim was able to get his racket on it and the ball just hit the net and dropped over for a lucky winner. He held up his hand with a gesture of sorry for the lucky bounce. "Love-fifteen," the referee announced. The next serve came up the line and Tim timed it perfectly hitting a forehand for a winner. "Love-thirty," was announced. Gunter smacked the next serve down the line for an ace. "Fifteen-thirty." Again Kruger served to Tim's backhand and he returned it weakly but the German went for too much on the volley hitting it out. "Fifteen-forty," The referee shouted. After five hours and fifteen minutes the small outer court crowd rose and cheered. Kruger hit another ace, for 30-40, still match point. Gunter put his first serve in the net, and then spun his second serve deep to Tim's backhand He sprang to the ball, set his tired feet and smacked the same two handed backhand that Kristy had taught him back in high school, down the line for a perfect passing shot winner. The referee announced, "Game, set, and match to Mr. Jacobson. He wins 4-6, 6-4, 3-6, 7-5, and 8-6." Tim marveled. He had just won a match at Wimbledon. He threw up his hands in triumph, and then jumped over the net to shake the hand of the tenth ranked player in the world.

After the match, Tim was interviewed by NBC's Bud Collins. "Tim, you seemed to have arrived at the French Open from out of nowhere and you won your first match at Wimbledon. What do you make of all this?"

"I'm just having a good time and trying to do my best."

"You briefly played Major League baseball, and you were known as the Omaha Kid. How does this compare?"

"Well, with my short time with the A's, I mostly sat on the bench and was part of a team. Here I'm playing, and out there by myself. This is more intense."

"Do people still call you the Omaha Kid?'

Tim laughed. "Well, maybe I'm not much of a kid any more, but if people remember me that way, sure why not?"

"Would you like to say anything to the people back home?"

He knew they would be watching, so he said, "I want to say hello to my sister in California and to my cousins in New York; also hi my Aunt Sophia and Uncle Tony."

*

On Tuesday, he awoke to a steady rain pouring down from the gray London sky. Luckily, he was not scheduled for a match, so he wouldn't have to wait through the rain delays. He decided to give his body a break and go sightseeing. In the morning he mounted of one of London's famous double decker tour buses. Inside his head he heard Joanie Mitchell's hit song about her not wanting to ride on the English buses "because there was no driver on the top." He smiled and sat back while the tour took him past Big Ben, Parliament and the Tower of London. Tim viewed the sights, fascinated as the guide explained how the former kings and queens beheaded their adversaries at the Tower, including two of Henry VIII's wives he no longer wanted. Tim pictured the Queen of Hearts in *Alice in Wonderland* saying "Off with her head!" No wonder we Americans decided to get rid of the monarchy, he thought. Maybe this history stuff *was* interesting.

By afternoon, the rain stopped and the tennis matches resumed. He retreated to the hotel to watch the BBC broadcasts, and saw his next opponent, the one and only John McEnroe, "decapitate" his unseated foe, like King Henry did to poor Ann Bolin. He hoped he would not be the next to fall to this American tennis monarch, King John of Queens New York.

*

Wednesday morning, Tim opened his eyes to a glorious English day. The early morning sunshine bathed the city in bright light. He was due to play at four that afternoon, so he wanted to get a good breakfast. Tim crossed the street, making sure to look right for the "wrong side of the road" English traffic, intending to eat at a Dutch pancake house. He noticed his picture on the front of the London tabloid newspaper, the one with a different topless page three girl every day. He paid the man a shilling and read the banner headline: "Poor American Orphan to Play Big Bad John." The article explained how Timothy Jacobson had lost his parents in a car crash. It went on to tell the readers that Tim's father was a war hero, stationed in England before storming Omaha Beach in France, thus explaining why Tim is called the "Omaha Kid." The writer then focused on John McEnroe, describing him as a brat, always behaving badly on the courts. He obviously wanted to set up a hero and an antihero for the coming match.

"Oh crap," Tim heard himself say out loud. After spending a few weeks here in London, he knew these papers sensationalized the news and the facts were not of primary importance to the publishers. They just wanted to sell newspapers.

When Tim arrived at the stadium that morning, reporters from all over the world were waiting for him. In the press room the questions came fast.

"When did his parents die? How did he feel about being an orphan? Was his dad really a war hero? Which did he like better, baseball or tennis? Which did he like best Omaha, New York or California?"

He felt like he was being grilled by the FBI and tried to be honest but keep his answers short. Some of the questions left him flustered like: "Was he Jewish?" That came from a reporter form Israel. Other questions left him confused: "Will you ever get married?" After a half hour, he looked at his watch and said, "Sorry guys, I need to get ready for my match."

Because Tim was playing the number two seed, the match was scheduled to play on Center Court. He walked out of a dark tunnel into the blazing sunshine. The mostly English crowd, having read the papers, cheered loudly for the son of a war hero. McEnroe followed him greeted by boos and divisive whistles.

The two players met at the net and Tim said, "Sorry John, I had nothing to do with that article."

"No one knows more about the English rags than I do. Don't worry about it. But I'm going to kick your butt anyway."

And so the head games begin, Tim thought.

During the match, McEnroe was on his best behavior; after all it was Wimbledon they were playing. Still, Tim struggled to concentrate. Center Court, the big crowd, the morning's distractions all affected his play. He felt like he was moving in mud, his feet always a step too slow for the action.

In spite of the friendly audience, Tim lost the first two sets 3-6, 2-6. He could not break the left handed McEnroe's serve and even had trouble with his own. In the third set he rallied, but still lost 5-7 to a great player. He left the grass courts behind, waving to the cheering spectators.

It was time to get out of England and retreat back home. He felt like he had been away too long. As he boarded the non-stop 747 to San Francisco, he thought, at least King John didn't get to cut off my head.

Chapter 30 Toronto
and New York City
August and September 1981

The Omaha Kid showed brilliance, his game was "on a roll." Playing in the Canadian Hard-Court Open Tournament in Toronto, Tim had beaten an international all-star list of opponents including Russell Simpson of New Zealand, Gene Mayer, Roscoe Tanner, and Harold Solomon of the U.S., Ilie Nastase of Romania, and the great Ivan Lendl of Czechoslovakia in the finals. The sponsor presented him with a check of $50,000, the biggest payday of his life.

*

When Tim flew into Kennedy airport after his big win in Canada, he felt an amazing sense of confidence. To expect to win the tournament the first time he plays at the U.S. Open wasn't realistic, but his ranking was his highest ever and with the Canadian prize money, he'd hired a coach and a trainer, just like the major players on the tour.

August in New York was hot and muggy. Often the air conditioning on subway cars broke down, leaving the millions of passengers feeling like stinky, sweaty sardines. After a day of exhausting tennis practice in Flushing Meadows, Tim was happy to transfer in Jamaica, Queens off the subway to the more comfortable cars of the Long Island Railroad which took him to Maria's house. It was the week before the Open and Tim, Maria and Sara picnicked by the swimming pool. The three lounged in their bathing suits, watching the evening fireflies blinking on, and talking easily about their lives.

"You're making that up," Sara said to Tim after he told them about his exploits with Brigitte.

"I couldn't make that up. I don't have that kind of imagination. Besides, no one would believe me."

Maria asked, "How did you feel when she told you it was over and her fiancé showed up?"

Tim said, "You know, I was a little melancholy, but on the whole I was ok. She was honest from the start. The romance was exciting. But I do miss her."

"More then you missed me after high school?" Sara swung her hips and made a kissing motion with her mouth. The three laughed.

"Obviously more than you missed me. When I traded sides in baseball it wasn't my choice. Who knew you would go over to the other team?" Then, he asked seriously, "What made you change sexually? Did you feel uncomfortable with me?"

"No, I enjoyed being with you. But you and I both knew we weren't in love. We were just two kids with raging hormones having a good time. To tell you the truth I never really wanted to be with another woman until Maria."

"What about you Maria?" Tim asked his cousin.

"I guess I was always gay, but I was in denial, I was so worried what Mom and Dad would think. I still am. That's why I'm still in the closet."

"Does Junior know?"

"No, and don't tell him."

"He won't find out from me. But how long do you think you can keep it a secret?"

"The family thinks that Sara and I are just good friends, roommates sharing expenses. Tim, you could help. Would you take Sara out and pretend you're on a date?"

"Just like old times, Sara?" Tim laughed.

Sara said, "This time you ain't getting lucky, Jocko. I'm not Brigitte."

*

Tim won his first match of the U.S. Open against veteran Stan Smith, one of Tim's heroes as a teenager. He had used a Stan Smith autographed wood model racquet back in his freshman year at Lynbrook High. He blew the future hall of famer off the court using a new style metal racquet in straight sets, 6-4, 6-3, and 6-1.

After the match, Tim expected to take the subway back to his hotel. As he exited the grounds, there were a horde of people waiting for him. He signed autographs for 15 minutes but more people kept arriving. One pretty teenaged girl pulled up her shirt and asked him to sign her bra. As he signed the undergarment, she kissed him on the cheek and screamed like he was a Beatle and it was still the sixties. Someone ripped off a piece of his shirt for a souvenir. Overwhelmed, he quickly retreated back to the gates realizing that he was now a star and in over his head. He remembered Reggie Jackson when he was with the A's and the crowds and groupies he attracted. He asked a security to call him a car. When he arrived at his hotel, he asked the front desk to change his name on the register to Joseph Corelli to keep any crazy fans from finding him.

*

Outside the new tennis facility was the Unisphere, a large globe like- model of the world, left over from the 1964 New York World's Fair. Tim's aunt and uncle had taken the family to the fair when they were kids. Maria, Tony Jr. and he had a ball on the rides and the exhibits. Just down the path was Shea Stadium home of the New York Mets where Tim and his friends spent hours watching soaking in baseball games. He knew this place well. He felt like he had an advantage. He was playing in New York City, his childhood home.

*

The packed crowd was on its feet going crazy. The jets taking off from nearby LaGuardia Air Port could not be heard over the din that poured down from the fans court side at the world's largest stadium in the world, U.S. Tennis Center at Flushing Meadows, New York City. This was something special! Native New Yorker, Timothy Jacobson had a 6-4, 6-3, 3-0 lead on the number one player in the world, Bjorn Borg. This was the match that was going to change Tim's life.

Tim looked up at his "friends" box. It overflowed with family and friends including his high school buddy Lonnie who yelled "Come on Omaha!" His new Australian coach, Jim Roche, held up his fist. Even he could not believe how well Tim was playing.

At Wimbledon, the spectators treated the tennis players with reverence, like gods that had come down from Mount Olympus. At the U.S. Open the players were cheered more like rock stars and Tim was about to become another Elvis or Mick Jagger. The New York crowd whooped it up chanting, "Omaha! Omaha!"

"Quiet please," the referee announced into the microphone above the ruckus of the fans. Just three more games and he would defeat the best tennis player in the world.

Tim took his time bouncing the tennis ball waiting for the noise to abate. He felt his adrenalin pulsing through his body as he smashed an ace down the center line at 130 mph. "Fifteen-love," the score was announced. Again the crowd went wild. Tim was ready and he spun a serve deep to Borg's backhand, who returned the ball crosscourt behind Tim who had come to the net for a volley. As Tim stretched back across his body awkwardly, his ankle gave way sending a shock wave of pain up his spine. He fell hard on the cement.

A hush came over the stadium as Tim grabbed his left leg and grimaced in pain. The referee came down from his chair and asked, "Mr. Jacobson are you all right?"

"I need the trainer."

The referee announced, "Time is out." He started his clock.

The U.S.T.A. trainer came running out and looked at Tim's ankle. It had already swollen almost to twice the normal size. Borg sat down, wiped the sweat off his brow and looked helplessly at his opponent.

"Ice it, tape it and put my shoe back on. I'm finishing this match." Tim told the trainer. He got to his feet and with two people supporting his weight, he limped to his chair.

After a few minutes treatment the referee said, "time."

Tim, his ankle wrapped tightly, limped over to the service line. He smacked his serve about half speed just above the net and Bjorn smacked an easy winner. The crowd booed the Swede, but he just shrugged implying, "What else can I do."

"Fifteen-thirty," The referee announced.

Tim tried gamely to hit his next serve but collapsed under his own weight. He looked up at the referee and shook his head, tears streaming down his cheeks. The referee said softly into the microphone, "It is my sad duty to announce Mr. Jacobson defaults. Mr. Borg wins the match 4-6, 3-6, 6-3, 6-0, 6-0, by default." The stunned, standing room only crowd was silent.

Bjorn Borg came around the net and offered Tim his hand to help him up. "I'm so sorry," he whispered in Tim's ear.

The trainer grabbed his other side and they eased him off the court. One person in the stands started clapping and the fans rose cheering loudly for the victor and the vanquished. He waved at the crowd wondering if he would ever hear fans cheer like this for him again.

Chapter 31 New York City
Autumn 1981 – February 1982

"So, what's up Doc?" Tim said with a laugh. "I always wanted to say that, you know, like Bugs Bunny."

The doctor did not even crack a smile. "Tim it is very serious. I need to run some more tests but I believe you tore another ligament. You probably need surgery."

"So bottom line, how long will I be out?"

"Out of your professional career as a tennis player?

"Yes."

"Tim you may never be able to play tennis again."

"What? No fucking way!" Tim's sudden anger spilled over towards Dr. Martin Cohn. "Is that your best bedside manner? Do you even know what you are talking about?"

"Sorry, I'll leave you alone to think about this."

"No, come back here you son of a bitch! Have you told my coach? Have you told anyone?"

"Not without your permission," he said as he walked away. Tim fumed. He soon realized it wasn't the doctor's fault. He probable left the room to let him cool down.

*

Tim lay on a gurney on the fifth floor of Mt. Sinai Hospital in Manhattan, his leg propped up with pillows. He stared out the window and saw the sun shining. I need to be out there, he thought. This can't be happening again. I was so close to the big time I could taste it.

Uncle Tony walked in the room with Maria. Tim noticed how old his uncle looked.

"How bad is it?" Uncle Tony asked.

"Bad."

"Tim, it's going to be all right." They will fix you right up, you'll see," Tony said trying to be helpful.

Tim could see his pain reflected in the concern on Maria's face. He realized it was not only from the physical pain in his leg but also the pain of facing an uncertain future. Another dream dashed. All his hard work to rehabilitate and become one of the world's best tennis players was for naught. His cousin reached out and held his hand. He felt her love. She was like the closest thing to a mother that he could remember. He held on tight.

*

Tim watched the U.S. Open finals from a hospital bed, his damaged leg having already had surgery. The doctor used the latest technique taking a ligament out of a cadaver and implanting it in Tim's ankle. Stainless steel screws held the bone together until it could fuse. Tim was told it was successful and he should be up walking as soon as it healed. When he asked if he would be able to play tennis again, Dr. Cohn said only, "Be patient and we shall see."

Tim found himself rooting for Borg against McEnroe. He didn't know why, he liked them both. Maybe it was because he knew he had gotten the better of the Swede and if Bjorn won, he felt that he would have been the champion. The final match was another amazing contest between the two future Hall of Famers. McEnroe won in five sets, avenging his loss at Wimbledon.

Maria showed up at his bed late during the match and they watched the last set together. After it was over she said, "I think you would have won."

"So do I. It felt like I couldn't lose."

She knew he was despondent. "Tim you're going to be all right. You know that."

"You know it's over. I'm 26 and it will take years for this to heal and for me to try to get back in shape. And that's if everything goes perfectly. The doctor hasn't even told me if I will be able to play tennis again at all."

"So let's set a realistic goal. What do you want to do for the rest of your life if you can't play professional tennis?"

"I don't know. Do you really expect me to tell you that right now?"

"Maybe not right now, I'll give you a few weeks to think about it. Then I'll be damned if I'm going to let you sulk! You need a goal to get you off your ass and start rehabilitation. Like you said, you're only 26. You have most of your life ahead of you. I know "The Omaha Kid" is better than that."

He smiled in spite of himself. "Ok, Maria, you did your psychologist job. Now can you just act like my big sister and feel a little sorry for me and let me feel a little sorry for myself?"

"Yeah, I'll let you feel a little sorry. After all, you could have been a contender!'" she said doing her best imitation of Marlon Brando. "You have two weeks. Then the sulking ends and the sun will start shining on you again, deal?"

"I guess...Ok, we have a deal."

*

The Los Angeles Dodgers Baseball team worker's compensation insurance company denied his claim to pay his medical expenses. The letter stated that since Tim had been able to play professional tennis, he had recovered from his baseball injury. His newly injured ankle was therefore not a covered injury. Lonnie checked into the claim.

Tim answered the phone in his hospital room. "Hello."

"Hi Omaha, It's Lonnie."

"What's up?"

"I looked into that medical situation for you. They really stepped in it this time. They always deny all claims first hoping the client just gives up. But I turned it around on them. Screw the insurance company; I went right to the Dodgers' management.

I reminded the team that this new injury was related to the first and never would have happened if not for that broken sprinkler in Albuquerque. The damages of you losing a professional tennis career would be enormous. I told them if we went to court I would ask for fifty million. I also reminded their lame ass attorneys that any trial would take place in New York City. Any jury might still not be happy about the fact that the Brooklyn Dodgers, left town. 'The Brooklyn bums', I can still remember when the papers called them that.

I digress. Bottom line, they acquiesced to paying all your mounting medical bills and any future costs. Further, they cut a settlement check of $1,500,000 to end any possible lawsuit. It's not a lifetime windfall, but enough for you to live comfortably for a while."

"That's great news. Thanks Lonnie. You're the man."

"Yeah, Tim, I only wish I could have gotten' you more. You've had some bad breaks. Damn, sorry I didn't mean your ankle, I meant…"

"Lonnie, I know. Thanks again."

"I'll be over to have you sign the paperwork."

"Good, bring Betsey. If I have to look at your ugly face I want to at least see your pretty wife."

"You damned orphan, I should have beat the crap out of you in grade school when I had the chance."

March arrived in New York but not the spring. The weather remained wintery, the temperature dipped, turned unseasonably cold with snow still sticking on the ground. The naked tree branches were reluctant to bud. Tim felt like a caged lion, staying on Long Island with Maria and Sara. He had made steady progress, moving from walking with crutches to limping on a tread mill. His only major outing was his daily physical therapy. He wanted access to the out-of-doors. It was time to go back home to California. Unfortunately, tragedy again intervened.

Uncle Tony suffered a massive heart attack and died on the evening of March 15th.

Tony Junior delivered the eulogy. He described how his father had made his fortune in the restaurant business and opened the door for JR's continued expansion of the organization to a multimillion dollar company. He started to tell what a great father the man had been but when he tried to talk about the adoption of Tim, his emotions got the best of him. He broke down crying, unable to continue.

Maria went up to her brother and hugged him. She said simply, "Dad was a wonderful man, generous and fair. I…We all loved him very much." Without anything else prepared, she stopped there and said, "Thank you all for coming."

As usual Tim felt relegated to the sidelines, a part of the family but not truly a son. He never quite fit as part of the family. He loved his uncle, but their relationship was never father and son. Tim felt devastated and confused. When JR faltered in his speech, he didn't feel comfortable enough with his family to step in and pinch hit.

At the funeral, Aunt Sophia looked like a ghost. Her psyche, already shaky, started to unravel. Maria told JR and Tim that Sophia had the classic signs of obsessive-compulsive disorder. Sophia only left the house on Sunday to go to church. The rest of her time was spent praying at her living room altar and bathing every few hours. The rest of the Lynbrook house was virtually unused. It was time to get her help. With the reluctant support of her younger brother and Tim, Maria took charge and found her mother a care home in nearby Valley Stream. JR decided to move his family out of Manhattan to his childhood home so that he would be located closer his mother.

A week had passed since the funeral. Tim was still staying with Maria. He was in the living room watching TV when Maria approached him.

"Tim, Dad is gone and Mom is obviously not in touch with reality. I'm tired of living a lie. I'm coming out and I want to tell JR. I'm inviting Cathy and JR to dinner and I would like you to be there for support."

"Of course, anything you want.

*

Maria knew better than to try and serve her brother Italian food when some of the best chefs for that cuisine were available to Tony, so she decided to try something entirely different. She found a recipe for Indian chicken curry. Sara and Maria spent the day in the kitchen preparing a feast.

JR arrived at his sister's house sleep deprived and emotionally raw from the effects of dealing with his father's death and the funeral. Maria went out of her way to be accommodating.

They all gathered at the dinner table. Tim loved the curry. His taste bud tingled from the mild heat. Tony hated it, barely touching the meal, moving it about like a kid avoiding his peas. Sara asked if he was finished. He nodded and said, "Maybe I'm just too European, but that was a little too unusual for my taste." He burped into his napkin as if to give his comment some emphasis.

As Maria served dessert she said, "JR, Cathy, I have something important to tell you." They both looked up at her. "You know Sara and I have been living together for a long time…We are more than friends."

Everyone looked at Tony. At first he didn't seem to understand. Then a look of disgust came to his face. "What the fuck?" he almost spit out. He pushed himself away from the table. "It's a good thing your father is dead and gone or you…well… come on Cathy it's time to get out of here."

Maria said, "JR, please let's talk about this. I'm still your sister and I love you."

"Who the fuck are you? You can't be my sister. I don't know you or want to know you! You're going to hell. And you, did you know this?" He asked looking at Tim.

"Yes, and I'm totally alright with it."

"Great a lesbo sister and a faggot California cousin, you deserve each other." JR never even looked at Sara, but grabbed the tight-lipped Cathy by her hand and pulled her out of the house, slamming the door as they left.

"Well, that went well," Tim said trying to break the tension.

Sara was sitting at the table crying. Maria ran out of the room and Tim followed. "It's ok, Maria." he said hugging her. "He'll come around. Give it time."

"Screw him...and her! Who need them?" She said wiping her eyes.

"Go to Sara, she needs you. You have each other and I'll stay with you guys as long as you like."

"Who needs you? You dammed California faggot." she said laughing and crying at the same time. She walked back to the table and put her arm around Sara. The two women kissed tenderly.

Sara turned to him and said. "Thanks Tim for being here for us."

He said, "I love both of you. Any time you need a California faggot, just let me know."

Chapter 33 Palo Alto, California
Summer 1982 – Spring 1983

July came and Tim found himself back working at The White Rabbit Bar in Palo Alto. He was walking, now without a cane, but after a quarter mile the pain would be too intense and he would have to stop. His new Stanford doctor assured him that he was recovering well and the pain should diminish. He joined a gym and swam to get himself back in shape. With the buoyancy of the water, he could walk and even jog on his ankle without pain.

Tim had moved in with Linda as she started her residency at Stanford Hospital. Linda was glad to have him back in her life.

"I miss watching you play tennis on television. I know it's hard for you, but you accomplished so much in so little time. No one can take that away from you," she said.

He felt better around her but the two did not get to spend much time together with her putting in crazy residency hours.

As the snow started to fall in the Sierra, Tim remembered being able to ski after his last recovery and how the ski boot held his ankle like a cast. He asked the doctor if he could try skiing again.

"I think you need to let the bone grow and heal a little longer." the surgeon replied. "Let's give it a little more time, maybe March."

That was just what he needed to hear. He picked up his training, his disposition improved, and then a new woman came into his life.

Linda met Katie during semester break when most students were away, home for Christmas. She was smart and sweet in that midwestern sort of way. He accent sounded from Wisconsin or Minnesota. Linda soon felt comfortable with Katie, even when Tim was not with her in the apartment.

Katie Anderson had a unique type of beauty. She was Eurasian and seemed to have the best features from both races. Her striking blue eyes and a red tint to her otherwise raven hair gave a hint to her mixed heritage.

When Tim was at work, Katie shared her story with Linda.

"My mother was a sixteen year old bargirl in Saigon when she met my dad, Sergeant John "Red" Anderson. He was a career soldier and fell in love with my mom, a Vietnamese war orphan. Within a month Red and Mie were married and he took leave to move her back to the States.

My Dad left his bride in Madison, Wisconsin not knowing she was pregnant. He went back to continue as an advisor to the South Vietnamese Army. Mom told me he was thrilled when he received the letter he was going to be a father. Unfortunately, he was killed in action in August the same month I was born, in September 1960."

*

Tim originally met Katie at the bar. The Stanford soccer team frequented the White Rabbit and they often interacted with Tim. Normally shy with men, Katie felt comfortable around Tim, even flirted with him. Her teammates noted her attraction and teased Katie.

Her friend Lois said, "So you apparently like Tim, why don't you go over and ask him out."

A corner of her lip rose up in a half smile. "You know I'm shy around boys, I could never do that."

"I know I've never seen you with a guy. I'm sure they ask you out all the time. What's up with that?"

Katie started to say something and stopped as if embarrassed.

"Come on, you can tell me. What are friends for?"

"You know I grew up in suburban Wisconsin, right."

"Yeah."

"Well the town was almost exclusively white. I was like the only Asian in my school. All the kids used to tease me. Call me stuff like slant eyes and gook."

"Kids can be so mean."

"Well many days I would go home in tears. But if I shared this with my mom, she would tell me in her broken English, "It Ok, you no tell on anyone get us in trouble. I became ashamed of her and ashamed of the Asian part of me. I wanted to be like everyone else."

"Oh Katie I'm sorry."

"Then came junior high and high school, the same boys that teased me started asking me out. I wanted so badly to fit in that I went on a few dates, but the pimple faced, hormone unbalanced jerks would just try to paw me. I felt abused, so I gave up on boys. I just wanted to study and play soccer. Luckily, I made lots of friends, my teammates. Playing soccer kind of saved me, helped my self-esteem.

"Did you ever want to date girls?"

Katie laughed. "No it's not like that. I think I am attracted to the bartender. Maybe it's because he is a little older, more mature."

"You know he is almost famous, played some pro baseball and tennis."

"Really."

"Really, and if you don't make your move soon, I'm going to go for it. I always thought he was good looking. Even before I met him, just seeing him play tennis on T.V."

"What do I say?"

"Ask about his nickname 'Omaha.' No wait; ask him about playing at Wimbledon."

Katie walked up to the bar and sat on a stool and smiled at Tim.

He had noticed this striking girl in the bar with her teammates before and was attracted by her distinctive beauty. She had always seemed unapproachable, ignoring any boy who asked her to dance or offered her a drink. He flirted with her like he did with a lot of girls in the bar, but never thought to ask her out. He figured she had a boyfriend, or she was gay.

He was surprised when she sat at the bar and asked, "Did you really play tennis at Wimbledon?"

"Yes, that I did. Can I get you something?" He asked while placing two mugs of beer on a tray for the waitress.

"What was it like?"

Knowing she was on the soccer team he said, "I figure it was a lot like you playing against Cal. You know the excited nervous energy before you start. Then you settle down as the game is played."

"Wow you're right that's about how I feel. Can I ask you another stupid question?"

"Ok."

"If your name is Tim, right, how come some of the people in the bar call you Omaha?"

He chuckled. "It's a nickname that goes back to high school and baseball."

"So you went to school in Omaha. I'm also from the Midwest."

"No, actually I went to school in suburban New York." She looked at him strangely. "I know the nickname only makes sense because I spent some early years in Omaha."

"I've never been to New York. What's it like?

"A little bit like San Francisco but bigger."

"I've never actually spent time in the city, you know between soccer and studying."

"I'm free tomorrow if you want to go." He said, while mixing another drink. Her flirtation had worked. He took the bait.

Now that she had reeled him hooked, she was scared. She hoped she hadn't caught a shark she couldn't handle. "Will you promise to behave? I usually don't date much."

"Scout's honor." He said holding up three fingers. Is eleven o'clock ok?"

She smiled at him. "Ok. Here's my address," she slipped a bar napkin onto an empty tray.

He picked it up, put the napkin his pocket and smiled.

*

Tim picked her up in the Jeep that had replaced his Mustang. It was a cool, breezy day in early December. The sun shined on them between rain storms. He took her to two of his favorite spots, lunch at the Cliff House and then a walk along the trail leading toward the Golden Gate Bridge. He limped along next to Katie, never trying to touch her, respecting his date's private space.

She flirting with him and touching his arm. They went out to the beach to watch the sunset. Sitting on a blanket, the two watched the sun dip behind the clouds from an approaching storm to the west. Colors of the rainbow were cast into the horizon, making it look like God was playing with his paint brush. Hundreds of birds flocked into the sky before their nightfall nesting.

Katie said, "this is awesome. I never knew a big city could be so full of nature's beauty. Thank you for a wonderful day, Mr. Omaha, Tim or whatever your name is." She giggled and leaned her body against his, seeking warmth.

"May I kiss you?" he asked.

"Yes."

They kissed tentatively and tenderly. She reached out and held his hand. When he took her home, he reached out to shake her hand. She kissed him lightly on the lips.

He asked, "Shall I call you?"

"I would be disappointed if you didn't."

*

Her mother was a Buddhist and they did not observe the Christian holiday, something she had always resented growing up in Middle America. So when Tim invited her over, she was very happy to have someone in her life in with whom to spend the holidays. Linda introduced her to Hanukah. Then, a few days later, they all celebrated Christmas. Tim and Katie exchanged little gifts.

Tim had to work on New Year's Eve, so he and Katie went to an early dinner together. He came home from work and found her waiting for him with a bottle of cheap champagne.

"I don't know anything about wine. I hope that this is ok."

He realized it probably cost her more then she could afford. "It's perfect."

They toasted the New Year and then Katie took Tim's hand and led him to his bedroom. She had told him about her lack of sexual experience so he asked, "Are you sure you're ready for this?"

Katie looked deeply into his brown eyes and replied simply, "Yes I want to make love with you."

*

Through January, Tim and Katie could not get enough of each other. Their desire burned with red hot intensity.

On Valentine's Day, the two went to a charming rustic inn at Half Moon Bay overlooking the ocean. Tim splurged and rented a suite that included a fireplace.

After putting down her valise, Katie pulled open the drapes to look at the ocean waves crashing down below the bluffs. "Tim it's wonderful, so romantic." She jumped into his arms and kissed him, then giggled with joy.

The steady rain didn't to bother the lovers as they went for a long walk along the cliffs, hand in hand. Tim ignored his bad ankle and Katie ignored his slight limp. She wore the gold heart necklace he had given her for Christmas. When he dressed that morning he sprinkled on her gift of cologne.

Returning drenched they stripped off their wet clothing and jumped into a hot shower in their suite. Later, toasty and warm, their toned bodies glowed in the shadows of the fire. They had a room service picnic splattering as much of the meal on each other as they did in their mouths. Their lovemaking started out playful and tender. Finally with uncontrollable craving, they consumed each other, satisfying a deep carnal hunger.

Tim listened to the rain on the roof as he snuggled with his sweet Katie. It had been a long time since he had been this happy, content.

"I may be falling in love with you."

Her Eurasian blue eyes opened and looked deeply into his. She felt like she could see into his soul.

"I love you too," she said, trying out the phrase, wanting desperately to believe it. She held on tight, not wanting the moment to end.

*

Katie soon found that her emotions were pulling-away from Tim. The fire she had for him smoldered. Free of her sexual inhibitions, she lost her emotional hang ups as well. Boys no longer intimidated her. She started talking to her male classmates, even flirting. When Billy Stewart from her chemistry study group asked her to go to lunch, she went with him. It would be ok with Tim, she thought. I'm just having lunch with a classmate. But the next night they went out for pizza and she found herself kissing Billy goodnight. She felt a little guilty, but mostly confused.

Some of the things that made Tim so attractive were starting to bother her. He was older. They didn't like the same music. He never attended college. Also, he had that stupid limp, it was so embarrassing.

*

The spring equinox came and the daytime hours began to win their annual battle with the night. Tim sat with Katie at a restaurant on University Avenue.

"Tim, I think we should go out with other people."

He looked at her with a questioning face. "Are you breaking up with me?"

"No...maybe. I don't know."

"What's wrong?"

"I love you and Linda. You're like family to me, but..."

"But what?" he asked his voice on edge.

"But I've never dated anyone else. I need some space."

He voiced a single laugh. I need space, he thought, I know what that means.

"Take all the space you need." He placed some money on the table and stood up to leave.

"Tim, don't be like that. I want you in my life. You're my friend." She reached for his hand.

He turned and walked away. So this is how it feels to have a broken heart. He was angry with her, at himself, at the world. It felt a lot like his the fall at the U.S. Open...when he couldn't get up.

Chapter 34 Lake Tahoe Area
Spring and Summer 1983

Tim dismounted at the top of Round House lift at Alpine Meadows Ski Resort. He could make out Lake Tahoe in spite of the low-hanging clouds. It felt good to be back in the Sierra. His venture into tennis had kept him away from skiing in his mountain refuge. At the top of the run he adjusted his goggles and pressed play on his Sony Walkman. *Tommy,* the Who rock opera blasted into his ears. It would be an easy run down the groomed-slope. He turned into the fall line, and started making controlled, flowing turns. It was like what they say about riding a bicycle, your body never forgets. A smile took over his face. "God this feels good," he said to the empty mountain.

At his last visit, his doctor told him. "You can go skiing but no black diamonds and just for a few hours a day. If your ankle becomes swollen or feels painful, stop immediately."

"Of course," Tim agreed.

He wanted to get out of town for a few days…away from Katie Anderson.

The days flew by and he didn't want to leave. His former boss offered Tim his old job back at the bar in Tahoe City. He took it and made arrangements to move back up to the mountains.

After an hour of skiing the ankle would start to throb. Not being able to attack the more challenging slopes, Tim looked for something else to occupy his time on the mountain. He started helping his old buddy, Steve, at the handicapped ski school. People who had just one leg, were paraplegic, or even blind were guided onto the hills. The former professional athlete quickly stopped feeling sorry for his relatively small problem and realized he had a lot in which to be thankful.

The snow turned slushy as spring progressed and the sun rose higher in the sky. By April, the locals were getting off the mountain by noon. Some resorts closed down. Steve met Tim for lunch and announced he was getting married to his longtime girlfriend, Nancy.

"Congratulations buddy. So, your life as we know it is over."

"Hey, I haven't been single for two years. We've been living together, you know. I'm not like someone I know, going off to Europe on adventures with groupies following him around."

"I happen to remember the days before Nancy, when all kinds of pretty babes were chasing you around."

"Well those days are almost over."

"What do you mean almost?"

"Want to come to my bachelor party?"

"Absolutely, just tell me when and where."

"How about May fourth in Sparks, Nevada? Six of us are going to the Mustang Ranch."

"Really?"

"Be there or be square."

"Ok," Tim replied, writing down the date on a napkin.

"Of course, nobody tells Nancy a word of this."

"Wild horses couldn't make me tell."

"Oh, I get it, Mustang Ranch, wild horses. Good one."

*

Late afternoon on the fourth of May, Tim joined Steve, Jim, his best man, Peter, and friends, Larry and Greg at the Silver Legacy Hotel in Reno for drinks, a lot of drinks. Then they took a limo to a strip club, and of course, they bought Steve the requisite lap dance, with not one but three of the women, for good luck.

They were feeling no pain when they exited the club and went back to the limo for the short drive to Sparks. Tim remembered the local joke. *Reno is so close to hell you can see sparks.*

They pulled up to the infamous Mustang Ranch whore house. Tim, never having been there, was expecting some grand house with an elegant madam dressed in a great gown to greet them at the door. Instead, what he found was a cluster of trashy trailers, with a sign over the door of the largest one, "The World's Famous Mustang Ranch." Below that were instructions to "Ring the bell and come in."

Inside was a dimly lit small bar room. The "ladies" responded to the bell like soldiers being called to inspection. Twelve women lined up in a row dressed, or what could be better described as scantily dressed, in various sexual fantasy outfits. The costumes ranged from a Dallas cheerleader cowgirl to sexy catholic school girl, complete with a short pleated skirt and her hair in pigtails. The agenda called for each man to pick a lady and buy her a drink before the woman would take him to one of the back rooms for sex at an agreed price.

Four of the guys picked a girl. The chosen lady latched onto an elbow or some other body part and with drink in hand, they exited the bar with their "gentleman," heading towards the garish back rooms. Tim decided he was not that drunk, or interested enough join the proceedings. He and Greg decided to stay at the bar, but the other "working" girls showed that escaping the festivities was not going to be so easy. Four of the rejected ladies approached them at the bar, imploring the men to buy them drinks while rubbing the insides of their legs hoping to change their minds and entice them to go to one of the back rooms.

Tim had never felt so turned off by a woman in his life. He paid one of the girls to join Steve and her associate in the back room for a threesome. Peter straggled back to the bar five minutes later. Steve was the last to return to the bar an hour later. Just as the six men were about to leave, the doorbell rang and three more men came into the trailer. The departing party goers were treated, or haunted, depending by their state of inebriation, by the sight of the same twelve women, lining up for the newcomers. It was definitely time to go.

Lake Tahoe and the snowcapped peaks of the high sierra formed a perfect backdrop to Steve and Nancy's outdoor wedding and reception. A group of ninety-four attended at the wedding. Tim was one of the few without a date. He wondered what Katie was doing. As he watched happy couples dance he missed her, with a yearning that almost ached. But he had a good time with his Tahoe friends. As far as Tim knew, Nancy never did find out about the bachelor party.

*

As summer arrived, Tim believed his ankle was better but hiking on the trail, it became painful after an hour or two. Coming down was harder than going up. His weight, pulled down by gravity, pounded his leg.

After a short time, the joint would swell, so he had to keep his journeys short. Afterward, he soaked his lower leg in ice to alleviate the swelling and help relieve the pain. Motrin became his constant friend.

On the evening of July third, Steve called Tim and invited him to water ski on Donner Lake early the next morning. After skiing, they could go for a bike ride over the pass on old U.S. Highway 40. Every Independence Day there was a great fireworks display at the lake and Steve thought it would be a great idea to watch the exhibition from the lookout at the top of the pass. Tim knew he shouldn't water ski so he offered to drive the boat.

The lake was like glass. There was no wind…perfect for water skiing. As the sun rose above the ridges of the mountains, Steve and Nancy took turns jumping off the dock immediately up on the single ski. They pushed rooster tails of water to the left and right as they turned in each direction. Each wore a wet suit top to defeat the chill of the alpine lake and air on that beautiful blue sky morning.

The turquoise of the lake shimmered, leaving an impression on Tim that he would never forget. He shot two rolls of film with his Olympus SLR camera in less than an hour, in an unsuccessful attempt to capture nature's beauty.

By eleven in the morning, the three had put the boat away and mounted their bikes. Tim's ankle proved no handicap when riding, hard work but pure joy. They assaulted the switchbacks going up the pass. The three friends climbed three thousand feet until they reached the top past the old bridge and spectacular views. They cruised past Sugar Bowl, staying on Donner summit, to picnic in the conifer forest.

Tim, Steve and Nancy stayed in the woods playing cards and reading books until late afternoon, arriving back at the top of the pass as the light started to fade. They watched, oohing and ahwing, the spectacular fireworks exploding below them at lake level. It was the perfect end to a fine mountain day.

Chapter 35 Lake Tahoe Area
May, 1984

It had just under two years since the U. S. Open Tennis Match with Borg. His limp was almost gone. It was time to test the ankle on the tennis court. In the winter of 1984 he had been back skiing at the top of the mountains, double diamonds with little pain. He continued to work at the handicapped ski school at Alpine Meadows and at the bar at night.

With his friend, John Robertson, a good recreational tennis player, Tim warmed up, rallying the ball back and forth. The strokes came naturally, but Tim's felt like his footwork to be slow a fraction of a step behind. If he hit softly, he could place the ball where he wanted, but when he went for a winner, he found himself out of position and the ball flew wildly. More importantly, the pain in his ankle was tolerable but the joint was stiff. There was no fluidity to his movement.

"How does it feel?" John asked.

"Like a bird trying to give milk."

John laughed, "Want to try and play a set?"

"Sure, I'm not here to dance. You serve."

Robertson drove his best serve down the middle and followed it to the net for a volley. Tim stretched and stroked a topspin lob over the amateur's head for a clean winner. John just shook his head and laughed. "That's right, I'm playing the freakin' Omaha Kid."

Tim shrugged his shoulders and smiled. "Lucky first shot."

"Lucky my ass; I couldn't hit that shot if I tried all week."

They finished the set and Tim won 6-2.

"So tell me again that you haven't played in thee years and have a bad ankle. You play amazing tennis," John said, flabbergasted.

"Thanks John, but I wouldn't have won a game against a top pro."

"Well that makes me feel better."

"You could see I couldn't hit anything on the line or with any power."

"Not really, but I'll take your word for it. No wonder people paid good money to watch you play. Come on, the first beer is on me."

Chapter 36 Northern California
Spring and Summer 1984

Linda graduated from Stanford Medical School and Katie Anderson earned her B.A. Tim received an invitation for both graduations in the mail. In spite of Tim's break up with Katie, his sister stayed good friends with his former girlfriend. Linda was so busy with her intense residency schedule, that she had little time to make new friends. Katie idolized the slightly older girl and the two spent time together.

It was through Katie that Linda made the connection that found her a job in the North Bay. Katie's friend, Lois Rubio, was another senior on the Stanford soccer team. Her parents owned the Sycamore Ridge Winery just north of St. Helena in the Napa Valley. The three women had spent some weekends visiting the Rubio Estate and, of course, tasting the well-known award winning family wine. Mr. and Mrs. Rubio were benefactors at the Queen of the Valley Hospital in Napa. They made sure young Dr. Jacobson was offered a job, not that it was hard for them to propose to the board that they hire the competent young woman with a Stanford medical degree.

Tim had run into Katie a few times during the past year. He finally felt like he was over their breakup. He cheered for both his sister and Katie when the girls went to the podium to receive their degrees. After the ceremonies he met another graduate, Lois Rubio, an attractive brunette with curves in all the right places. Her days playing forward on the soccer team had toned her body. Wow! Tim thought, seeing her with Linda and Katie.

"Wow!" Lois said to Katie. "You may remember I told you I had a crush on him when I was still in high school and saw him on television playing tennis at Wimbledon. You don't mind if I..."

"No not at all. It's past history." Katie brought the two of them together.

"So you must be the famous Omaha Kid I've been hearing about," Lois said as she shook Tim's hand. He looked like a mountain man with a neatly trimmed beard and slightly longish dark brown hair. He had that "raccoon eyes" ski tan and looked in pretty good shape. Sparks flew.

Linda and Katie watched the two of them devour each other with their eyes.

Katie whispered to Linda, "I think your brother has forgotten I even exist."

Linda whispered back, "Hey you had your shot."

Mr. and Mrs. Rubio planned go out for a special celebratory dinner with their daughter. Lois asked if they could make it a party and invite her friends.

It was an eclectic group. There were Lois and her upper-class California parents, Eurasian Katie, with her Vietnamese born mother, and the family of orphaned Linda, the new Jewish doctor, her Catholic brother Tim, and their Aunt Mae and Uncle Willy. To add to the cultural diversity, the Palo Alto restaurant was East Indian. The guests ordered beer from Germany-and California wine.

Mr. Rubio proposed the first toast. "To the three lovely new graduates, look out world."

During dinner Tim and Lois sneaked glances at each other. Tim knew a little about Lois from Katie and Linda. She was smart, graduating from Stanford "with honors" as a business major. Among the first girls benefiting from Title Nine, the gender equity athletic law, gained great confidence as a co-captain of the twice NCAA championship soccer team. She told her friends that the fight for sexual equality was over and she was among the winners. The heiress of a very successful wine business knew what she wanted and was proficient at getting it.

As she told Katie, Lois had a crush on The Omaha Kid in high school, watching him play tennis on television at Wimbledon and the U.S. Open. She whispered to her friend, "He's even better looking in person."

After the meal, the parents retreated to their hotels and left the young people to party. They went to the White Rabbit. The locals were all glad to see their former bartender and wanted to catch up with the Omaha Kid, but he found a table in the back with the graduates.

Lois took Tim in hand and pulled him to the dance floor. His time tending bar paid off. He knew his dance moves and spun her, across the floor, showing no problems with his ankle. The music slowed down and the couple wrapped their arms around each other moving to the Eagle's ballad, *There's a New Kid in Town*, their bodies fitting together like they were made for each other.

"You're a great dancer." She whispered in his ear.

"Thanks, you're not so bad yourself."

"How would you like to get out of here and go back to my place?"

He looked over at his sister and Katie sitting at the table. Two men were already making their moves talking to them, drinks in hand. "Do you think they will miss us?"

She smiled seductively at her handsome new friend. "Not tonight; they won't."

*

After graduation Lois Rubio moved back to the Napa Valley and went to work at her family winery in the marketing department. Seeking some independence from her parents, she did not move back to her parent's estate but rented a house in Yountville with her friend Dr. Linda Jacobson. Tim came to visit them often. He and Lois continued to date.

*

Mr. and Mrs. Rubio told Lois they were not enamored with their daughter's new boyfriend. Frankie Rubio took exception to Tim for two reasons. One was Tim's lack of a college education. The second reason was based on a wrong premise. He believed that Mr. Jacobson was Jewish like his sister. He did not believe he was prejudiced but did not want Lois to get seriously involved with a man who was not a Catholic. What would happen if they got married and had children? He had no way of knowing Tim was actually brought up with a similar Italian American Catholic background as his daughter. Lois never even thought to bring up the subject with Tim.

Tim and Lois started hitting tennis balls together at the Silverado Country Club when he was in town. Lois had become a member upon returning to the Napa Valley. The connections she made there could be important for her job with the winery. For the first time in years she found herself not on a soccer team, so she needed another outlet for her physical activity. In high school, Lois had played on the tennis team in the fall and soccer in the spring. She returned to the sport, and enjoyed playing the game. It was also fun to have a hobby in common with Tim.

*

In the late morning, fog held onto the western hills of the Napa Valley but to the east at the Silverado Country club basked in sunshine. The first Saturday in July, Tim and Lois teamed up to play doubles against Linda and her current boyfriend Doug, who she knew from her Stanford days. Tim held his game in check to allow the others to stay competitive, but they all knew that if he wanted to he could take the match over at any time. His ankle still hurt, but with the good weather helping to keep his muscles loose, his athletic ability returned to about ninety percent. The amazing speed of his youth had dissipated but even at less than his best, he was still an athletic marvel.

They sat for drinks and lunch at the club after the match. The men ordered beer and the women had white wine as they waited for the server to bring their food.

"So when are you moving here?" Linda asked her brother knowing he had been thinking about coming down from the Sierra.

"Probably as soon as I can get a job."

Doug chipped in, "Tim, this place needs tennis pro. Snider is leaving for San Diego. You would be perfect."

"What makes you think they would hire me?"

"Are you kidding me? Your match against Borg at the Open is legendary. The Omaha Kid's accomplishments as a Bay Area hero are right up there with Joe Montana or Reggie Jackson."

Tim gave him a funny look and shook his head.

Doug reset, "Ok, maybe not Joe Montana, how about Dwight Clark?"

"If you say so," Tim replied.

Lois said, "I know you were busy playing that match in New York, so you don't know how many people in Northern California were watching, rooting for you."

"Were you?"

"Of course, dummy, that's when my crush began."

Tim wound up getting the job as the club's tennis pro. He found an apartment in Napa near the Junior College and settled in close to his new girlfriend and his sister.

*

Once Tim-settled in Napa, Maria and Sara decided to come for a visit.-After a few days of sightseeing and wine tasting, the visitors sat in Tim's living room where Linda joined them for a drink before dinner.

Tim asked, "So are you two still in love?"

Sara looked over at Maria and said, "Very much so, I think we're closer now than ever."

Maria nodded in agreement with her mate. She asked Linda, "What about you and that Doug, is it serious?"

"I'm so busy with work. My first full year as a doctor, I barely have time for romance. He lives in Palo Alto, so it's hard to see each other very often."

"What does he do there?" Maria asked.

"Works for one of those new hi-tech startups; an engineer."

"Stanford engineer, good job, maybe he's a keeper. How do you like your new job delivering babies at the hospital?" Sara asked Linda.

"Love it. But if you had my job you wouldn't be gay. I see too many heads crowning out of vaginas," Linda said with a smirk on her lips.

"That never stopped a male doctor from wanting to get into one of those baby makers," Maria reminded her cousin.

"Good point," Linda said, laughing.

"Hey, how did this conversation turn into girl talk?" Tim asked.

"I was getting to you Tim. So tell me, how serious are you with the new flame, Lois?"

Tim looked at Linda. "This all stays in this room, ok."

Linda said, "You're my brother. I'm not going to tell Lois anything you don't want me to."

Tim was silent for a moment then he said, "Maria, I've always been able to talk to you about stuff like this…I don't know. I really like her a lot. It's all good. The sex is great, lots of passion, but I feel like we are both holding back emotionally. I've been burned at love the last few times so I want to take it slow."

"And her? How do you think she feels?" Maria continued with her probing.

"Well, she never has said she loves me. Maybe she is waiting for me to say it. Also, she is a lot younger, I'm not sure she is ready to settle down. There is something else; I get the feeling that her Dad doesn't like me. He's never said anything, just seems a bit put off, and maybe Lois picks up the vibe."

"Well if you're happy, maybe you should just give it time." Maria concluded.

"Yeah," he said thoughtfully. "Ok, enough of this heavy crap. Let's go pick up my lady, go to dinner and have some fun."

"We made reservations at The French Laundry. Is that ok?" Sara asked.

"Only if you're buying. I'm only a tennis coach these days."

Maria said, "come on let's splurge, my treat. I'm on vacation, and we didn't have to pay for a hotel."

*

After picking up Lois, the four went to dinner. They sat outside on a beautiful August, Yountville evening. The sun was dipping low over the western hills just a the fog was approaching from the ocean. Colors splashed in the sky.

Tim said, "It's sad that JR's still not talking to you two."

"The worst part is not seeing Joey. I love and miss the little guy."

"And Aunt Sophia is still in the care home in Valley Stream?"

"Yes, but she is doing better. I think she would like to see you Timmy."

"Only the girl I grew up with would still call me Timmy. Does Aunt Sophia know anything about you two being together?"

"No, no, no, no, no! She would have a special place in her Catholic hell for me and my Jewish lesbo."

Lois tried to follow the conversation, but was confused. She turned to Linda for help. "Why did Tim grow up with Maria and who is Aunt Sophia?"

"You and Tim never talked about this?"

"No."

Linda looked at her brother sideways and said, "How come men never talk about the important stuff with their girlfriends? Don't try and answer that Maria, you shrink, it was a rhetorical question. Ok, Lois, here are the Cliff Notes. Our parents died in a car wreck. Mom was Catholic and Dad was Jewish. The aunts and uncles fought over us, so Tim went with My Uncle Tony and Aunt Sophia, while I went with my father's side of the family."

Lois thought for a minute adding it all up. "So Tim, you're not Jewish?"

"Not really Catholic either."

"But you were brought up Catholic?"

"Yup, just like you."

"Holy crap! Really, you two were split up like that? And then you were brought up in different religions. I think this is amazing. Someone should write a book about all this."

*

Jim Tarpley took lessons from Tim all summer and his game started to look impressive. The high school junior showed a lot of promise. In August, he won a local teen tournament. On a water break during his lesson he told Tim, "Mr. Jacobson, my high school needs a tennis coach. No teacher is qualified or wants to do it."

"I told you to call me Tim."

"Ok Tim, we still need a coach. Would you be interested?"

Tim thought about when he played high school tennis and his lack of good coaching. "What makes you think they would hire me? I'm not a professional teacher."

"I knew you were going to ask me that. My principal, Mr. Johnson is looking for a walk-on coach in tennis and baseball. He asked me to talk to you. This is his card. He said that if you were interested to call him."

Tim took the card from the boy. "It might be fun to coach baseball. I still love the game."

After an interview with Mr. Johnson, Tim took the part-time low paying job as both the tennis and baseball coach at East Napa High School. He continued to work at the country club as well.

Chapter 37 Napa, California
May 1985

The scoreboard showed two outs in the ninth inning and the Petaluma High School runners took their leads off both first and second base. The Trojans played against the East Napa Bobcats baseball team for the section championships. Coach Jacobson called time out and strolled to the mound. He still walked with a slight limp making him look from a distance, older than his 30-year. At this level, unlike the big leagues, the whole team could gather during a time out and Tim called everybody on the team in around him.

"Ok," he said without a smile, "how many of you want pepperoni on your pizza after the game?"

The boys looked at him quizzically. "Come on hands, up if you want pepperoni." More than half raised their hands.

"Do you know why I'm asking you this? We have practiced this situation so many times that I don't have to tell you what to do. You know, just relax. Think about what you have to do if the ball is hit to you. Now Roger, don't forget to check the runners in the stretch and make good pitches. Then we can all get out of here and eat some pizza." The coach turned and walked back to the dugout.

Roger Dorel fired a fastball on the outside of the plate and the Petaluma batter hit the ball hard to right field. Jim Tarpley, who was also the number one tennis player for the school, came charging in, played the ball on one hop and fired a strike to the catcher. The Petaluma runner, trying to score from second never had a chance. He was out by ten feet. Three outs, game over and East Napa High had its first sectional championship. The players sprang into the air and then they ran in to the mound to do a big group hug.

Tim watched from the dugout with a big smile on his face. This felt really good. The he hopped up the steps to remind his team to line up to shake hands with the Petaluma players. All of a sudden the sun seemed a little brighter in the sky and Tim adjusted his sunglasses. At least that would be what he told the players, instead of the fact that he had to wipe a tear of joy from his eye. After all, as Tom Hanks said in the movie, *A League of Our Own*, "There is no crying in baseball."

The Omaha Kid loved coaching. It was almost as much fun as playing. That fall the tennis team won eight of their eleven matches in spite of only having one senior. They got better as the year progressed, winning their last five.

In spring his baseball squad played outstanding team ball. They were great at the fundamentals, not allowing the other teams to get any easy runs. If Tim had one weakness as a baseball coach it was teaching pitching, never having played the position. So he called in Sam Rayburn, a pitcher and teammate from his Modesto A's days. Rayburn lived close by in Vallejo. Tim's former teammate had a great curve ball and probably would have been in the majors if not for a torn rotator cuff. Sam was happy to help.

After pizza with the boys, Tim met Lois for a victory celebration. She was coming from work, dressed smartly in a navy blue skirt with a matching jacket, white blouse and a string of pearls around her neck. She gave her boyfriend a kiss and then ordered a bottle of sparkling wine from a neighbor's winery. Lois had dated Tim for almost a year, but neither had said those three words that make a relationship serious.

"You look beautiful," Tim said. He was dressed much more casually than Lois, in a short sleeve golf-style shirt with East Napa High emblazed on the breast, coaching shorts, and tennis shoes. They looked like an odd couple, but she liked his unassuming athletic look.

"Thank you and congratulations. What a year you had coaching! I'm so proud of you. Here's to the East Napa High Bobcats." They clinked glasses and each took a sip.

"Yum, that's very good, Tim said.

Well into their celebration and superficial conversation, Lois said to Tim, "I have news. I'm going to France next week. We are looking to do some kind of marketing deal with a Bordeaux winery. You could meet me there and we could make it a vacation, go to Italy or Greece."

Tim thought about it. He knew traveling with Lois would be well above his budget as club tennis pro and a high school walk-on coach. He had reserves saved from his Dodger settlement. Most of that money was tied up in long term annuities, but he thought he had enough fluid cash to swing a trip if costs could be kept reasonable.

"When?" he asked.

"I should be done with my work in Bordeaux by the middle of July. Then we can meet in Paris."

"I guess I'd better get my passport renewed. You know I have some friends in Paris. I would like to see them."

"I remember you told me you stayed with some people during the French Open. It would be fun to meet real Parisians."

The next day Tim called Paul and Cynthia. They said they looked forward to seeing him again. He was also relieved when they told him Brigitte would not be there. She was off playing on the circuit. Being with Lois and seeing Brigitte would just be too strange.

Chapter 38 Europe
Summer, 1985

They met at the Hotel Virnet at the Champs Elysees in Paris. Tim flew overnight and arrived blurry eyed and exhausted. Lois greeted him with a kiss and allowed him to sleep until the afternoon while she went out shopping.

That evening they met Tim's old friends, Cynthia and Paul for dinner at Pavillon Le Diven restaurant near the hotel. Lois listened intently to the conversation about tennis and heard them relive Tim's 1980 French Open experience. Tactfully, they left Brigitte out of the story.

"How long have you two been together?" Cynthia asked.

"Just over a year," Lois answered, happy to rejoin the conversation.

"Where do you go next?" Paul asked.

"Italy, we both have ancestors there." Lois said.

Paul asked, "Have you been there before?"

"No," said Lois. "But we are really looking forward to it. By the way this shrimp dish is incredible!"

"I think you two are going to have a lot of fun." Cynthia winked at Tim as if to tell him that he found a good one.

After dinner, the sun was setting and the evening sky glowed behind the Eiffel Tower. Paul and Cynthia led Lois and Tim towards the Place de la Concorde. It was the 14th of July, Bastille Day, the celebration of the French Revolution and the birth of the nation's first democracy. Towering speakers had been set up in the park. Adjoining avenues were closed, filled with thousands of people giving off a vive like they wanted again to storm the Bastille and reawake the passion of the revolution itself. As night fell on the City of Lights, the crowd became even more restless and started to clap in rhythm, whistle and shout. Suddenly music burst from the speakers. Fireworks exploded turning the night's blackness into a cascade of colors. The musical and explosive display awed the multitudes covering street. For over an hour, the coordinated show filled the sky and left Parisians and visitors breathless.

When the program ended, the couples kissed on the cheeks, and said their goodbyes. Lois and Tim walked back to the hotel hand in hand. "Now I know why they call Paris the city of love." Lois said. "It's been a while since we have been together and I can't wait to get you back to our room."

Back at the hotel they matched the intensity of the fireworks in their lovemaking. When the passion subsided the two held each other in the afterglow. There were tears in Lois's eyes.

"Are you crying?" Tim asked her, feeling the wet tears on his chest but not being able to see them in the darkened room.

"Yes, I'm happy," she said and held him tighter.

*

The next morning they were on a train heading south for Italy. They stopped in Switzerland and spent two days exploring the Alps. Then the couple went to Florence to see Michelangelo's David. They stood there for quite a while just gaping at the masterpiece. Lois wanted to reach out and touch the marble. "What do you think?"

"It's truly amazing." He knew it was wrong before he said it but his sense of humor could not be denied. "You know I've seen quite a few nudes in the Oakland A's locker room. I won't mention any names but David's not packing as much…*heat* as some of my ex-teammates."

"I can't take you anywhere."

"Don't tell me you weren't thinking about his endowment."

Lois shook her head, but she giggled in spite of herself.

The statue of David showed to be an amazing work of art, but the rest of Florence bedazzled them. The city, the home of the Renaissance showed off its assets. They spent two days in this wounding about the town, where Princes and Dukes once gathered the riches of the known world. The art and architecture kept them captivated. While they ~~relaxed their tired feet sipping~~ espressos in the Plaza del la Signore, Lois said, "I think that Florence just might be the most beautiful city in the world."

From Florence, in a rented car, they drove to the Italian Riviera. The couple stopped when they found a beautiful bed and breakfast overlooking a secluded beach on the Ligurian Sea and took a break from sightseeing,-spending two glorious days playing on the beach. Both of them were happy that the European beaches allowed women to go topless. Lois tried to lose her tan lines and Tim made sure he was wearing his dark sunglasses hiding his wandering eyes.

They befriended another American couple, Joe and Betty Garcia from New Mexico and ate dinner together. Joe spoke fluent Spanish and could communicate with many of the locals. After their meal, they walked along the beach, watching the horizon darken as the sun sank behind the cliffs that towered above the shoreline. They came upon a bonfire started by two local men using driftwood. The natives waved at the two passing couples and signaled them to come and enjoy the fire.

Joe started talking to the local men and learned that their names were Lorenzo and Romeo. Tim was tempted to ask Romeo "wherefore art thou" but he restrained himself. Upon learning that the four newcomers were American, Lorenzo said, "I be in America." He then excitedly told Joe that he was in the *something* and did *something*. Joe asked the man to slow down, so he could try to understand him. Joe nodded his head. He explained that Lorenzo had been in the Merchant Marine and had been to San Francisco. The Italian pointed to Tim and Lois and said, "California." Tim pointed to Lois and himself and said, "San Francisco."

Lorenzo ran up the beach and disappeared for a few minutes. When he came back, he had a bottle of Jim Beam whiskey that he had brought back from his trip to America and wanted to share it with them. Tim nodded. It was his turn to run back up to his hotel to grab a good bottle of Italian wine. They had a party on the beach sharing the whiskey and wine as they watched the fire glow, its reflection shimmering on the tranquil sea. The six of them proceeded to get stinking drunk.

Romeo kept trying to pass his cigarette to the Americans to share but they declined. He felt a little insulted. Joe told the Italian that they did not smoke because they were athletes. Romeo said defiantly, "Me athlete!" He proceeded to prove it by taking his soccer ball and juggling it with his feet. When Romeo kept the ball in the air for a full minute, the inebriated Americans were very impressed and clapped for the man, but they still did not want to share his cigarette.

The next morning Tim and Lois woke up with head splitting hangovers. Tim's mouth felt like cotton and his head felt like it had been hit with a hammer.

Lois shivering after a cold shower said, "I may never drink again in my life."

"We have to drink wine with meals or they will throw us out of the country."

She laughed, "I have to drink wine or they will throw me out of the family."

The couple met Joe and Betty at a late breakfast and those two looked just as bad as they felt. After a full belly of eggs, toast, sausage and lots of strong coffee, the fog around their brains lifted a little, just enough for them to say goodbye to their new friends and head down the coast towards the nation's capital, Rome.

Lois noticed the sign as they crossed the Rubicon River. "My Dad told me that my paternal great-grandfather grew up near this river before going to America. Being here gives me a strange feeling, like I'm coming to a second home. Does that make any sense?"

"Yeah babe, I guess it's like the way I feel about New York. I don't feel quite that way about Italy. Maybe it's because I'm only half Italian. We mutts belong in the U.S.A."

As they entered Rome, the traffic flow picked up with cars weaving right and left, disregarding stop signs and many intersections had traffic circles instead of lights where each auto competed to get into any possible opening. It appeared to Tim that the locals believed that traffic signs and laws were a suggestion rather than a command. With the crazy drivers, the heavy traffic and his hangover Tim felt his body's tension increase. He gripped the wheel hard and his headache returned. "These guys make New York cab drivers look good and sane. I always thought that was impossible."

After two solid hours of creeping and horns honking they found the Hotel Champagne Garden. A grand old classical building centrally located to see many treasures of the city, and just blocks from the ancient Roman Forum. First class all the way, a valet met them at the car. Tim explained to him it was a rental and it had to be returned that day.

"No problem sir. I will take care of that for you, just leave the keys," the valet said.

After checking in, the couple was taken to their suite, furnished in princely style, lush with lots of rich velvet, with deep royal crimsons and purples.

"This place is impressive," Tim said, as he tipped the uniformed bell boy. "Can we afford it?"

"Don't worry about it. I have some wine business to do in Rome, so my family's company will pay for the room on the expense account."

"I feel a little uncomfortable about that, like I'm a kept man."

"You should be so lucky."

"I'm serious."

"Honey, I wasn't going to tell you this until the trip was over because I didn't want to complicate things right now, but my father wants to hire you to be part of the company. It would be a big raise in pay from your tennis pro job at Silverado and you could still have time to coach high school."

"Really?" Tim's mind raced; he was confused and suddenly uncomfortable.

"What are you thinking?"

"I was thinking that your Dad didn't seem to like me."

"That was before."

He raised the volume of his voice. "Before, when he thought I was Jewish and not a *Pisano* like him?

Lois did not back down. "That's unfair."

"Is it really? Think about it. When was the change? It was after you found out that Linda and I were orphans and brought up separately. You told him about that, didn't you?"

"Yes, but that doesn't mean he is prejudiced. He loves Linda."

"Yeah, but Linda isn't a potential mate for his darling daughter."

Her body language changed. The former captain of the Stanford soccer team stood hands on hips leaning forward. "You must understand that my parents would feel uncomfortable about me dating a man from a different religion, no matter what that religion is. I can't control what my parents think any more then you could have controlled your aunt and uncle. Personally, I don't care if you are a Hindu, Muslim, Buddhist or whatever!"

Tim took an step back and a minute to calm down. "Sorry honey, I'm tired from driving. I guess my background makes me hypersensitive to this kind of crap. Religious differences almost destroyed my family. For gosh sake, my parents are buried in different cemeteries--one Jewish, the other one Catholic."

"I didn't know that." Lois took a step back and found tears in her eyes, knowing his parents died in a terrible crash.

"I'm sorry. This is not your fault. It's my shit. Let's enjoy our vacation, ok?"

They hugged. Physically and mentally the two were exhausted. The late night party on the beach, the long drive and this small spat left them emotionally depleted.

Lois kissed him. "My hangover is gone."

He still had a little headache but came over to the bed and massaged her back. After a few minutes, she turned and faced him, looking deep into his eyes. They made love and fell fast asleep entwined in each other's arms.

*

Tim and Lois woke up early, refreshed and revitalized and ready to tour Rome. They went to the Sistine Chapel where Michelangelo's ceiling left them feeling awed. At the Roman Forum, Tim did his Julius Caesar imitation for Lois. He stood on the steps to the Senate and said, "I came, I saw, I conquered. Sorry, Brutus the army has all the knives it needs." Then he pretended to be stabbed and fell down. "Where is Mark Anthony when you need him?"

Lois smiled, amused. "Don't quit your day time job," she said without thinking. Then she realized how those words pertained to his job offer by her Father. "No, I didn't mean that. But..."

Tim started laughing and then so did Lois. They both laughed so hard that it brought tears to their eyes.

Lois took his hand. "This romantic vacation stuff is tricky."

"Just don't make me laugh anymore. Hey, we're in Rome; we need to get some pasta."

"Sounds like a plan."

*

Two places they toured in Rome made Tim particularly reflective. Outside the Coliseum, Tim thought about his professional baseball and tennis career. He felt was strange coincidence that the only major league home field he played in was also called the Coliseum. He wondered. Did fate bring him to this spot for self-reflection? Was he just a modern day gladiator? Did they have games like baseball and tennis during the Roman Empire? He had no idea. Maybe the Romans would have made him a soldier, part of a legion, without a chance to be an athlete.

Then there was The Vatican, the center of power and reverence for the Catholic Church. Visiting the building caused Tim to think about his relationship with Christianity. It was so intertwined with his family relationships. He shook his head thinking about Aunt Sophia's religious neurosis. The Catholic Church's stand on homosexuality felt archaic to him. The Church's dogma had complicated Maria and JR's relationship, and that angered him. He couldn't look at the building without feeling that the office of the Pope, a designation that was left over from the Middle Ages, was screwing up his cousins' lives in the twenty-first century.

He turned to Lois and said, "How would you feel if I didn't fly home with you to California but stopped in New York? I need to see my aunt and my cousins."

"Your *Pisano* crazy side of the family, I'm fine with that. Babe, take care of what you need to do."

"Hey, they aren't all crazy. There is Maria."

Lois said with a bit of tongue–in–cheek humor. "What, your sane, lesbian, almost-sister-cousin? Thank God for Maria."

"Amen."

Chapter 39 Long Island, New York
August, 1985

The pilot announced the final approach to JFK International Airport. Tim looked out of the window as the plane left the Atlantic behind and flew over the south side of Long Island. He could almost pick out his childhood home. He suddenly remembered that thunderous noise as a kid, the sound of the jets taking off above his Lynbrook home if the wind conditions were right. Tim had almost forgotten that childhood memory, when the engines were louder than the crack of the bat against the ball. His flight landed, he got off the big 747, and he took a taxi for the short ride to Maria's house.

Sara came to the door and gave Tim a big hug. "Here, let me help you with your stuff. You know where the guest room is. We'll go back there."

"Where is Maria?"

"She was running a group in Woodmere, should be home any minute. Are you tired?"

"Yeah, been up most of the night. Just slept a little. But I'm wired on coffee. Maybe I can take a nap later."

"Sounds like a good idea. You hungry?"

"No, I ate breakfast on the plane."

After he stored his luggage they sat in the living room.

Sara said, "We were surprised you called from Italy to say you were coming. We didn't expect you."

"I know, change of plans. During my trip I felt like I needed to see the family…clear some stuff up."

Maria came in the front door and when she saw Tim, she let out a whoop and jumped into her cousin's arms.

"It's so good to see you, Tim. Are you tired? Want to go to bed for a while?"

"No, maybe later, I'm good for now."

They made small talk for a while, and then Maria asked him. "So what was so important that we warranted a special visitation?"

Tim smiled. "Boy, you go right for the important stuff, don't you?"

"I guess it comes with my occupation." Tim kept silent for a moment so Maria probed, "Tim, tell me what's on your mind. Do you want Sara to leave?"

"No, Sara, you're fine." He paused for a while. Then he told them about Lois's father's job offer, the argument with Lois and all the religious confusion that the trip to the Vatican stirred.

"You realize that this is not about Lois or her dad, but how you react to their behavior," Maria said. Sara watched their interaction with a sense of curiosity, but stayed quiet in the background.

"What do you mean?" he asked.

"You can't control anybody else's actions, only your own. If you try to change someone so you can be happy with them, you are doomed to failure."

"What if they want to change?"

"Wonderful, work with them. The real question is: what do *you* want to do?"

"Good question."

"Let's start with the job offer. Do you think you might want it?"

"I'm not sure; the higher pay would be nice. I'm not making that much as a tennis pro and little more than nothing as a high school coach."

"Do you want to work for Lois' family?"

"Now you've hit the problem." He squirmed in his seat.

"There is always something else you could do."

"But I love coaching and if I get another fulltime job, I can't do that... unless I went back to bartending, which I really don't want to do."

"So it comes back to: What *do* you want to do?"

"Hell, I guess I want to do what I'm doing. Screw the lousy paycheck. After all, I do have my annuity from baseball."

"Ok, Tim, sounds like you have a plan for now. Now on to the next important question, do you love her?"

He laughed. "Another good question." His face looked like he was almost in agony.

"Remember that letter I told you about, my dad's letter about love at first sight. Since I read that I thought that would happen to me. I would instantly know. But with Lois my feelings are always evolving. I had been holding back but I love her a little more all the time."

"Let's play a little game. You don't mind if Sara works with me? She often works in groups with me. I think she can be helpful here."

"Sure."

"Make believe Lois is sitting in that chair." Maria pointed to Sara. "What would you say to her?"

"Lois, I want to love you."

Sara smiled at him and said, "You want to, is that all I get."

"Lois, I think I love you."

"Still weak," Sara said.

"How did you feel when you said that?" Maria asked Tim.

"Uncomfortable."

"Maybe you're not ready for this next step yet. What about her, has she told you she loves you?"

"No."

"Maybe you both need more time. Being in a loving relationship is not as easy as falling in love."

"Ok."

"How do you feel now?" Maria asked.

"Tired and a little sad."

"I think you need a nap. Then later we can go out to dinner. We can continue this discussion then if you want. Maybe we can also figure out why you might have a problem with The Church, like their stand on homosexuality."

"My problem or yours?"

"How 'bout my mom's?"

"Yeah, that would be a good place to start."

*

Despite JR's harsh words to Tim the last time they were together, they were still on speaking terms, but just barely. They had some brief conversations over the phone, with Tim mostly inquiring about Joey and Aunt Sophia. JR still refused to speak to Maria.

Tim went to his childhood home in Lynbrook to visit JR and his family. He spent some time visiting with Joey, who was very excited to see his uncle, the former professional athlete. He even had two copies of Tim's rookie baseball cards. The boy played catch and Uncle Tim showed him how to throw a curve ball. Tim returned to the living room to speak to JR.

"Don't you think this has gone on long enough between you and Maria?" He asked the cousin who while they were growing up together, had respected Tim as his older brother.

"Don't start, Tim. Stay out of this."

"I tried to, but this impasse is not good for the family and Aunt Sophia is not getting any better. You two need to work together."

"She should've thought of that before she took up with that woman."

"Why do you care so much?"

"Because she is *my* sister."

Tim ignored the jab implying that Tim, after all, wasn't really part of the family. "Yes, she is, that's my point exactly. She needs you and you need her. What she does with her sex life is not your business."

"It is when I have a young child to be influenced by her."

"You don't really think being gay is contagious, like Joey is going to catch it, do you?"

"Well AIDS is contagious. Maybe that's God's way of showing everyone that gay people are sinners."

"I hope you don't really believe that. What is breast cancer? Is it God's way of showing that motherhood is a sin? And what about all the straight people who get AIDS, like Arthur Ash and half of Africa?"

"I just know that homosexuality is wrong!"

"Even if you believe that, do you remember Jesus saying, "Let he who has not sinned throw the first stone.""

"Wow, you actually remember some of the bible stuff from when Mom took you to church. You probably haven't been back since."

Tim ignored the provocation, and turned the focus back on the priority issue. "Junior, why are you so angry at me and Maria?"

"I'm not angry and quit calling me Junior! Nobody calls me fuckin' Junior anymore!" he yelled. Then he stopped and laughed, "Ok maybe I am a little angry."

"That's the first time I've seen you laugh all day. JR came over and hugged Tim. Tears streamed from his eyes. "I think Mom's like she is because of Maria being gay."

"Do you really think that?"

"I don't know," JR said, wiping his eyes with his shirtsleeves.

Tim said, "Joey misses his Aunt Maria and I think you miss her too. What does Cathy think?"

"She thinks I'm an idiot. She would like us to get back together, be a family again."

"There you go. Will you think about it? You don't have to socialize and be buddies. Just be nice to each other."

"I'll think about it."

"Maybe Maria knows a good therapist you could go see."

"Ok, butt face, you made your point. I don't want to have to beat the crap out of you."

"Yeah little brother, just because you weigh more than me now, don't think you have the advantage. I still can kick your ass, Junior!"

"Ok, I guess you can call me Junior."

"Yeah, and you can call me butt face."

They laughed.

Two days later Tim flew back to California. He felt a freedom, like he did when he was as a kid and the final bell rang on the last day of school.

Chapter 40 Napa Valley, California
April 1, 1987

Storms dominated the winter of 1986-1987. But by April first, blue replaced gray, the sky cleared and the sun warmed the countryside. The grape vines were no longer naked; their new green shoots stretched out above the golden mustard. Buds appeared on trees and then came the flowers teeming with bees.

On this beautiful spring day, Tim felt invigorated by the smell of the crisp clean air as he hiked in Bothe State Park just north of St. Helena. Lois dressed in shorts, a tee shirt and hiking boots, accompanied him up Redwood trail. Tim thought that Lois was even more beautiful than the day he had met her. When she graduated from college, she was very pretty, but still looked girlish, not quite in full bloom. Now she added a self-confidence which gave her an inner beauty that accentuated her natural good looks.

They walked mostly without talking, enjoying their exertion as the trail started to climb up towards Coyote Peak. The two had moved in together in the fall and were at the point of their relationship that they were totally comfortable with silence. Neither felt compelled to talk just to fill in the blanks in their conversation.

Lois had told him how proud she was of him. She didn't care how much money he was making. He was amazingly successful as a high school coach, both in tennis and baseball. The East Napa tennis team had won championships the last two years and two of the individuals he trained in tennis went on to win the section tournaments.

It was his work with the baseball team that attracted the attention of the whole east side of the City of Napa. Baseball is not usually a high school sport of notoriety but each home game attracted large crowds. At the end of the season the high school had another baseball section championship trophy sitting in the case outside of the gym. Four players in three years had been drafted by major league teams and many others had earned scholarships to big college programs.

Aunt Sophia died that in January. Lois accompanied Tim to the funeral, and they stayed with Maria and Sara. Tim was grateful to see that Maria and JR had reconciled. Brother and sister were still not close, but they were talking and Maria visited Joey often. It was also welcome news to find out that Cathy was pregnant again.

Maria had shared with Tim her conflicted joy with the news of her brother's upcoming baby. With her committed relationship with Sara she realized she would probably never be a mother, something she yearned for with a feeling of desperation. She told him that no agency would approve of a gay couple adopting.

That last trip to New York had brought Lois and Tim closer. They sat with Maria and Sara and talked for hours. Lois and Maria formed a bond of friendship. They also spent time with JR, Cathy and Joey. Lois could identify with the parallels of Tim's family's roots and her Italian-American background.

When they reached the peak, they sat on a flat rock and held hands as they looked over the valley and the vines reaching up towards the far hills. Tim reached down like he was picking up an interesting rock.

"Lois, look at this nugget. I think it might have some gold in it."

She looked in his hand. It was the last thing she expected to see. It was an engagement ring. Tim dropped to a knee. "Will you marry me?"

Tears welled up in her eyes, "I...I...yes!"

"I love you," he said for the first time to her. He waited to be sure that when he said those special words, he really did love her like his father loved his mother in the letter.

"I love you too," she said wrapping her arms around him. They kissed affectionately. "I feel like I'm at the top of the world."

"You and me babe, we're at the top of the world."

As they drove back down to Napa late in the afternoon, they stopped at Sunshine Market in St. Helena to buy sandwiches and salads for a picnic dinner. At Rutherford they turned off Highway 29 and cut over to the Silverado Trail to take them back to their apartment.

"This better not be an April fool's joke, or you will be singing soprano with the boy's choir."

"No joke, Sweetie, although now that you mentioned it I wish I had planned some kind of gag."

"I think I'll hold off telling my parents. April first is not the day to spring this on them. Are you going to tell Linda?"

"Who do you think helped me pick out the ring? Do you like it?"

"It's perfect."

When they got to the apartment, there was a young woman sitting outside. Tim thought, ok, here comes the April fool's day joke.

As the couple approached the girl, she stood up, turned towards Tim and asked, "Are you Timothy Jacobson?"

"Yes." Tim said, a smile on his face, wondering which of his students were setting him up for this joke.

"My name is Marilyn Aliceson. I'm Jo Lynn's daughter from Modesto. I believe you are my father."

The smile left Tim's face replaced by his jaw dropping open. As Lois watched the encounter, she saw the change in her new fiancé. "Tim, what is going on? Is this a joke?"

"The girl said, "Lady, I can assure you this ain't no joke."

Tim just stood there, not knowing what to say or do. "What makes you think I'm your father?" he finally asked.

"My mother told me all my life who my father was. She had newspaper clippings of you as a baseball and tennis player. She blames you for her screwed up drug addicted life. She said if it wasn't for you she never would have had me. She could've done something else, like maybe attract a good husband instead of the assholes she always dated. You're the Omaha Kid, right?"

"I've been called that." He didn't know what to say to Lois or this girl. "Do you want to come in? Obviously we need to talk."

"Yeah, that would be good. I've been waiting out here for a while and I'm pregnant so it ain't easy to stand here."

"You're pregnant?" Tim asked further stupefied.

"Yeah, that's why I'm here."

Lois looked at Tim. She was shaking and her knees were weak. "Tim, who is Jo Lynn? Why don't I know that you have a daughter?"

"You don't know about this because I didn't know about this. Let's go inside."

Tim sat on the couch next to Lois. He reached for his fiancé's hand but she pulled it back away from him. Marilyn sat in the chair across from them.

Tim said, "I didn't know about you. Jo Lynn refused my help, told me that she was going to get an abortion." Lois cringed when he said abortion. She appeared to be getting more uncomfortable by the minute.

"She told me something like that," the teenage girl said.

"How do I know I am your father? I don't want to sound crude but your mother was sexually active before me."

"That don't surprise me. She likes to screw around. To tell you the truth, she is a fuckin' crack whore. I haven't seen the bitch in months. She ran off with some guy, leaving me alone in the apartment without paying the rent, so I just got evicted. And to answer your question, I'm ok taking a blood test. See if we match."

Lois could not listen to this anymore without asking, "Tim who is Jo Lynn?"

"I went out with her a few times when I was 18 and in the minor leagues in Modesto. She told me she was on birth control, and then told me she was pregnant. When I told her I wasn't ready to get married, she didn't want to have anything to do with me. I never knew she had a baby. I'm sorry Marilyn."

The girl said, "Listen I ain't got no problem with you. I just need a place to stay 'till I have the baby, ya' know... your grandchild. Then I can get some welfare and I'll be gone."

Lois had heard enough for the day. "She can stay in my room. I'm going to go…home for now. Give you some time…to get to know your daughter."

"Lois I…" A look from Lois cut him off. He knew she didn't want to discuss all this now.

He tried a different avenue. "I love you." he said to Lois, pleading with his eyes for her not to leave.

"I'll call you," she said, and walked out the door.

He took a few minutes. Could it have been only earlier that afternoon that they had been happy in love? He looked at the girl in front of him. She had platinum bleached blond hair and full red lipstick on her lips. She wore lots of eye liner and looked to have false eyelashes. She was slim, but with full hips and breasts. He didn't have to ask, he did the math. Tim dated Jo Lynn fifteen years earlier.

"How did you find me?" Tim asked her.

"It wasn't hard. I followed your career. You have always been kind of a fantasy hero to me. I imagined that you stayed with my mother and took me to Paris, London and New York when you played tennis. The farthest I've been from Modesto 'till now was Frisco, just once, when one of my mother's boyfriends took us to go to see the Giants play at Candlestick. I liked him, so of course it was the last time he came around. You know my mother named me after Marilyn Monroe because she married Joe DiMaggio, her baseball player. Of course that didn't last long. Did it? I think I look like the actress. Don't you? Oh yeah, your question, there was an article about you and East Napa High in the Modesto Bee."

Tim realized that the girl was trying to look like her namesake, with the platinum blond hair and false eyelashes. She almost pulled it off.

"What's your due date?"

"September fifth."

"Do you need a doctor or anything?"

"I'm good, but I'll need a place to deliver. Don't worry. I've got a MediCal card."

He picked up the phone.

"Who you calling?"

"My sister, she is an OBGYN at the local hospital. We are going to get you a full physical. Ok?"

"Fine with me."

Chapter 41 Napa Valley, California
Autumn 1987

Lois returned his engagement ring. She told him it was not over. She still loved him, but she needed a time out to see if they could get all this drama behind them. Tim called JR and Maria in New York to tell them the story about Marilyn. They were almost as shocked as he was. Maria promised that she was going to come out to California when the due date was closer.

At an appointment in her office, Linda asked the girl if she wanted to know the sex of the baby before her delivery.

"Sure," she told her new aunt."

"It's a girl."

"Ok." She said indifferently.

Linda asked, "where are you planning to live after you have her?"

Marilyn frowned. She gave Linda a look that said; girl, you just keep out of my business. Instead she said, trying to be nice, "I'm still working that out."

Linda got the hint. This adolescent did not want to be friends. Still she tried to break the ice a little. "Do you have any ideas for a name?"

"I'll ask Tim what he thinks I should name her."

"Don't you want to choose the baby's name?"

"I know I won't name her Jo Lynn."

Later, Tim suggested "Roberta" after the baby's paternal great grandmother.

"Sounds ok to me," Marilyn said, seeming not to care one way or another.

*

On September seventh, 1987, Roberta Sophia Aliceson was born six pounds five ounces. The baby was healthy, but Marilyn refused to nurse her newborn girl.

"I heard it makes your boobs sag," she said. Nothing that Linda said would change the teenaged mother's mind.

Marilyn and Roberta were sent home to Tim's apartment after they were discharged from the hospital. He was busy with tennis practice but as promised, Maria and Sara arrived from New York to help out. They arrived in Napa a day before mother and daughter came home. The two women went out to shop for an hour leaving Marilyn home with the baby. When they came back Marilyn was gone, leaving little Roberta alone sleeping in her crib. A letter was left for Tim:

> Dear Tim,
> You weren't there for me when I grew up. I ain't blaming you just tellin you. You can give the baby more than I can. My boyfriend picked me up. No name. I ain't tellin you where I'm goin. Give little Roberta what I can't. Thanks for helping me out.
>
> Marilyn.

They had a meeting, Tim, Linda, Maria and Sara to decide what to do.

Tim said, "Maria I know how badly you want to be a mother. Do you
want the baby?"

Maria said, "You're the baby's legal grandfather. Don't you want her?"

Tim sighed, "It's not a matter of what I want. In a weird way, I think Marilyn was right." Who can provide best for Roberta's needs? Linda and I well…we don't know what we are going to do. If it comes down to you or me, I think that you and Sara could do a better job right now. Do you want her?"

"Yes, but I don't think they will legally allow Sara and me to adopt."

"I think there may be a way. What if I am the legal guardian but you will actually raise the baby. Legally, you might have to move to California, because of the guardianship issue. If things change for gay couples, you could adopt. Would you do that?" He looked at Sara and Maria. "Do you two want to talk about it? Take some time?"

Maria looked longingly at her partner. She said, "This may be the answer to our prayers."

Sara nodded, "There is nothing to talk about. We want the baby."

"Are you sure?" He asked Maria.

"Yes, absolutely, Tim this is something I've only been able to dream about."

"Good, thank you. Let's get a good lawyer," Tim suggested.

Linda said, "I've got it covered. I know just the right guy from my Stanford days."

*

Tim decided to enroll in his first college classes and work on getting a degree, thinking that since he was coaching at the high school level, it might be a good idea to become a physical education teacher. He realized this would be a multi-year commitment so he continued to work at the club as the tennis pro. It was strange going to classes at Napa Valley Junior College with young men that he had coached in high school the last two years. His desire to improve his circumstances outweighed his discomfort of starting college in his thirties with his former students as classmates.

Tim hoped that Lois would call him and renew their relationship. Each day that passed without hearing from her. When he tried to call she did not answer, so he left massages. Linda told him that Lois was under great pressure by her parents, mostly her father, to end their romance. His sister told him that Lois hadn't completely decided what to do. She was confused. Lois was still unnerved with the idea that his daughter had shown up on his doorstep and needed time to sort through her feelings. Tim decided to initiate communications rather than wait for her to call him. He phoned and Lois agreed to meet for lunch.

They met at a cafe in American Canyon away from most people that might know them. They wanted some privacy. The two sat in a corner booth in the back.

Tim started with a little levity. "It feels like we're spies on a clandestine mission meeting like this. All we need are some dark sunglasses."

She smiled at him, "I've missed you."

"I've missed you too. So are you ready to come home?"

"I don't think I can."

"Lois, this all happened when I was eighteen, years ago, ancient history and I love you."

"No, it happened *now* to me. Tim, I love you. I think I always will, but..."

"But what?"

"But I'm not comfortable. I've lost the feeling that I was safe with you."

"We haven't changed. I'm still the same guy."

"But the whole thing was so...sordid, like I was living in some kind of daytime soap opera."

"So tell me, what do you want to do? Is it, are we over?"

"Maybe just for now. Let's give it some time," she said, tears in her eyes.

Chapter 42 Napa Valley, California
November, 1990

Maria Corelli could not remember ever being this fulfilled. She felt like she had it all. Sara, her partner, was a wonderful stay at home mom to their daughter, allowing her to work full time with her growing practice in the city of Napa. Roberta had her second birthday and now acted out the behavior of a "terrible two." Everything in the house was "mine," even the cat, Sylvester. The two women had spent a great deal of time child proofing the house, but Sara followed the girl around like a pull toy trying to keep the curious child out of trouble.

Roberta now had the last name of Corelli. She was still officially under Tim's guardianship, but in reality Sara and Maria were her parents. Tim lived just a mile away. He spent more time at his cousin's house then his own apartment. He couldn't get enough of the little girl.

Tim knocked twice on the door and walked into the house. He had a key but the front door was usually open and he could come and go any time he wanted.

"Anybody home?" He yelled from the entryway.

"Unc Tim." Roberta came running ungracefully to him. She couldn't quite say uncle yet, and he was to be called Uncle Tim, not grandpa. It was just easier that way for everyone. Tim fell to his knees as the girl wrapped her arms around his neck.

Sara followed the toddler into the room. "Tim, thank goodness, I need a break. Will you watch her while I go to the store for some food?"

"Absolutely, what are we having?"

"Maria and I are having pork chops. I don't suppose you want to stay for dinner? but I guess you want to stay for dinner."

"You're so intuitive."

"Fine, I trade cooking for you to get away from the little rascal for an hour."

"Deal, please get some potatoes and bread for me also. If I had to eat what you girls nibble on, I would starve."

"Ok," Sara yelled back as she went out the door.

He then turned his full attention back to Roberta. "Who wants a horsey ride?"

"Me, me."

"What was I going to do?"

"Unc Tim, I WANT HORSEY RIDE!"

"Ok, you don't have to yell. Come hop on. Ok, ready cowgirl? Let's go catch the bad guy."

Twenty minutes later Maria walked in. "I see you're babysitting."

"Yup, and we just captured the outlaw, Ma'am."

"Mommy M!" Roberta yelled and ran over to her mother.

Tim chuckled, "she is so fickle, it was all about me until Mommy M got home."

Tim, Maria and Sara knew that Roberta would have some unique problems in social settings and when she started school. Few gay couples raised children, but Roberta would always know she had two mothers that loved her. They decided to tell her when she was old enough to understand, her uncle was really her grandpa.

A little while later after Maria settled in. Roberta watched Snow White, and Tim sat on the couch across from his cousin.

"Maria sometimes I worry about that girl. Do you think she will feel abandoned by her biological parents? You know I always felt like I didn't belong."

"I think one mistake my parents made with you was, although they loved you, they would never tell you that they did. You had to be the good Catholic boy or forget about getting anything thing positive from my mom. I know that was hard for you. It's not that she didn't love you, she did. That is why she tried so hard to save your soul. I think deep down she believed your parents got what they deserved for marrying outside their faith."

"Wow."

"So, Roberta needs unconditional love from the three of us even when we are upset with her. We need to make any discipline not about her, but her behavior."

"I think I understand. It's not going to be easy is it?"

"Hell no, I don't think being a parent is ever easy. Now I have a different question for you. Did you miss your parents?"

"Yes, all the time."

"Even though you never really remembered much about them."

"I think that was part of the problem. In my mind they were flawless. Everything would have been perfect if they lived.

"Well we know Roberta won't feel that way. She will probably blame her biological mother for all her problems. Maybe when she is older we should talk to her about Marilyn, her flaws and the choice she made."

The phone rang and Maria answered it, taking the call in her study, leaving Tim to contemplate their talk.

She came out a little while later with a surprised look on her face. "You'll never guess who that was."

"Jesus, I don't have a clue."

"Good guess. It's someone who just thinks he's Jesus. It was JR. He wants to come and visit us for Christmas."

"Holy crap, Maria that's wonderful."

"I know, be careful what you wish for, you just might get it."

*

JR's visit turned out to be lovely. Maria and Tony did not acquiesce to a formal truce. They never even had the sexuality talk. Both pretended the whole conflict never happened and an armistice evolved.

For her part Cathy acted delighted to have her sister-in-law and Sara back in her life. She left Joey and new daughter Teresa with a surprised JR, while she took off with Maria and Sari to Christmas shop in San Francisco. He agreed reluctantly, only because Tim was going to come over and watch football.

Joey said. "Do I really have to play all day with a stupid little girl?"

JR responded. "That girl is your part of your family. You need to be nice to your cousin."

Joey started to play with Roberta. She followed him around like a puppy dog. Tim and JR had one eye each on the games on television on one watching out for the kids.

Joey, to their surprise never came back to complain. At the end of the day, he said, "You know what Dad; she wasn't bad for a girl."

The days together flew by as the family went sightseeing, dining, shopping and wine tasting. Tony was especially enthralled with the wine tasting and the gourmet restaurants. He always thought about how to compete and make his eateries better.

Christmas morning Linda and Tim arrived at Maria's house early, before eight and walked into the unlocked door. "Hello, we're here." Tim announced.

Roberta came running and jumping up and down with excitement. "Santa came, Santa came. She grabbed each by the hand, leading them to the tree.

Maria said, "Coffee's on the counter."

"Great, thanks." Tim said. He poured two cups, one black for Linda and he put milk and sugar in his.

"Ok, who goes first? JR asked, wearing a big smile.

Roberta and Joey yelled in unison, "Me!"

Maria suggested. "Let's let Joey go first, he's the guest."

Roberta groaned but said, "Oh...Ok."

When their turns came each kid tore into the next present. The grownups were almost as excited watching the children's joy of the festivities. The adults opened their gifts with a little more patience but almost as much pleasure. It was their first family Christmas together since Linda and Tim came to New York when Uncle Tony was sick and first time together with this group for Roberta and Sara. Everyone appeared to have a ball.

Latter in the day, Tony admitted to Maria. "You look like you are doing OK here. I'm glad I came. I like this place."

Maria said, "I'm so happy your here."

Tim stood in the kitchen overhearing the conversation. He thought, it's a freeking Christmas miracle! What's next peace between Israel and Palestine?

Chapter 43 Napa Valley, California
Spring 1991

Tim attended two years of Napa Valley Junior College, then another two of an accelerated program at Chatsworth College while coaching tennis and baseball at East Napa. He continued working as a tennis pro at the club. It was an amazing juggling act and after all the effort, Tim was ready to receive his Baccalaureate degree and his teaching credential.

Chatsworth College specialized in teacher education and had locations in almost every large community, with classrooms in mini-malls. To Tim, this diploma-from the school next to the mattress discount store was as important as a degree from Stanford or Harvard. In many ways, starting college late and working full time made his degree a more worthy achievement than degrees of the more prestigious universities. The Chatsworth College ceremony had only fifteen other students, but he thought it was important enough to wear a cap and gown.

When they announced his name, Linda, Maria and Sara cheered. The sudden noise scared Roberta and she screamed and almost started to cry but when she saw everyone clapping, she joined in.

The jubilant group all went out to celebrate. All noticed that Lois was absent. After the breakup they'd stayed on friendly terms for a while but it became awkward to see each other. Lois talked infrequently with Linda, still friends, barely. Tim heard rumors that Lois was dating this lawyer or that doctor, but didn't see her. He'd invited her to his graduation, but never received a confirmation one way or the other. He really had been too busy to date, at least that's what he told everyone.

*

Ginger Collins was an art teacher at East Napa High School. She had short light brown hair, a pretty face and a great smile. When Tim was on the school campus he always dressed the same, in blue shorts and a blue or gold tennis shirt…the school colors. "East Napa Bobcats" was stenciled above the pocket of his shirt. As the weather got colder, he just threw coaching sweats over his outfit. Ginger, true to her artistic nature, dressed in all colors of the rainbow. For years when they met on campus, they had teased and flirted with each other.

Tim stopped by the faculty room to get a cup of coffee before baseball practice, Ginger dressed in a pink cotton sleeveless blouse and a knee length purple skirt with matching purple beads around her neck, was eating a late lunch. Her usual smile greeted him.

"Tim congratulations on getting your degree. I hear you are going to be a full time teacher next year."

"It's been talked about but I haven't been formally offered the job yet."

"We all know you will get it. With Joe Johnson is retiring and with your record with the teams, it's a done deal."

He knew the students loved Ginger. She displayed an amazing effort to show off their artwork. Ginger an accomplished artist sold her oil paintings often at a pricey Saint Helena gallery. She had full control of her classes, which appeared to him to be organized chaos. She was often at his games with a fancy camera taking pictures for the school yearbook, which she was in charge of publishing.

"Are you free to get some coffee later?" Tim asked. She looked at him with a funny expression. "Sorry, was that too forward?"

"No, it was just the last thing I expected. I have a better idea. Let me take you to dinner, my treat, a graduation gift."

"I couldn't take advantage of you like that."

Her usual smile came back. "Tell you what. This one is on me and if we do it again it's your turn."

"Ok, where would you like to go?"

"How 'bout you meet me at Mustard's at seven."

"Sounds nice."

*

Tim hadn't been out with a woman for almost four years. It was fun and exciting to be out with Ginger. First dates were always an adventure. He felt like he was doing fine with the small talk part of the exam.

Being a coach or a teacher and living in the same town is a little like being a sports star. Tim was always looking over his shoulder for students or former students that knew him. Privacy was difficult. He remembered when he was just starting at East Napa High and was seen out with Lois. The next day members of his baseball team would rib him asking, "Who was that hot babe you were out with Mr. Jacobson?" Since then, he tried to be careful about being seen in public. They both hoped that being up in Yountville was far enough from the school to allow them to escape being noticed.

"So, what do you like to do besides baseball and tennis?"

"I like football too," he said tongue in cheek.

"No, really Tim."

"Well, you're going to think I'm just saying this, but I like art."

"No, really Tim," she said again deadpan, not even smiling with her mouth, but her eyes gave her away.

"Hey, I went to the Louvre! I even have a postcard of the Mona Lisa to prove it."

"Wow, a serious art collector," she said, her mouth returning to its smile. It was hard for Tim not to like this woman. "When were you in Paris?"

"The first time in 1980."

"I love Paris. It's a great place for an artist. Were you there by yourself?"

"You're humbling me now. Most of the people I deal with at the club know I was there to play tennis in the French Open."

"Sorry, I'm not a sports fan."

"That's ok. It's kind of refreshing to meet someone who doesn't know my history. Let's just say for now I went for the art."

Ginger laughed. "Ok. Prove to me you like art."

"You want to see the postcard?"

"No, I want you to go to the De Young Museum in San Francisco with me Saturday."

"So you're not sick of me yet."

"No, we have plenty of time for that."

"I have two tennis lessons to teach at the club until noon. Can we go after that?"

"It will be a little hurried, but we could make it work."

"Ok, it will be my turn to treat. I'll pick you up after tennis."

They couldn't avoid it. Within a week, everyone at East Napa High School knew they went out together.

*

For seven years Tim's baseball team had been the talk of the town. The worst that his team had ever finished was second place. The five section championship trophies that his teams won stood in the case outside the gym. They would not add one this year. Victor Garcia, the team's best pitcher, developed tendonitis in his elbow and had to be shut down for the season. The starting shortstop and team's best player, Bud Norwood, was declared ineligible because of poor grades. Two other starting players were busted for cocaine at a party. Both were juniors.

Tim met with the two young men and told them about his former roommate, Nate Johnson, and how he lost his life to the drug. He suspended the two from playing the rest of the year, but kept them on the team for practice.

"Everyone deserves a second chance. Do you want to be screw ups your senior year or leaders of the team? I want a written answer from each of you on my desk by next Tuesday. Ok boys, go to practice." Without these top four players the team finished in fifth place.

Chapter 44 Napa Valley, California
September, 1991

Linda and Tim went out for Chinese food in downtown Napa. He ordered Kung Pau chicken extra spicy and she had Mongolian prawns with lots of steamed rice. They shared their dishes, something they had done often over the years.

Linda smiled at her brother. "I have news," she said eyes sparkling.

He looked up from his food and stopped moving the chopsticks to his mouth.

"Kip and I are getting married." She had been dating another doctor for about a year, a Japanese American, Kip Tamori.

"Masel tov. So you finally met his parents?"

"Actually I wanted you to be the first to know. He is going to fly down to San Diego to tell his parents this weekend."

"How do you think that will go?"

"Well, traditionally Japanese-American parents are not so great with inter-racial marriages. So he has been telling them that he is dating a JAP, not telling them that it stands for "Jewish American Princess."

"Ha ha very funny. So really, how well do you actually think they will deal with this?"

"We're about to find out, but I feel it must be in our genes, marrying outside our ethnic group. You know, like Mom and Dad."

"Yeah, that worked out so well."

"It would have if they stayed alive. Besides it's almost a new century, this racist stuff has to end sometime. California is the perfect place for an ethnically mixed family."

"Sis, you're preaching to the choir."

"So to change the subject, how are you and Ginger doing?"

"I like her a lot. It's been fun this summer."

"That's all, just fun?"

"So far, give it time. I don't think I am ready to fall in love again so soon."

"Going to invite her to the wedding?" Linda inquired.

"Wow, my kid sister a bride. When will it be?"

"We're looking at October, before Thanksgiving."

"That's soon."

"You're telling me. I've got a lot to do. But we don't want a long engagement. I love him, Tim."

"I'm really happy for you."

"You didn't answer my question about inviting Ginger to come with you. Are you ok with me inviting Lois to the wedding?"

"At one time you were together all the time, really good friends. You should invite her if you want. Do you think she will come?"

"Maybe."

He was quiet, looking far away for a minute. Then he finished his meal in silence. Just the thought of Lois made him uncomfortable.

Linda asked. "Want to have some dessert?"

Tim's attention came back to his sister. "You never get dessert."

"It is your last day at the country club. Monday's your first day teaching. I thought you might want to talk some more."

"Thanks, Sis, but I'm good. Do you need to talk some more?"

"Not today." She stood up. "Bye, love you."

He got up and kissed her on the cheek. "Love you too. Bye."

Chapter 45 Saint Helena, California
October 20, 1991

How did I let things get so messed up? Lois Rubio asked herself. She had been trying on dresses all day realizing that she wanted to impress him. She loved him. She never stopped loving him. Damn him, damn the freaking Omaha Kid!

A week earlier she had broken up with Will. William Joseph Higgins, the Harvard educated lawyer. He was smart, from a good family with money, Catholic, even played a pretty good game of tennis, everything she wanted in a man. Or was it everything her father wanted in a man?

They were never officially engaged, Will and Lois. He asked. She answered, "I need more time. I'll let you know." A year later he was still waiting for an answer. They had been a couple so long that at wine functions her dad introduced him as her fiancé. Mr. Rubio may have not seen her cringe when he said that but Will noticed. Yet he loved her and wanted to give her all the time she needed. She hoped that she would lose her feelings for Tim and find herself in love with Will.

When Tim's graduation invitation came in the mail, she knew she couldn't show up at the function with Will. So she decided to ignore the whole thing and pretend she wasn't so proud of Tim. And pretend she wasn't still in love with him. So why did she check all the box scores of his high school baseball games in the Napa Register? Why did she secretly go by his apartment and watch little Roberta and him play together. One time he almost caught her. No matter how much she tried to deny it, she just couldn't get over the man.

This woman who had been confident all her life was so indecisive when it came to her romance with Tim and now with Will. Why couldn't she either declare her love for Tim or move on and commit to her new suitor.

Was she a coward? She wondered. Why couldn't she just come out and tell her dad, "I don't care if he had a baby with someone else, I still love him?"

*

That last night together, Will and Lois went out for dinner in Calistoga. That day Lois's wedding invitation arrived in the mail. She showed it to Will while they were waiting for their entrée. She bit her lip. He of course knew about Tim, and his sister Linda, the doctor. He had been introduced to her at a wine function and had seen her many times. Lois had never introduced him to her former boyfriend.

"Are we going to go?" He asked.

She answered, "I don't know."

"She was such a good friend, why wouldn't you go?"

"What? She said, not focusing, lost in thought. She looked back at Will for a second. "Sorry, what did you say?"

He gave Lois with a frown. "Where did you go?

"Just thinking."

He asked again, "If you and Linda were such good friends, why wouldn't you go? Is it because of him?"

"Are you jealous?"

"Should I be?"

"Don't you lawyers always say never ask a question if you may not like the answer."

"Is this one of those times? You still love him, don't you?"

She didn't answer for a good long moment. "Unfortunately I believe I do."

Will signaled the waiter, slipped him a hundred dollar bill and said, "Please cancel our order. This should cover everything." He turned to Lois and said coldly, I'll take you home."

In the car, she said with tears in her eyes, "Sorry, Will. You have been so nice, so patient…"

The rest of the trip was in silence. He dropped her at the front door of the Rubio estate.

"Goodbye Lois," he said with finality.

"Good…" before she could finish, he was gone.

She walked into the house in a daze.

Her mother took one look at her and asked, "Are you alright?"

"No. I just broke up with Will. I'm still in love with Tim and it's too late. He has found someone new. I…I've been such an idiot!"

Chapter 46 Yountville, California
November 2, 1991

Tim found tears coming to his as he watched his little sister walk down the aisle. He couldn't believe how beautiful she looked all dressed in white. Kip appeared handsome in his formal tuxedo with tails. The Tamori's presided regally.

Kip's parents were reluctant at first, but soon Mr. and Mrs. Tamori accepted their son's choice for a bride. After all, his father told him, "this was the United States not Japan." Their parents were in the relocation camps during World War II because of discrimination.

What could be more American than to have their son, the doctor, choose another doctor who was a Caucasian to be his bride? Yet Kip's family was Christian and there was the whole Jewish thing, and the minister was a Buddhist and they were at a winery not in a church. Trying to keep up with modern American society was all so confusing. Yet seeing their son happy, with his beautiful bride, filled them with pride.

*

The reception took place at Granite Rock Winery near Yountville. Tim wore a sports jacket and tie for one of the few times in his life. Ginger wore a taupe-colored, knee-length, sleeveless dress with glittery matching high heels. Right away, Tim noticed that Lois was there without a date. She wore a simple short black dress with a gold necklace and black pumps. He tried to ignore Lois but he couldn't help it. He stole glances at her all evening.

Finally, Ginger said, "I know you want to talk to her. I understand the situation. Go."

Tim looked at his new girlfriend and asked, "How do you know…"

"Women know these things. It comes from years of gossip."

He approached Lois with trepidation.

"How are you?" he said as he came to her table.

She almost looked through him. "I practiced what I was going to say to you if I had a chance and now I don't know how to say it."

"What do you want to say?" He asked, encouraging her.

"Tim, I'm so sorry. You needed me and I wigged out."

"You…"

"No. Let me finish. I was confused, then angry, then sorry. My stupid parents didn't help. They got me more worked up, more confused. After I sent back your ring I couldn't face you except for that one time. I tried to see you again, but I was not so brave. Then I tried to move on, was almost engaged to a lawyer. Was going to marry him …but he wasn't…you."

"Now I don't know what to say," Tim said softly.

"Tim I still love you." Tears were streaming down her face destroying her make up.

"Lois, I just came to say hello. I'm here with someone, and I can't do this now." He looked back to his table and Ginger was gone. "Lois don't leave. I have to check on my date."

"I'll be here, I won't leave this time."

He ran back to his table. Ginger's belongings were gone. He checked the restroom, maybe she had gone there. Then Maria came over to him and said, "Ginger told me to tell you she is leaving. She will see you at school. She said not to worry, that she's a big girl. It's been fun." Then Maria added. "Good luck Tim."

He kissed his cousin on the cheek. "Thanks."

He slowly went back to Lois. She looked at him longingly. A slow song was playing. He led her to the dance floor and encircled her with his arms. They danced. He whispered in her ear, "I never stopped loving you."

*

The next week Tim saw Ginger at school in the teacher's lounge. He wanted to hide but knew he owed her an explanation. He walked over to her and before he could say anything, she held up her hand.

"Don't you dare apologize. I knew you were in love with her the moment you walked into the wedding. Tim, it's not my first time around the block. I've broken up with men before. I just want to know, are you two back together?"

He didn't want to look her in the eye. "I believe we are."

Ginger laughed. I'm glad. We had a good time, but I knew something was missing. Now I know and we both can go on from here."

"Ginger you are an amazing woman."

"Yeah well it's fun to be noble. You want the bitchy side of me?"

"No that's Ok, I'll pass."

"Good, we're going to be working together. I would like us to feel comfortable around each other."

"Should we hug?"

"I think that would be too much."

"Ok then, I'm just going to go out to the ball field."

"Oh Tim, one last thing."

"If you marry Lois I want to be invited. You owe me a good time at a wedding. If a Rubio gets hitched it would be quite an event. I would like to be there."

"I promise. You will get the first invitation." He did the Boy Scout three finger thing again.

Sycamore Ridge

Chapter 47 Napa Valley, California
June, 1992

The contrast between Linda's and Lois's weddings told a lot about the difference between the backgrounds of the two women's families. Linda's wedding at the small Granite Rock Winery was a lovely but simple affair. The Jacobson family was middle class, monetarily comfortable, but not extravagant. The food, music and ambiance was excellent, and high quality but not conspicuous.

The Rubio family spared no expense for their only daughter. The multi-million dollar Sycamore Ridge Winery was decked out with all the fineries that money could buy. It was a community event, the "who's who" of the Napa Valley attended. A string quartet played as the guests arrived. For Tim's part, his side of the aisle would include his family, good friends from both coasts, many of the faculty of East Napa High School and even some former major and minor league ball players he still called friends. Lonnie was an usher. Steve, Tim's ski buddy, was his best man. Ginger was there with her new boyfriend, a fellow artist who would be taking pictures of the event. Katie still friends with soccer buddy Lois, worked for Apple arrived with her husband and two children.

The ceremony and reception took place outdoors, with the lavish grounds of the vineyard providing the backdrop. A lovely choppah, a trellis of wood adorned with flowers, was built for the couple's bower. Although they were having a Catholic wedding, this adornment was something borrowed from the tradition of Tim's Jewish half. It made him feel good to have something from his biological father's side of the family.

The weather could not have been more beautiful, as high wispy clouds filtered the bright sunshine with a temperature in the low eighties. The view from the cliffs overlooking the valley was spectacular. The party goers could see endless rows of vines ripe with a bounty of wine grapes. Newcomers from back east attending the wedding marveled at the scenery.

Tim felt he understood why Lois's parents had been so careful about letting him get close to their daughter. He was not just marrying Lois or even her family, but was becoming part of a legacy. He felt a little uncomfortable about taking on this responsibility but realized he did not have to change his nature. The Rubio's were not superior, just blessed with an inheritance, like the nobility from their home country of Italy.

Lois walked down the aisle, looking like a model from a wedding magazine, her strapless lace dress exposed her tanned shoulders. A gold necklace that glimmered in the bright sunshine adorned her neckline. A crown of flowers that matched perfectly with her bouquet sat on top of her flowing hair. The petals strewn in the aisle by five-year-old Roberta, the flower girl, accented the colors. The Catholic priest from Saint Helena Catholic Church performed the nuptials. In compliance with the wishes of Lois and Tim he did not hold a formal mass, just a simple ceremony.

Along with the religious requirements, Lois and Tim exchanged vows that they wrote. Lois highlighted the promise to stay with her husband in sickness, health and especially when he needed her. Tim said that he would work every day to be true to her love.

When the priest said, "I now pronounce you man and wife" they kissed and a popular local rock band played "All You Need Is Love," by the Beatles. Everyone joined in singing to the new Mr. and Mrs. Jacobson. After the song, the newlyweds were taken away for pictures, and the band continued to play as the corks popped and the party started in earnest.

Tim walked up to his new father-in-law, stuck out his hand to shake and said, "Mr. Rubio…"

"No son, no more Mr. Rubio for you, call me Dad or Frankie."

"Ok, er…Frankie… How about Frank?"

"That would be fine."

"I just want to tell you that I'm going to do my best to make you proud…"

"Stop right there Tim. I want you to know I'm very proud of you. What you have done, completing your education, ten championships coaching high school tennis and baseball teams. I'm impressed."

Tim felt a frog in his throat. "Thank you Mr…Frank. That means a lot coming from you."

"Besides having you in the family has already paid off for the winery," Mr. Rubio said with a laugh, your cousin JR is changing his wine menu in the Corelli family national restaurant chain from Bordeaux wines to Napa Valley wines highlighting The Sycamore Ridge label."

Chapter 48 Asia
June and July 1992

The newlyweds left for a working honeymoon. Work for Lois, then play. She had a presentation in Tokyo to make on behalf of the winery. Tim was left on his own for two days in the huge Japanese city. Tokyo struck Tim like an upside down New York. The language was impossible. Luckily most of the people he dealt with spoke some English. He explored the best he could without Lois. In the evening they got back together and went out to the best sushi and local restaurants they could find.

When Lois completed her work in Japan, the honeymooners took off for Thailand. They were able to rent a car with a private driver and personal guide, and pay for a night of lodging, for less than the cost of a resort hotel room in Hawaii. They rode elephants in the northern jungle, visited the Buddhist temples, saw the infamous World War II Bridge over the River Kwai, and shopped and toured in Bangkok. In parts of the capital, when they went out in the evening, girls would approach Tim and offer themselves for sexual favors. When he tried to explain to one of the girls that Lois was his wife, she replied that "he need wife number two to make more fun."

Lois teasing him asked, "You're sure I'm going to be enough for you Stud?"

"You know they have male prostitutes here also."

Lois laughed and hooked her arm with his. "You're all I want babe."

One thing they both could enjoy after a hard day of touring was a Thai foot massage. There was always a massage parlor close by to work out the daily kinks. The practitioners would spend an hour on each of them as they sat together in large comfortable reclining chairs. The masseuse started by washing their feet, massaging up their legs, their backs, their arms and finished with their heads.

The honeymooners finished their trip on a beautiful tropical beach in the south near Phuket. They swam, snorkeled, rode bikes and just hung out on the sun-splashed beach. They had rented a private cabin in a cove just above the turquoise ocean water where they could find shade, read and make love.

On their last night on the island Lois and Tim walked, holding hands, along the shoreline to what had become their favorite restaurant, a quarter mile down the beach. They sat at a table on the shore and watched the sunset as the waves crashed just yards from their bare feet. They shared a meal of snapper stir fried with fresh green beans, seasoned with garlic and basil, and a second course of spicy green curry prawns with lots of cold Thai beer.

After the great meal, Mr. and Mrs. Jacobson retreated to their room with its king-size bed covered in mosquito netting, for a final round of honeymoon love making. For Tim, love making felt somehow different now that he was married to Lois. Their love was sacred with body and soul linked for a lifetime. He caressed and kissed every inch of her. When she raked his chest hair with her scarlet fingernails, his passions met hers. In sweaty embrace he confessed. "I love you completely."

Lois cried tears of joy. "I'm very happy, my love."

The next morning, they went to visit a small secluded Wat, a Thai Buddhist temple, up a steep trail on a cliff overlooking the ocean, the view magnificent. One elderly monk lived in solitude at the tiny bamboo temple. They had been told that he was a healer and a visionary. Catching their breath, they entered the sacred place. They brought a gift of fruit for the monk and bowed their heads in reverence to the golden Buddha sitting on a platform in the shrine. The monk blessed the couple. He did not speak English, but used gestures to communicate. He pointed to Lois and made a hand sign of her rocking a cradle. She said to him, "No, I'm not going to have a baby."

The monk just smiled and shook his head knowingly.

Chapter 49 Northern California
Summer 1992 to Spring 1993

Tim waited parked in the car above the rocky cliffs and the surging waves of the ocean just north of Bodega Bay. The typical July blanket of fog hugged the rocky coast obscuring the view as Lois meet Jodie Miller at her house. Mrs. Miller facilitated the committee for the Coastal Land Trust. The environmental group hoped to use the Sycamore Ridge Winery grounds to hold a charity auction to raise money. Lois was working out the details including a donation of wine. It was a way for the winery to give back to the Northern California community.

As Tim waited for his wife, he watched as a bumble bee moved from one flower, taking the nectar and carrying the pollen to impregnate another. He had the radio tuned to the San Francisco Giants game with Lon Simmons describing the action. Lois finally returned. They had planned this getaway hoping the weather would be clear and they would have a romantic lunch at the Tides Restaurant overlooking the bay.

"Ready honey?" he asked.

"Let's go get lunch. Too bad the fog's so thick."

"I'm looking forward to the fresh oysters they farm in Tamales Bay."

Lois normally loved oysters but today the thought of the mollusks made her nauseous. She waited for trip to the bay to tell Tim about the test she had at the doctor's office the day earlier. They drove the short way to the Tides. The two walked in. Garlic and other spices and the smell of ocean permeated the restaurant. Tim's mouth watered. Lois excused herself and rushed to the bathroom, where she threw up her breakfast. She washed out her mouth and fixed her makeup and placed a stick of gum in her mouth to defeat the putrid smell. Tim was already seated when she came to the table.

"Honey I'm not very hungry.

"Is everything alright? You look a little pale."

Her stomach did flip flops. In spite of her queasy belly, she looked at him with love.

"Tim, we're going to have a baby."

He dropped his menu, stood up and hugged his wife. "Hell yes!" Then he gave Lois a big kiss in the middle of the restaurant. "It's ok folks we are going to have a baby."

People at the other tables gave the couple a round of applause.

"You are such a ham." She said laughing.

"Are you sure? How do you know?"

"The doctor told me yesterday."

"Yesterday, and you waited to tell me?"

"I thought I would be more special telling you here."

"This is wonderful. So I guess you don't want oysters."

"Please don't say that word or I'm going to be sick again."

"Is it okay if I eat something?"

"Absolutely."

"Is there anything you want?"

"Actually, Chocolate ice cream sounds good. It might settle my stomach."

Tim signaled for the waitress. "She wants to start with dessert. Can you please take this away and bring the lady some chocolate ice cream?"

"Congratulations you two," the waitress said, smiling. "I'll bring that ice cream right away."

*

Tim went back to teaching school and coaching tennis at East Napa in the fall. The tennis team looked good with Tommy Carlton leading the way as the number one singles player. Carlton, now in his junior year, had taken tennis lessons from Tim at the club since he was five, and Tim was hopeful the powerful 17-year-old might go far.

Tim wrapped up practice early and drove up to Saint Helena where Lois wanted to show him a house. He cruised up the Silverado Trail, followed her directions, from town up a hill to an impressive Victorian style house overlooking the valley. He found Lois inside with the real estate agent. The house proved to be a small mansion with five bedrooms, three baths, and the impressive hallway led to a large great room, big enough for entertaining many guests. The modern kitchen could easily accommodate a chef and a helper. The large backyard faced an immaculately trimmed green lawn fenced off from wild hillside. The enclosed swimming pool had a rock waterfall and a hot tub with room for eight.

"Honey, this place is huge. With the price of real estate here up valley this place must cost at least over a million or two," Tim said, in slight shock.

"You may have noticed that my parents did not give us a wedding gift. They want to buy this place for us. The owners are moving to Southern California and they are motivated to sell. It's a steal. With my job in marketing, Dad wants me to have a place big enough to entertain potential clients. Of course they want us to be happy with it. Do you like it?"

"What's not to like?" He felt a twinge of guilt. The house with a price tag no teacher would earn in a lifetime.

"You know "Oma" It has plenty of room for many more kids," she said with a twinkle in her eyes. She stated to call him this pet name after they got married.

"It's wonderful but are you sure. We might feel obliged to you parents."

"Tim, my parents want to do this. We all are part of the family now."

He shrugged his shoulders. He felt overawed but nodded his head. "I guess it's alright."

"I think we want it," Lois said to the agent. "Can you meet me and my father at the winery tomorrow?"

"What time would be good for you? She asked, taking out her appointment bool

"Ten? Lois inquired."

"Yes that works." The agent smiled.

*

A steady rain beat down on the roof, and the large fireplace blazed, warming the partially furnished living room. The Christmas lights cast a cheery glow in the windows, and lighted reindeer grazed the front lawn.

Linda, Kip, Maria, Sara and, of course, six-year-old Roberta visited to celebrate Hanukkah. Linda, although not very religious, still wanted to share her traditions with her family.

The adults were gathered around the fire talking after lighting the Menorah. Roberta watched a Disney videotape in the next room. Linda and Lois rekindled their friendship since becoming sisters-in-law.

"I so envious we want a baby," Linda confessed to Lois.

"Well Sis, keep trying. If you're not successful at least you'll have a good time." Tim said with a twinkle in his eye.

Sara groaned. "You know your sense of humor hasn't gotten much better since high school."

"Easy girl, you might hurt his feelings," Maria said to her partner.

Lois joined the fray. "Impossible, don't you know he doesn't have any."

"I just don't get no respect."

Just then Lois yelped in pain, with a questioning look on her face.

Tim asked, "Honey, are you ok?"

"I'm not sure. I just had a sharp pain in my belly, but I think I'm all right." Just after saying that, she doubled over in pain. "There it is again," she said breathlessly. A spot of blood could be seen coming through her jeans.

Linda sprang catlike across the room to Lois's aid and examined her.

"Tim, call the St. Helena Hospital Emergency Room. Tell them I'm coming with a medical emergency. Maria, get me that blanket." She pointed to the throw on the couch. "Kip we can be there in a couple of minutes, faster than the ambulance. Get the keys, let's go!"

Tim sat paralyzed, shock registering across his face.

"Tim *now*!" Linda commanded as she and Maria bundled Lois toward the door.

*

Two hours later, Linda returned to her family. Kip waited with his brother-in-law, while Maria and Sara took Roberta home.

Linda took Tim's hand and said, "Lois and the baby are going to be fine. We still have to run some more tests but I think it's a very mild form of what we call marginal placenta previa. In other words, the baby is too low, but not seriously. Lois will probably need bed-rest and no strong physical exertion until the birth. One other thing, *he* looks fine."

It took a few moments for Tim to figure out what she had just told him. "Did you say *he* looks fine?"

"I did," she said with a smile.

"A boy."

"Yup, you're going to have a son, Tim." She hugged her brother.

He kissed her cheek, so relieved, eyes misty. "Thanks Sis...I..."

"You can go see her now," she said.

Lois came home from the hospital in just a few days, before Christmas. Loretta Rubio moved into the guest room to care for her daughter, especially during the day when Tim was at work. Lois moved to a bedroom on the first floor to avoid the stairs when she was allowed out of bed.

In the evenings, the three talked about everything from politics to baseball. Tim was surprised by Loretta's view on religion. He knew she was very involved with Saint Helena Catholic Church, but she often disagreed with the dogma of Rome. Like many American Catholics, she differed with the Pope about birth control, gay rights and even abortion. Yet she was very careful with whom she shared her views. She understood the politics of living in a small town and its implications to the popularity of their wine business. One political issue she did not hide was her commitment to the environment. She was an active member of the Napa Land Trust and the Nature Conservancy. Tim realized his mother in law was different from his Aunt Sophia. Her views were not that different from his. She could be a friend and an ally. He felt less trapped in the grandeur of the house.

*

In early March the vineyards were still awash with the golden yellow glow of mustard. The oak and sycamore trees along the river budded with baby green leaves. The winter rains had retreated north to Washington and Oregon, and sunshine bathed the valley in warmth. Two articles appeared in the local papers' columns:

The Saint Helena Star
March 4, 1993
Local girl and former Saint Helena High School soccer star Lois (Rubio) Jacobson gave birth to a baby boy yesterday.

Lawrence Frank Jacobson was delivered by C-Section at Queen of the Valley Hospital and is a healthy 8lbs 2 oz boy. He is the first grandchild of Sycamore Ridge Winery owners, Frank and Loretta Rubio. The baptism is schedule for May 25th at Saint Helena Catholic Church.

The Napa Register
March 4, 1993

East Napa High School coach, teacher, former A's major league baseball player and Silverado Country Club Tennis Pro, Tim Jacobson became a father yesterday. His wife, Lois gave birth to Lawrence Frank Jacobson at Queen of the Valley Hospital. Coach Jacobson's tennis and baseball teams have won 15 section championships.

After delivering the baby, Linda delivered her news in Lois's room at the hospital. Tim held little Larry. "Guess what guys? Linda said. "I'm following your lead. I'm pregnant."

Tim said, "Mosel Tov."

Lois, still in bed "threw" her sister-in-law an air kiss, "Congratulations!" She said and held her arms out for the baby.

Tim, all smiles but terrified that he might do something wrong like drop the baby, handed him over. He couldn't remember ever being this happy.

In the two years that passed since Larry was born, Lois returned to the land of the healthy, but the placenta previa pregnancy had damaged her uterus and she now was unlikely to have another baby. Linda put her on a preventive dose of birth control pills.

Larry, a healthy and happy toddler, drove his parents crazy. The little boy had to explore everything, just a step from disaster. The couple hired a full-time live-in nanny, Teresa. Tim and Lois encouraged the young lady to speak Spanish with Larry, giving him a head start on becoming bilingual.

Their house became a home filled with beautiful furniture, artwork and most importantly love. For the most part, the couple got along really well. When they faced a problem, Cousin Maria was always there to help them work it out.

Tim continued to be very successful as the high school tennis and baseball coach. In the past two years the school won one section championship in each sport and a second place in tennis, and-losing by just one run in the section finals in baseball the last year.

One early Saturday morning in late June, Tim and Lois decided to take their tennis rackets out to Crane Park and rally the ball around. Tim's damaged ankle had always caused him some pain when he played, but if he limited himself to one set, the residual effects were not bad. Ibuprofen became a good friend.

Tim proposed that he only get one serve and they play a set. They had tried this handicap before and he had always won. Lois agreed anyway. She loved the competition. He was up three games to one when he hit a poor serve and she jumped all over it, smacking the ball deep to his backhand. He moved quickly to his left, hit the shot and planted his foot to move back to center court. His ankle exploded in pain. He dropped his racquet and sat down holding his leg in the air.

"Are you all right?" Lois asked from the other side of the net.

"No!" he said simply, sucking air to deal with the stabbing pain in his leg.

Lois ran to him and saw that his ankle was already swollen.

"Hold on Oma."

She put a towel under his head for support, then sprinted to her tennis bag, pulled out her cell phone and dialed 911. She asked them to send an ambulance as quickly as possible.

He was rushed to Saint Helena Hospital. Lois got a bad vive flashing back to her last time in this room during her pregnancy emergency. They gave him morphine and took him to get x-rays.

"Your husband needs immediate surgery. His ankle bone has broken almost in two where the screws were attached to hold on the replaced ligament. I've never done a surgery this complex. He needs a specialist. We're transferring him to Stanford."

Three hours later, Tim arrived at Stanford Medical Center. Linda couldn't join them, since she had babies to deliver, so she sent Kip to help them maneuver through the system and give advice.

A team of two top surgeons came out to talk to Kip and Lois. Kip knew one of the doctors from his Stanford residency, Michael Samson. Michael addressed them.

"I wish I had good news to tell you but I don't want to sugar coat it. I'll try to make this simple. The bone is in bad shape. We can use a new technique the FDA just approved. If you agree, we can replace the ankle bone with titanium and attach a new ligament from a cadaver."

Lois asked, "Have you ever done this?"

"No, few doctors have, but I've replaced many hips and knees, it's the same idea. I'm sorry but I need to tell you, I don't think he will be able to play tennis. He may not be able to run again."

Lois covered the cheeks of her face with her hands and gasped. "No, can't you do anything else?"

"I wish I could."

"What about skiing?" she asked hoping against hope that he would still be able to enjoy at least one of his outdoor passions.

"Doubtful," Michael said. "We should tell him. He is on strong pain killers and is hurting. He may not be totally able to understand what is going on. I think you are going to have to help him choose. I see that you have his medical power of attorney."

"What do you think, Kip?"

"It's really beyond my expertise, but Michael is one of the best."

Lois shrugged her shoulders with a look of resignation on her face. "Let's do what we need to do." They met with Tim who was waiting on the gurney in the examination room a morphine drip attached to his arm. He was groggy so Lois decided to go through with the operation. When the surgeon left her, she broke down and cried.

Chapter 51 Napa Valley and
Palo Alto, California
September 1996

Tim was angry at God. The Roman gods, the Indian gods, fate, at whatever deity he could name his anger surfaced. Just when things were going well his damned ankle rebelled. Without the injury the Omaha Kid could have been a major leaguer or could have been a great tennis player. It just all seemed so unfair. Why? He yelled in silence to the gods. He had been so close to becoming a star. Now his painful deformity went beyond ending his athletic career to an attack on his love of an outdoor existence. Could he ever have a normal life? Would he be able to hike in the woods? At this point he couldn't even play catch with his son.

The beautiful weather, with autumn leaves spinning the colors of the rainbow, teased his sense, giving him a greater feeling of being trapped. It was hard to care about anything. For twenty-three hours a day he retreated into his bedroom overwhelmed by his disability and his pain. The one hour total out of his room was spent with Lois and Larry at the table during meals. A few times a week Lois would drive him down to the park to be pushed around in his wheelchair. He had about given up walking because of the pain in his ankle heightened with any activity. Going to work was out of the question. How could he teach PE outdoors on his feet all day? The tennis and baseball teams suffered without him. Both finished with a losing record. Tim zoned out watching the flat screen TV mounted across from his bed.

*

He found it hard to believe. When he came out of surgery a year earlier the doctors told him he may never be able to play tennis or run again. He went through the steps of grieving: denial, anger, bargaining, depression, but not acceptance. Never acceptance! It was better to be angry.

Tim believed if he tried hard enough he would be able to run and play again. He religiously went to physical therapy. He went to the club and swam laps. He tried acupuncture, massage and even prayer. But the best he could do after months of-therapy was walk, the pain showing on his face. He displayed a severe limp and used a cane. The pain refused to go away. Dr. Samson, his surgeon, said that everything looked fine; he should be feeling better soon. When the pain did not retreat, the doctor shrugged his shoulders and said, "I've done all I can now, it's-up to your body to heal."

He angrily threw out his tennis racquets and skis. He retreated to his room and the pain pills. First, Tim used hydrocodone, then Percocet and finally OxyContin. Still the pain would not leave him. He spent each day more stoned than the one before. Because of the medication, it was unsafe for him to drive. Bad daytime television became his only friend. His once finely tuned body turned flaccid. His muscle tone degenerated and his skin paled.

Lois pleaded with him to do something. His anger gave way to depression. He felt worthless, less than half a man. When his wife got angry, he retreated further and cried openly, unable to mount a defense to his wife's anger with his condition. Lois remembered her vows to stand by her man in sickness and in bad times. Tim tested her resolve.

Linda and Maria finally suggested a possible answer to Tim. Linda heard about a chronic pain clinic in Palo Alto run by a former Stanford doctor. Maria talked him into going for an appointment. Lois drove him to Stanford for a full evaluation of his mental and physical state. After hours of examination he was invited to meet the clinic's founder, Dr. Weinberg, and the psychologist Dr. Helen Prince. Tim entered the room skeptical about the whole proceedings. He felt like he had been down too many dead ends.

Dr. Weinberg said, "You are an excellent candidate for this program. It's a six week commitment. You will stay in a hotel here. You can go home for a visit after the third week."

Dr. Prince saw the skepticism on his face. "You can do this," she said. But it won't be easy. You have to really want it."

Tim shrugged his shoulders. He still wasn't convinced.

Dr. Weinberg turned to him and said, "I'll bet you a steak dinner this program will give you your life back."

"Will I play tennis again?"

"I can't say that. You know that's improbable, but what is it worth to you to rejoin the world?"

Lois turned to him with pleading eyes. "Say yes."

He considered it for a few moments. Maybe it could work, he thought. What do I have to lose? "I hope to be buying you a steak," Tim finally said to Dr. Weinberg.

Chapter 52 Palo Alto, California
October to November 1996

The Weinberg Clinic was located just across the Stanford Campus in the heart of a social and industrial revolution. Palo Alto had become the high-tech mecca for the world. Companies like Google, HP and Apple headquartered in the Silicon Valley with Stanford University providing many of the minds for technical innovation. The clinic embraced innovation.

People in the pain program from out of the local area stayed at the Marriot Residence Inn on El Camino Real in Palo Alto. Tim still knew people in the area from his bartending days but he wanted to be fully committed to improving his physical condition so he decided not to call them while he was in the program. The clinic told him to leave his wheelchair at home. He moved around on crutches.

Lois stayed with him that first night in the hotel. They used the evening as a romantic get-away, their first in over a year. The couple went out for Vietnamese food. The hot curry reminded them of their honeymoon trip to Thailand. Tim's use of prescription pain medication had destroyed his libido. The curry and being away from home helped to wake up his sexual desires and when the couple returned to the hotel they made love for the first time in months. When Lois left the next morning she kissed Tim goodbye with hope in her heart.

Tim took on the pain clinic like he was playing in the World Series. He was going to give it his best shot, knowing this might be his last chance to get his life back. He didn't want to swing and miss at the opportunity.

They started the first morning in the conference room which served the clinic as a classroom, with office chair gathered around a big table. To an outsider, the room may have looked like a corporate training or product development room rather than a place of healing. Dr. Helen Prince, the psychologist, passed out a three ring binder full of material. Four women and two men sat around the table.

Helen began, "This is your textbook and your workbook; bring it with you every day. Open to page one and you will see your schedule, three hours in class and two hours of physical therapy every day. You need to start moving."

"Now, we are going to go around the room and introduce ourselves, but remember we are all here because of chronic pain so don't dwell on that. Let's start with you." Dr. Prince nodded to the red haired woman on her left.

"I'm Samantha Stone. I'm a nurse and I strained my back lifting patients. I live in San Leandro. I'm divorced and have a 15-year-old son who is staying with his father in Redding." Samantha thin, pretty looked to be in her early forties. She turned to her left to look at the next patient.

"I'm Kathy Montanez from the Mission district in San Francisco. I work for a supermarket and hurt my forearm from stacking shelves everyday. It doesn't want to get better and I miss working. It's been over a year. I'm a single mother, although my six year old son sometimes stays with his father." Kathy brown haired, dark complicated and looked to be in her late twenties.

The next man, an Afro-American, appeared to be about 30-years-old. "Hi, I am Don Weathers, from Sacramento. I'm a high school English teacher. I hurt my back eight years ago, refereeing a basketball game. I've had two surgeries, but they didn't do much good. I'm divorced, have a ten-year-old son and a seven-year-old daughter, both live with their mother in Roseville."

"Hi, I'm Brenda Wolf. I'll be fifty tomorrow, can I say that?" She looked at Dr. Prince.

"Of course," the psychologist said. "Happy birthday and welcome. Go on."

"Well, I'm married and have three kids. I got hurt working at the cannery in Oakdale. It's my back also. I guess that's it." She seemed shy and shrugged her shoulders.

"Thanks Brenda." Dr. Prince said trying to be encouraging.

An Asian-American woman sat next to Tim. She said, "Hi everyone, I'm Sharron Lee. I work as a firefighter and live in Santa Cruz. I broke two vertebrae in my upper back when a burning wall collapsed. They want me to retire, but …well we'll see. Oh yeah, I'm married, no kids."

Finally they came to Tim. He wanted to keep it simple.

"I broke my ankle on a sprinkler playing baseball, reinjured it playing tennis and broke it a third time, again on the tennis court. I've had a few surgeries, but now it just refuses to get better." He inferred that the stricken joint had a mind of its own. "I'm married and have a three-year-old son."

"Thanks everyone. Take a break. Then we're back in here for another hour before you go to 'Functional' physical therapy."

Debra Weinberg, the physical therapist, joined Helen Prince for the next session. The clients were told that this was unusual. Most of the time the classroom sessions had only one instructor, but this was an important introductory class and both professionals presented material. Tim learned that Debra was the daughter of Dr. Weinberg. Debra told the group to open the book to page 10, which had a diagram of the body's nervous system. Tim had studied the nerves in his college anatomy classes to become a physical education teacher. Yet he didn't know what Debra was about to tell them.

"How many of you know the difference between acute and chronic pain?" Only the firefighter, Sharron Lee, raised her hand. Debra just shook her head.

"This always amazes me that no one ever explains this to you." She continued, "Ok now this is important for you all to understand. Acute pain occurs when your body is injured. It is a warning sign that something is wrong. If you grab a hot pan and you get burned, the signal is sent through the nerves to the brain that something is wrong and you drop the pan. The acute pain stays with you until your hand is healed. Let me repeat that important part. The pain is supposed to stop when the injury is healed. In some unusual cases, the nerves do not stop firing. The nervous system stays on even when the body is healed. That is *chronic pain*. That is what all of you have."

"Does everyone understand? Are there any questions?"

Don asked, "So this is why I have pain? The nervous system is stuck in the on position?"

"Exactly," Debra replied.

"Why does this happen?" Sharron the firefighter asked.

"That, we do not know," The physical therapist said.

Helen stepped forward. "How many of you have been told by someone that this pain is all in your mind, that it is a psychological condition?" The whole class raised their hand.

"Let me tell you right now. This is *not* a psychological condition. You are not crazy. Well, maybe you are crazy but about something else." That got some chuckles from the class. "Chronic pain is a real medical condition. Your pain nerves will not quit firing even though they should."

"Medication just masks the condition. It does not stop it. But a side effect of your pain medication can cause you to stop being active. That is the worst thing you can do. Activity lessens the pain. We can not tell you that we can make your pain go away, but here you can learn methods to help lessen the effects of pain on your body and mind. We want to improve the quality of your life. When you are ready, Dr. Weinberg will work with you to lower the levels of your pain medication."

Brenda Wolf raised her hand. "What about medical marijuana?"

Dr. Prince answered, "It also covers up the pain and usually causes a lack of motivation to move. We don't recommend it for people with chronic pain."

The lecture left Tim wondering, why hasn't anyone told me this before? All the doctors have done for me is to give me pain medication. He looked around the room. A powerful sense of understanding came to him. These people are my teammates. This is probably the most important game I will ever play. I have the best coaching here at the clinic that money can buy. I can do this. I can win this game!

After the classroom they moved to the small gymnasium room. Martin, a licensed trainer, joined Debra in running the physical component of the program. The two instructors introduced them to "Functional" class. It was unlike any physical therapy he had done before. The clients kept their own charts and were in charge of their own program. Each exercise was geared to getting them to function in the real world, from pushing a shopping cart to lifting a box off the ground.

Don, with his bad back, even made it one of his goals to be able to bend down enough to pick up his dog's poop from the ground. Debra set up an exercise where he would practice bending over with a plastic bag and pick up plastic poo-poo you can buy in a party store. Other students found an individual program to fit their needs. Tim aggravated his pain just walking, and pushing off was excruciating, so the moving the cart platform became job one. He also worked to relearn climbing stairs.

Later in the day they would have a second, more traditional physical therapy session that included lifting dumbbells, riding on a stationary bike and walking or running on a treadmill.

*

Just like on any ball team, some people become close companions. Tim became particularly good friends with Don, the English teacher and Sharon, the firefighter. After class, they started to hang out together. They went out to dinner and often went back to one of their rooms and talked for long periods of time. Tim remembered his baseball days in the minor leagues and how enjoyable it was to spend time with teammates. These people, like his minor league cohorts, shared the common goal of winning. Pain replaced the opposing team as the enemy. To win they had to improve their physical and mental condition to bring it to the next level. No one else in his life could relate to what he was going through, but these people knew. They all had a shared experience with pain. They understood what it took to fight the battle against pain and the everyday struggle to try and get their lives back.

*

Improvement came slowly to Tim, but it came steadily. By the end of week three he could walk a few blocks with little pain. They were taught the importance of pacing exercise. Doing too much could cause a "flare up" of pain, sending the individual into a backwards spiral. The athlete in Tim wanted to train harder, but he had to guard against that impulse.

On the third Friday, it was visitor's day at the clinic. During the last session of the day the client's family, or in some cases, close friends were invited in to see some of the things that they were learning.

Lois came early to participate in a couples counseling session with Dr. Prince. Lois related how she had been angry at Tim when it looked like he had given up. "He never would have let the athletes on his teams do that when they were behind."

Tim admitted with tears in his eyes, "I had given up, because I didn't know what to do. I was lost. Sometimes even the best players need good coaching to get better."

As the session neared the end, Dr. Prince asked Lois how she felt now. "Are you still as angry?"

Tears streamed down her eyes and Dr. Prince passed her a box of Kleenex.

"No, I finally have some hope. I'm proud of his progress."

"Tim, how are you feeling?" The doctor asked.

"Relieved," he said as Lois passed him the box. "I know I let my family down. But I'm getting better and I have…a plan."

"Good," Helen said. "It sounds like you two are making headway."

As they walked out of the room Lois reached out and grabbed his hand. Helen watched them hug and cry on each other's shoulders.

Lois whispered in his ear, "I love you so much."

"Thanks honey, I needed to hear that."

*

Lois took him home for the weekend. Saturday they spent the day together as a family picnicking in the park. Tim had missed little Larry intensely. A big smile found the boy's face as he walked hand-in-hand with his dad. As they ambled down the sidewalk, they sang, "Take me out to the ball game. Take me out with the crowd..." That night Tim and Lois snuggled like newlyweds and made love. Tim almost forgot about his pain, at least for a one glorious day.

*

It was Thursday of week four and Dr. Prince ran the group therapy session. They had been talking about depression and how it had gripped all of them at times. Don asked if he could read a poem about the subject, something he had written in the depths of despair.

Helen replied, "If you think it would be helpful, sure."

He recited:

Dark Blues Behind the Looking Glass

The sun refused to shine
Dark clouds follow me around
Pain racks my body
Gravity is pulling me to the ground.

I'm falling down the rabbit hole
Spinning to a place so bad
Nobody wants to follow
Not even the hatter so mad.

I ask Alice for some of her pills

Hoping to keep my head
But my depression continues
So I refuse to get out of bed.

Here even the Cheshire cat
Refused to send me a smile
The deck of cards shuffles by
And I have fallen another mile.

The Queen of Hearts
Is trumped by the evil black King.
Will the sun ever shine again?
Will it ever be spring?

"Don I'm impressed," Dr. Prince said with genuine admiration. "It is cathartic to write about you pain. Now that you expressed your feelings it's time to move on. Your next poem needs to be about moving beyond your pain."

The others in the group were nodding their heads. They all had been down that hole. Samantha had tears in her eyes.

Sharron said, "I can so relate to that even if I could never write it. Maybe if I'd had an English teacher like you, I would have had better grades."

Tim felt the poem deep down inside him, a frog stuck in his throat, but the jock code of giving someone shit for being sensitive kicked in. "So Don, I think you been watching too much of the Disney channel on drugs," he smiled at his friend.

"Thanks Tim, I knew you would understand."

Dr. Prince said, "I don't want you all to dwell on the depression. I brought this up to be a learning tool. What have we learned we can do to break up these feelings? Don, what can you do when you feel like you're falling down the *rabbit hole*?"

"I can write."

"Good. Sharron?"

"Listen to music."

The psychologist continued around the room. Tim suggested that he could watch a ball game. The group continued to address this subject.

Later, Tim asked Don for a copy of the poem. He framed it and put it on the wall in the room with his sports trophies like another team he defeated.

*

Week five came and Tim felt better than he had for over a year. He was down to one Percocet a day. The pain in his ankle stayed with him, but it did not dominate his mind. The warm days of late October gave way to the beginnings of the Northern California winter. High clouds gathered overhead hinting of rain as the hotel shuttle took the group to the clinic on the second to the last Monday. Tim read the newspaper headlines that foretold of the next day's election. It looked like Clinton would be reelected despite that whole intern scandal. By mail, Tim had already voted.

In the first session, Dr. Prince had the group fill out an inventory explaining their plans after the program. They would discuss it later in the day. Tim studied the sheet. He had thought about what he was going to do when he left this cocoon, but hadn't come up with a good solution to his physical limitations. Teaching PE all day despite his progress seemed beyond his grasp. He excused himself from class and pulled out his cell phone.

"Mr. Rubio, this is Tim."

"Tim, please call me Frankie. How are you doing at that clinic? Lois told me you're getting better"

"I'm doing much better thank you. As a matter of fact, that's why I'm calling. You made me an offer once to work for you in marketing at the winery before I became a teacher. Are you still willing to give me a job?"

"Absolutely, but have you talked this over with Lois?" his father-in-law asked.

"I wanted to ask you about it first. I thought it would be better if you and I could work something out before I talked to her. I still want to coach high school baseball in the spring. I could take unpaid time off, if that would be all right with you."

"With your record as a baseball coach, your continued involvement would only be an asset to the winery. It's a great idea. I would consider it a community service."

"That's great, Mr. Rubio."

"How many times have I told you to call me Frankie?"

"Well, you are going to be my boss now."

"I'm still Larry's grandfather."

Tim laughed. "Thanks, Frank you won't regret this."

"I know how hard you work. I've seen what you've done coaching. And Tim...welcome back to the world of the living."

*

The following Saturday Don, Sharron and Tim walked together on the Stanford campus. They passed the tennis courts where Tim played years earlier. It had rained the last two days but on this late November afternoon, students crowded the courts to play. Tim felt a yearning as he watched the players pound the ball.

"I remember watching you do that on TV," Don told Tim. "How do you feel watching this?"

Tim said. "There is some sadness, but right now I'm happy just to be out walking again."

Sharron said, "I heard in group that you played tennis. I didn't know you were good enough to play on television."

Don said, "Yes, he was at Wimbledon and the U.S. Open one year. If I remember right, that's when you first hurt your ankle."

"Actually, the first time was playing baseball in Albuquerque. The U.S. Open was the second. It seems like a long time ago."

"It was, you old timer," Don said.

Tim said, "I guess my athletic career would be over now even if I never got injured. I never thought about that before."

As they walked back to the hotel, they passed a bike shop. "Do you mind if we go in here for a minute?" Tim asked.

"Not at all," Sharron said." Don nodded.

The three walked in. Tim spent a half an hour a day during physical therapy on the stationary bike and he realized that cycling was a good way to get exercise without putting too much pressure on his ankle. If skiing and playing tennis were beyond his capabilities, maybe he could find a new outdoor passion. He thought about cruising on a two wheeler past the vineyards on the Silverado Trail. He bought himself a nice bicycle and had it sent home.

*

Lois came for his "graduation" from the clinic. She gave him a big kiss on the lips. "I've missed you." He answered by sweeping her in his arms and giving her a real kiss bodies locked in embrace. They walked to lunch smiling, holding hands like newlyweds.

The program wound down after lunch with Helen, Debra and Martin presenting each of the clients a diploma and a short speech of individual encouragement. Tim found it hard to say goodbye. It reminded him of the end of a season in baseball when you cleaned out your locker and bid farewell to your teammates. He knew he would see Don and Sharron again; they had made a date to come up to Saint Helena for a visit.

Tim and Lois left right away, wanting to beat rush hour out of the South Bay. Lois did the driving. She knew the route from Palo Alto to Napa well from her college days, when she commuted back home from Stanford for holidays.

Soon they were whipping up the Silverado Trail. Tim allowed himself to gaze at the lovely late autumn leaves ablaze in vineyards that extended from the valley floor to the edges of the hills. The beauty touched his soul. He could see it again, anew, feeling almost like a tourist, but this was home.

Little Larry, hearing his parents approaching, was waiting in the front hallway when Tim walked in the front door. He yelled, "Daddy!" and ran to his father.

Tim scooped him up in his arms, gave the boy a bear hug and *walked* him into the living room barely limping.

"I have something for you," Tim went to his luggage and pulled out a rubber ball. "Catch!" He tossed the ball underhanded to the little guy. Larry caught it one handed, wound up and threw the ball overhand back toward his father. The ball went over Tim's outstretched arms, smashed up against the wall and bounced back, almost hitting Tim in the backside of his head. Tim laughed out loud. "You have quite an arm there Larry."

Lois watched, in love with her two guys, but she said, "Ok you two take it outside."

Out into the backyard they went. Father and son played catch for the first time.

Chapter 53   Northern California
Spring to Autumn 2002

Thing went well for Tim for ten good years. His success coaching the East Napa High School Bobcats baseball team became legendary. In the spring of 2002 they won their eleventh section championship for the Omaha Kid That summer he started feeling weak and listless. He tried to push through it, thinking it was just fatigue or maybe he had a flu virus he was fighting off. As the summer wore on his condition did not improve and he started to feel muscle aches all over. He decided to see Kip, by then his regular doctor, who set him up to take a series of tests.

Kip called Tim and asked him to come see him and bring Lois.

"It can't be good that he wants you to come with me," Tim said to Lois when they made the appointment. When the two arrived at the office, the receptionist showed them into a private room in the back. Kip came in accompanied by Linda.

Tim looked at their solemn faces and asked, "Ok, Kip, what's going on? Linda why are you here?"

Kip and Linda stood while Tim and Lois sat in front of them. Kip took a deep breath and said. "There is no easy way to tell you this. Tim, you have ALS, better known as Lou Gehrig's disease."

"No, that's not possible." Lois screamed, "He…has, was… fine."

Tim was in shock. He felt like he had been hit with a sledge hammer. "What…What do I do?"

Linda came over and hugged her sister-in-law. They cried in each other's arms.

"Kip said, "There is nothing for you to do differently, right now. But the disease is progressive and there is no cure. I wish I had better news. Read the material I am giving you. There are some anti-viral drugs I will give you and will start you on some steroid treatments to help you keep your muscle mass as healthy as possible."

Tim was thoughtful for a minute. "So I have a progressive nerve disease that will get worse and eventually take my life. He smiled. Also I have HIV and cancer."

Kip gave his brother-in-law a funny look. "Nobody mentioned cancer or HIV."

"Finally some good news." He said laughing at his fate.

*

Word spread quickly to the rest of Tim's family. JR , Cathy and the kids came to visit from New York. Maria, Sara and Roberta spent a lot of time with Tim. He told them that the lessons he learned from the Weinberg pain program was helping him greatly in dealing with this new diagnosis. As usual, Maria became his sounding board. His deterioration evolved and he went downhill quickly. It was hard for his friends and family to watch.

*

East Napa High School declared the November 12, 2003 home football game as Tim Jacobson day. They soon realized that with all the alumni wanting tickets, there would not be enough room in the small high school stadium for the crowd. Extra bleaches were order and placed in the gaps. Ticket sales would be donated to the Tim Jacobson scholarship fund. The grant would be given each year to one student that has showed the best combination of athletic ability and outstanding grades, picked by a facility committee.

The day of the game a breeze kicked up blowing the autumn leaves in bunches throughout the stadium. The parking lot was full and people were bussed in from church parking lots. When every space in the stadium was filled with a standing crowd, Lois pushed Tim out onto the field in a wheelchair.

Tim looked out to a paid crowd of 19,221 the most ever at a Napa County football game. Tim used a walker to stand up from a wheelchair in front of the microphone. A standing ovation started and continued unabated. For Tim it brought to mind the movie, *Pride of the Yankees*, which he was about to reference.

Tim leaned in and said, "Thank you so much." The huge crowd hushed to almost total silence. "I want to thank you all for coming." His voice echoed around the concrete structure. "I also want to thank all the people at East Napa High School who organized this. It is wonderful that we were able to raise money for a combined academic and sports scholarship. That you are doing it in my name is a great honor.

"Being up here in these circumstances reminds me of the movie I think that many of us have seen about Lou Gehrig. I can't quite quote him and say I am the luckiest man on the face of the earth, because I love my life and would like to be able to stay with you all a bit longer.

"I have lived long enough to know I am a very lucky man. I used to think I was unlucky. Just before I made it to Major League baseball, I hurt my ankle and had to give up that dream. Then I felt like I was about to be a star in professional tennis but was injured again. Now I realize that those setbacks were not bad breaks, but something to put me on the road to my destiny. Instead of an athletic career, I became a coach at East Napa High School. Teaching boys to become men was so much more important than a World Series ring or a Wimbledon trophy.

"Besides, how many major leaguers can say they hit a thousand? Ok, it was only one hit in one at bat but it still goes down in the record books. And how many tennis players can say they lost to Borg and McEnroe at major tournaments in one year? Oh yeah, probably a bunch. That might not be such a good example. As that Saturday Night Live lady, Rosanne Rosanna Dana, used to say; 'Never mind.'" That brought a few chuckles from the crowd, through the tears.

"What made me even luckier is that I learned what is really important. Like the love of a good woman who stands by you when the going gets tough. I want to thank my wife Lois for teaching me what true love is. I want to that my cousin Maria was always there for me, even when we were little kids, living like brother and sister. The rest of my family is incredible, especially my sister Linda. I thank them all. I've also had good friends enriching my life. Thank you as well.

"I want to close by saying something I had to learn the hard way. Enjoy every day you get to play on this earth. Don't worry about what you don't have, but count your blessings for what you have. If you swing and miss, get ready for the next pitch. Let go of your regrets and enjoy the game of life. Thank you all."

During Tim's speech there was an eerie quiet in the stadium. The love and respect for the man had the large crowd hushed, tuned in to every word. When Coach Jacobson finished and sat back down into the wheelchair the crowd rose as one and mild applause turned into a rousing standing ovation. Finally the large crowd started chanting, just a murmur at first then in a full voiced din that reminded Tim of the U.S. Open so many years earlier. . Omaha, Omaha, Omaha… It continued unabated until reached the locker room that was his second home for so many years.

Tim Jacobson died in June of 2007 just after the end of the high school baseball season. The boys on that team dedicated that year to him and it was the last section championship the school has won.

Postscript
Berkeley and Saint Helena, California
Summer, 2007

I'm Roberta Corelli and I loved my grandfather, my dear Uncle Tim. He gave me his love and provided a positive male role model. I wrote this story you have just read. I hope you enjoyed it. His life was so interesting it had to be told.

This postscript is my personal testimonial to him. I wanted to tell it to you using my voice.

We spread Uncle Tim's ashes on the hill under the Sycamore trees where he and Aunt Lois were married. The Omaha Kid perished with bravery and a sense of calm. I know because I watched with both my moms, Sara and Maria, my Aunt Linda, uncle Kip and my courageous Aunt Lois. I didn't cry at his bed until Uncle Kip said, "He's gone." Then I sobbed for a long time.

I am now a twenty-two-year-old student at U.C. Berkeley majoring in literature. When I graduated from East Napa High, the teacher the committee named me to win the Tim Jacobson Scholarship Award, better known as the Omaha. I know it sounds like nepotism but the teachers' committee listed three reasons for the choice:

1. Second highest GPA in the class.
2. Captain of the Bobcat soccer team and leading scorer.
3. Won the section championship in tennis singles.

I was tremendously proud to win the award named after my grandfather. I believe my sports prowess was inherited from him.

I love the diversity in my family. I think it gives us a unique flavor. My gay mothers, Jews, Catholics, Japanese, and if you include my biological mother's genetics some Okie and America Indian showing we are true American mutts. What more can a modern American girl as for? I have no regrets that I never heard from my biological mother, Marilyn. I'm sharing this because she was a small but important part of the Omaha Kid's story.

I've done a lot of research for this book. Thanks to the internet, I have been able to find and interview most of the major characters in this story, from France, Omaha, New York and California, including spending many hours with Uncle Tim before he died. With some people the interviews were brief but with others like Brigitte Moldaur, many hours were spent on the phone talking laughing and even some crying. Thank you all of them for their help in making this book possible. I may have taken some literary liberties filling in the blanks for the sake of the story, please forgive any inaccuracies. Yet I wanted to stay factual as much as possible to the true adventures of the Omaha Kid.

Just before I finished writing this memoir I went with my Aunt Lois to Omaha, Nebraska to watch Cousin Larry play in the Little League World Series. Larry was a lanky but well-toned fourteen-years-old. In the final game with the championship on the line, Larry came to bat. The bases were loaded, two outs, score tied in the bottom of the ninth. He worked the count full. The pitcher went into a full wind up and a fastball flew towards the plate. Larry turned his hips into the swing, the wrists and hands followed looking like...like his father. The metal bat gave off a loud *"thunk"* as it connected with the ball. The sound echoed in my mind. As Larry jogged around the bases, I could almost see the Omaha Kid jogging with his son headed for home.

ACKNOWLEDGEMENTS

I have many to thank for the successful development of this novel:

- Marla Hansen Martin for her edit of my rough draft and invaluable advice
- The Solstice Writing group for their advice and critique
- Kathleen Paterson for her early edit and feedback
- Dan Kaufman for his timely critique
- David Corbett for his teaching at the Mendocino Writers' Conference
- Ana Manwaring for her writing classes and professional edit
- Chris Lamala for his helpful critiques.
- Dorothy Mackay-Collins for her critique and support
- Mary O'Leary for proof reading and support
- Nancy Howell for proof reading
- Jenny Pessereau for editing and proof reading
- Colleen Winters for giving me continual support and patience that allows me to write

I thank you all.

About the Author:

Nathaniel Robert Winters "Bob" was born in Brooklyn in and grew up mostly in Valley Stream, New York a suburban town on Long Island. After serving a tour of duty in the Navy he fell in love with Northern California and made the area his home. He graduated from Sonoma State University and achieved a Master's in Education from California State University Stanislaus. He enjoyed the opportunity to be a high school history and science teacher for the Turlock School District for 33 years. For many years an avid skier and tennis player, he also coached baseball and soccer. He currently lives in Saint Helena, a small town in the wine growing region of Napa Valley with his wife, son and dog. Bob has an affinity for nature and loves to travel. His family has hosted foreign exchange students from France, the Czech Republic and Russia.

Despite having Parkinson's disease, he has written fifteen books in the last ten years.

The books of Nathaniel Robert Winters

Something for everyone:

The Substitute a children's Winter holiday story

Roger Raintree's 7th Grade Blues Young adult:

A modern early teen adventure with relevant lessons to be learned in each chapte

Finding shelter from the Cold   Young Adult and adults that have a love of dogs: — Ice age fictional story about wolves becoming dogs. Its source was an ABC nature film using DNA evidence. Will remind the reader of Jack London's Call of the Wild

Adult Novels: ***The Adventures of the Omaha Kid-*** Romance, adventure, sports, triumph and tragedy

Penngrove Ponderosa- Story of Sonoma State students in the early 70's—sex, drugs with the shadow of Vietnam in the background

Sci-fi***: Past the Future***—Space ships, baby factories, Clones, Time machines just for starters. Will Dave save the world?

Black Knight of Berkeley—Hero Murder Mystery

Poetry and short stories:

The Poet I Didn't Know and

Another Revolution

Fictionalized biography

Rumors about my Father,

No Place for a Wallflower

Legend of Heath Angelo

Not Quite Kosher-Memoir

Heavenly Bodies and other Diversions- Stories, poems